THESE SCANDALOUS STREETS 2

A Novel By Tranay Adams

These Scandalous Streets 2: A Thug & His Bride
/ Tranay Adams-1st ed. © 2015
Editor: Sunny Giovanni
Interior Design: Tranay Adams
Publisher: Tranay Adams

CONTENTS

CHAPTER ONE

Malakai and Bizeal each had one of Crazy's arms over their shoulders as they helped his drunken ass through the double glass doors of the restaurant, Rizzo's. The girls brought up their rear. When they made it outside their chauffer, who was leaning against their limo taking a smoke break, dropped his cigarette to the sidewalk and mashed it out under his cheap patent leather shoe. He stepped to the back passenger door and opened it.

"Yo, y'all holding?" a haggard looking fiend inquired, scratching his neck. He was in a tattered white T-shirt that was stained yellow around the collar and dirty jeans that had tears at the knees.

"Tyrone, you see where the fuck we at? Your ass needs to bounce," Bizeal asked heatedly.

"Oh, my bad, but a nigga out here jonesin." The fiend's mouth moved like he was chewing something, but it was empty. He needed a fix badly. "I'm tryna cop a twenty, but I'ma couple dollas short, can you help me out?" he pulled out a few crumbled bills and some loose change from his pocket.

"You believe this nigga?" Bizeal looked to Malakai then turned back to Tyrone. "I'm not gonna tell you again, homeboy. Bounce or get bounced, mothafucka!"

"Alright, look," Tyrone stuffed his money back into his pocket. "What if I had some information for you? I'm talking about some real top-secret shit." He rubbed his hands together and looked around cautiously, making sure that no one was watching him about to sell his bit of knowledge.

"You got Crazy, man? 'Cause I'ma 'bout to put the beats on this nigga." Bizeal looked to Malakai with a hard face. He was dying to put them hands on him.

"Nah, chill lets' see what he has to say," he looked to the crack head. "Speak, nigga, and you bet not be wasting my time."

Tyrone looked around to make sure no one was listening to what he was about to say. "I know who it was that smoked your folks."

"Who?" the hustler's brows furrowed. His crew had splattered many niggaz around the city during the war for control of drug territory, but they had yet to have any casualties on their end, so he wondered who these folks his smoked-out ass was talking about.

The fiend leaned in closer so only Malakai could hear him. What was said pissed him the fuck off. He frowned and squared his jaws. Murder flashed in his eyes, and he busted the crack head in his mouth. Bwap! Specs of blood flew as he went sailing backwards into the limo, sliding down to the sidewalk.

"I see you gotta death wish."

He looked around to make sure no one was watching him as he whipped out his head bussa, cocking one into its chamber. Tyrone's eyes bugged and he wished he would have kept his mouth shut. It was too late now. The nigga should have never parted his goddamn lips. Malakai threw open the backdoor of the limousine and pulled his scrawny black ass inside, dazed and moaning. Bizeal came right behind him, closing the backseat door shut as he climbed inside.

"Go ahead, nigga, say some more fly shit, so I can give you a vasectomy." Malakai dared the crack head, pushing his gun into his crotch. His eyes were wide and glassy as he looked down to the steel pressed into his crotum then into the eyes of the man holding it. They were dark and madness dancing in them.

"I'm serious, man. I could tell you!" the junky was frightened.

"Tell 'em what?" Crazy slurred, climbing inside the limo. He looked from the smoker to his homeboy, gripping his shiny black tool.

"Shhhhh!" Malakai held a finger to his lips, hushing his friend. His eyes never wavered though. Nah, they were concentrated on who he deemed was the biggest piece of shit to have ever been oozed from between a woman's legs.

"Man, this fool done wet himself." Bizeal frowned, seeing the wet spot expanding at his lap.

"Ugh." Crazy turned his head in disgust.

Looking into the hustler's eyes, Tyrone knew he meant business. He wanted to back pedal and say what he knew was just word of mouth, but then he'd be gambling with his manhood. And with a 40. cal underneath his nut sack he wasn't willing to try his luck. Swallowing hard he decided to tell the upstart all that he knew. "Okay. I'll tell you…"

Malakai brought his ear to the crack head's lips, listening attentively to what he was being told. After adhering the story his eyelids snapped open, and his mouth went slack.

"What's up, Mal?" Bizeal frowned.

"Fuck he say?" Crazy's face twisted.

Malakai drugged Tyrone out of the back of the limousine, letting him drop to the pavement hard. He winced when he bumped the back of his head on the sidewalk but scrambled to his feet hastily. He was about to run when the crack peddler snatched him back by the collar of his shirt, ripping it a little further. *Schhhhrippp!* He forcefully turned him around so that he'd be facing him. Staring deep into the windows of his soul he said, "Get the hell outta here and don't chu breathe a word of what chu just told me to anyone! Ya hear?" his face contracted with anger, and he gritted, shaking the crack head by his collar, causing his head to bob violently.

"Yeah! Yes!" Tyrone swallowed his spit and nodded his head rapidly.

"Get the fuck outta here!" he kicked him in his ass as he made to run off. He fell out in the middle of the street, scrambled upon his feet and took off running.

Urrrrrrk! Honkkkk!

A Toyota pickup truck nearly hit his bony ass but he managed to escape unscathed.

"What's up, man?" Bizeal inquired of Malakai, approaching his brother from another.

"What that nigga tell you?" Crazy wanted to know, coming to stand beside Bizeal, forehead wrinkled.

Malakai leaned up against the limousine with his head hung, running his hand down his face. He looked like he had been dealt the most devastating news in his life. His eyelids stretched wide open, lips forming a tight line; he blew hot air from his nostrils.

"Babe," Dakeemia place a comforting hand on his shoulder, a concerned expression written across her face. "What did that crack head tell you?"

Finally, Malakai lifted his head and looked at his girl. "I know who murdered my brother."

"What?" surprise enveloped her face, and she looked closer into his face.

"Who?" Bizeal asked, dying to know who it was that had touched his extended family.

"Who did it? Tell me and we can go get this nigga now." Crazy gripped his shoulder, staring into his eyes. He loved Blessyn just as much as he loved Malakai. Whoever took the rapper hurt his man and he wanted them dead behind it.

Malakai stood upright. He closed his eyes and massaged the bridge of his nose, taking a deep breath, exhaling. His eyes were glassy and bleeding hurt. Licking his lips, he cleared his throat and gave them the name,

"That mothafucka'z dead!" Crazy slammed his fist down upon the trunk of the limo, denting it.

"Hold up, are you sure that it was him?" Bizeal questioned. "I mean, what good is the word of a crack head?"

"I hear what chu saying, homeboy, but what fucking reason does that smoker have to lie for?"

"I can't say for sure," he responded. "But if you press a strap to a nigga'z nut sack I'm quite sure he'll dream up some shit to tell you, too."

"Too bad you let 'em go 'cause we could have tortured his smoked out ass 'til he told us what we wanted to know."

"So you believe 'em then?" Bizeal wanted to know.

"Baby, please tell me you don't believe that fool," Dakeemia slipped her hands around Malakai's waist and laid her head against his chest.

"Yeahhh," he nodded staring straight ahead and thinking about what the junkie had told him. "I don't know why but the story he told me sounded believable enough."

"Even if it is true, I still don't understand…why would Showtime have yo' brother killed?"

***

It was eleven o'clock at night when Blessyn pulled up to the park banging Scarface's Smile in his purple Lamborghini with the peanut butter interior. He executed the engine and hopped out clad in camouflage fatigues and matching cap, swagged the fuck out. He took a drink of his lemon Snapple as he advanced in Showtime's direction, his iced out cross and Jesus piece swinging from left to right. The lights of the park hit the jewelry and made its diamonds twinkle like the stars in space.

Blessyn stopped before Showtime and took another drink of his Snapple. He screwed the top back on the bottle and slapped hands with the CEO of his label.

"What's up, fam?" he addressed him.

"You know, the streets are talking," Showtime began, massaging his chin with a jeweled hand. "And they're saying you're severing ties with Big Willie after this next album." He cleared his throat with a fist to his mouth. "Now, I'm not one to take what a few niggaz say and run with it 'cause that ain't never been my style. Nah, I'd rather hear it straight from the horse's mouth."

Blessyn looked him dead in his eyes without so much as blinking an eye. "Yeah, I plan on making a move." He spoke as if it wasn't a big deal.

"Say what?" the multimillionaire's forehead wrinkled. He couldn't believe that one of the biggest stars on his label was saying that he was about to cut out on him especially since he'd given him his big break.

Blessyn looked Showtime dead in his eyes, speaking loud and clear. "After this next joint, I'm out. I took a few meetings with A1 Entertainment and they're talking about: two albums, 1.5 mill. I keep all of my publishing and my masters."

"So, you leave me to find out about it like this through word of mouth?" Showtime asked hurt, eyes having grown glassy. He looked at the rapper like he was his little brother so this revelation cut him deeper than any scalpel could. "I thought me and you were 'pose to be better than this. I thought we were family."

"I was gone tell you, my nigga, but with us celebrating this new album going double platinum. And seeing how happy you were, I didn't know how to come at chu about it, ya feel me? I was just waiting for the right time for us to sit down and chop it up, real spit."

Showtime nodded and gripped Blessyn's shoulder, placing his hand on the back of his neck. "Come here." He managed a weak smile as he embraced him, tears streaming down his cheeks. "You broke my heart," he whispered into the rap star's ear and pecked him on the cheek. Right after, he shoved him backwards and walked off.

Hearing movement at his back, Blessyn whipped around and met a dark figure. He held his arm over his brow trying to see the face of who it was standing in the darkness, straining his eyes. Abruptly, the mysterious person pointed something at him that he couldn't make out but his heart told him that it was a gun. Realizing that his life was in danger, Blessyn's eyes bulged and he gasped. All he saw was muzzle flashes before his pupils as a handgun rang out in the night. Two bullets flew: one exploded his Snapple bottle while the other struck him high in the chest. He stumbled backwards and fell on his back with his leg lying at an awkward angle, gasping for air. Blessyn's eyes wondered around in his head like he didn't know where he was or what had hit him. He heard the gunman's footsteps as he approached him, gun leveled at his dome piece.

Poc!

A bullet to the skull sent him spiraling into darkness where he'd never be heard from again. The gunman removed the jewelry and cash from his person. He then turned to Showtime who had his arms stretched wide open. He gripped his handgun, aimed, and pulled the trigger twice, dropping him.

"Aw, fuck!" Showtime cursed, touching his shoulder and coming away with blood.

"Did they pass through?" Keith kneeled down, checking his boss's wounds.

He'd shot him in the shoulder and arm.

"Yeah, they went right through, but this shit hurt." He replied while grimacing.

"Gimmie your watch, your necklace, and any cash you have." Keith told him.

Showtime gave him what he'd asked for and pulled his cell from his suit. He flipped it open and said, "You better get out of here. I'm about to call Los Angeles's finest. Don't forget to toss the burner and torch the car." He reminded him.

"I'm on it." Keith told him, hopping into his whip.

Present

Malakai rode shotgun with Dakeemia whipping the big body truck, occasionally glancing over at him. After the crack head had told him who was behind his brother's murder, he was all the way fucked up. He exchanged daps and hug with his niggaz and he and wifey moved out. He'd told Dakeemia that he wasn't going to shack up with her that night. More than ever he wanted to be in his grandmother's arms crying like a big baby how he used to when he was a little boy. It was something about being in her embrace that made him feel better. He needed to be held up against her ample bosoms and listening to her heart beat as she hummed a soothing tune to him.

Malakai stared straight ahead wearing the same face that Mitch had in Paid in Full when he his little brother, Sunny's severed finger was mailed to him. His eyes were pink and glassy, tears constantly flowing down his cheeks. He was tight lipped and his nostrils were flaring. Not only was he hot, he was also hurting. When his thoughts came back from visualizing how his brother was murdered in cold blood that night, his eyes wandered up seeing his grandmother's complex coming up ahead. Dakeemia didn't even bring the truck to a complete stop before Malakai was throwing open the front passenger door and jumping down into the street. He ran as fast as he could en route toward his grandmother's complex. His eyes misted with tears and floated in the wind as he hauled ass. He shoved a middle aged man aside that was emerging through the entrance gate with a Greyhound on the leash. The man looked at his black ass like he was crazy. Malakai broke down the path and cleared the staircase in a couple of bounds. Bending the corner, he continued his way toward his grandmother's unit. Once he reached the door he fished around inside of his pocket for the keys, when he found them he hurried to unlock the door but ended up dropping the keys. He snatched them back up and tried the door again. He was so discombobulated that he tried to open up the door with several of the wrong keys. Realizing this, he calmed down as best as he could before deciding on the key that he felt would open the door. Click, he heard the door as it opened. He turned the knob and threw open the door, darting inside of the unit.

As soon as he invaded the condo his sense of smell was pleasured by the scent of chicken frying inside of the kitchen. He could hear the sound of the bird crackling and popping as it sizzled in the grease. His grandmother singing about Jesus Christ drew his attention.

"Momma?" he called out to her.

"I'm in here, Mal!" she called back out to him. "You're just in time for dinner. I'm cooking fried chicken, cornbread, yams, greens and macaroni & cheese."

Hearing the woman he affectionately called momma inside of the kitchen, he ran inside of there and found her wiping her hands off on her apron.

"Momma," he called out to her again and she looked up. Worry lines went across her forehead when she saw the hurt in his eyes and the tears cascading down his cheeks. His bottom lip trembled and she saw his knees buckle. She was concerned now because she hadn't seen him like that since he was a little boy.

"What's wrong, baby?" she said as she approached him.

"Momma." He ran over to her and dropped down to his knees, hugging her around her waist. He buried his face in her bosoms and bawled like a new born baby. Surprised, she looked down at him and tears stung her eyes, rimming her eyelids. It hurt her heart to see her precious baby boy like this. She didn't know what was bothering him but she wanted to stop it whatever it was.

"What's wrong, baby?"

"He killed him, momma, he really kiiiiilled hiiiiiim!" He broke down screaming and hollering. He snorted the snot back up his left nostril and whimpered.

"Who are you talking about, sugah?" Her forehead wrinkled.

He pulled himself together as best as he could, looking up into her face. His body shuddered as it was rocked by emotions.

"Showtime…he…he…he killed Blessyn."

His revelation didn't even surprise her because she around knew in her heart that Showtime's rotten ass was the one that stole her oldest grand baby's life.

"It's gonna be alright. You hear me, baby? It's gonna be alright," she said holding up his chin with a curled finger as she stared down into his crying eyes.

"Hold me, momma…oh God…please, just hold me." His voice cracked with his emotions, needing and wanting to be embraced by her.

With that said, she threw one of her chunky arms around him and caressed his head with her other hand. She tilted her head back and allowed tears to stream down her cheeks as she sang a song that slowly began to sooth him.

An hour later

Malakai sat inside of the kitchen at the table facing his grandmother. They both had cups of hot apple cider tea sitting before them. While Mrs. Williams took the occasional sip of hers, he just sat there staring ahead and twisting his cup around. The pinkness in his eyes had lessened, but the dry white streaks down his cheeks let on to him crying earlier that night.

"Mal, let me ask you something, and I want chu to be completely honest with me, okay?" she said after taking a sip of her tea.

His eyes wandered up and met hers. He nodded his agreement. "Now that chu know who it was that had a hand in killing your brother, will you seek revenge?"

"I suppose you'd want me to leave this in the Lords hands, huh, momma?" he asked, looking her in the eyes like he already knew what she was about to say.

"Nope." She licked her lips having taken another sip and clearing her throat. "Not this time, baby boy. If you don't get a hold of that bastard, then I will."

He frowned and coiled his neck, eyes narrowing because he couldn't believe his ears. As long as he'd been living his grandmother had followed the words of the Bible, but now she was talking about killing, something that the God Almighty forbid. "I know why you're looking at me like that, sugah, but what the Lord has planned for that scumbag once he's left this earth may not be enough for me. Uh uh, ya see, I need to know that justice has been served while he's still here living and breathing," she said with glassy eyes, jabbing her chubby finger into the table top. "You hear what I'm saying to ya, son?"

"Yes, ma'am." He conceded.

"Well, what do you planning on doing?" she inquired with seriousness.

Malakai looked down at his cup of tea and then back up her. Taking a deep breath he said, "Absolutely nothing," He picked up the cup and finally took a sip. "I'm going to leave the fate of Showtime in God's hands.

He stared her dead in her eyes as he tilted the cup, watching her reaction. He knew that she was trying to bait him into admitting that he was going to kill Showtime and Keith, and there wasn't any way that he was falling for that shit. As soon as he would have told her his plans she would have gave him this entire lecture about why he shouldn't. He wasn't trying to hear that shit because as far as he was concerned, those two mothafuckas had it coming.

"Good boy." She nodded approvingly, but looking somewhat disappointed.

"I'ma call it a night, momma." Sitting the cup down, he stepped around the table and kissed her on the cheek. With that action, he went off into his bedroom for a good night's rest.

Malakai didn't know it yet but his grandmother had something in mind for Showtime. She'd be damn if he got to live the rest of his life in peace. Not when he had a hand in her oldest grandson's murder.

CHAPTER TWO

Treasure took Tyson by the face and kissed him, hard and passionately. They made out going up the stairs and into her bedroom, where he fell on top of her on the bed. He removed her Steve Madden sandals and pulled off her skinny jeans. Using his teeth, he pulled her panties down, revealing her bald vagina. Tyson stood face to face with the pussy like a boxer would his opponent in the center of the ring before a heavy weight championship fight. He took his time admiring it, as if it was the painting on the ceiling of the Sistine Chapel. It was hands down the most beautiful love-box he'd ever laid eyes on. He looked from her pussy to its owner who was giggling and smiling. He smiled back. Holding her legs apart, he brought his hot, wet mouth to her sex, penetrating it with his tongue and allowing it to slither between her walls. Treasure flinched and hissed. Closing her eyes, she allowed Tyson to make love to her with his mouth. His oral skills took her to a paradise of pleasure she had no idea existed. The Low Bottom's thug had the princess of R&B Soul talking in tongues. He couldn't believe his ears, the jargon sounded like the language Martians used to communicate with one another. Her moans let him know that he was handling his business, which drove him to work her clit even harder.

Tyson brought his head up from Treasure's honey pot trailing a length of saliva from it to his lips. He wiped his mouth with the back of his hand and looked to her V. It was oozing with her juices and jumping at the same time. Her thick caramel legs shook uncontrollably. He smiled at his handiwork, thinking the Pussy Crazy had struck again. Tyson stood to his knees, unbuckling his red belt and unzipping his camouflage cargo shorts. He pulled his boxer-briefs down exposing his erection. His dick was so hard that it damn near touched his stomach. He'd barely gotten the condom on before Treasure had grabbed his hardness and guided him inside of her.

"Mmmmmm." His eyes rolled and he shuddered, even through the rubber he could feel the warmth and moisture of her sex. He moved his love muscle in a circular motion at a slow and steady pace, and then he hit her with the long strokes. He was pushing and pulling his thick length from her womb.

"Ahhhh, ssssss." Treasure's eyes fluttered as his girth massaged the walls of her slick tunnel. He'd grind in her passionate rhythm and pull back until only the tip of his dick was inside of her before pushing all of him back in, going balls deep. Only his nut sack would be hanging out of her. A sheen of sweat formed on his forehead as he laid it down. The sheen of sweat soon turned into beads as he worked Treasure from his side, holding up her right leg and forming a human scissor.

"You like how that feels, baby?" he asked with slit eyes, his face was that of a man who'd just entered Heaven.

"Yessss," she spoke sensually with a grimacing face and shut eyes, feeling his hardened meat sliding in and out of her aisle of love.

"Grrrrr!" His brows furrowed and he clenched his jaws, showcasing his teeth. Feeling himself about to explode, he gripped her hips so tight that she winced. His slow and steady pace had increased and he began to pound her with such intensity that he soon shot his load. "Ughhhh!" Tension released his body like a pair of strong hands and relief washed over his face. Exhausted, Tyson laid his head against her back. He sweated, smiled and panted all at the same time. "Haa! Haa! Haa! Haa!"

Treasure turned over in bed to face her lover. He grabbed her hand and brought it to his lips, kissing it as he stared into her eyes, happily. She stared back into his with a fulfilled expression. Suddenly, seriousness came over her.

She cleared her throat and began, "Tyson."

"Yeah?" he asked, eyes closed as he gently kissed her hand as if it were her lips. She curled her finger and tilted his chin up so that he'd be looking into her eyes. "What's up?" a line formed across his forehead when he noticed the dead serious ass look on her face.

"Call me crazy but I think…" She looked down as she trailed off.

"You think what?" he encouraged her, tilting her chin up like she'd done his. Staring into her face he could tell that she was quite nervous which made him eager to hear exactly what she had to say.

"I think…I think I'm in love with you."

"That's funny, 'cause I know I'm in love with chu."

They both smiled and shared a long, deep, sensual, loving kiss.

An hour later

When Tyson's eyes fluttered open he found himself lying in a different position in bed. This wasn't anything new to him being that he'd always had been a bad sleeper. Feeling movement at his back, he turned over in bed and met the back of the woman he was madly in love with.

"Babe…" he nudged her. "Babe…" he nudged her again and again, trying to wake her.

Treasure stirred a little and responded back groggily. "Yes, sweetie?" she kept her eyes closed.

"You sleep?"

"Shiiiid, you think I'm not after the way you put it down?" She cracked a smile and grabbed him by his wrist, pulling his arm around her. He nestled his head against the back of hers and kissed her tenderly on the back of her neck. He was thirsty but decided to wait until she had fallen back asleep before venturing out. She looked so peaceful in her slumber that he didn't want to wake her, so he slipped his arms from out of her possession. Next, he slid out of bed and threw on his camouflage cargo shorts, buckling the red canvas belt that held them up on his waistline.

When Tyson emerged from out of the bedroom pulling the door shut behind him, he was surprised to find Skylar posted up inside of the hallway with her arms folded across her chest. She wore a kimono and her blonde individual braids were sprawled over her face and shoulders. Her smiling lips said I know what you've been up to as she tapped her French tipped nails against the side of her elbow.

Skylar had decided to take it back home earlier that night leaving the fellas having a ball at King Henry's gentlemen's club. All of that tit and ass had her horny and she be damned if she was going to pay one of those stripper hoes to come up off the pussy. Little momma was a lot of things but a trick wasn't one of them.

"So, uhhh, what were y'all doing up in there?" she inquired.

"Shit, just watching a movie," he said nonchalantly, scratching his chiseled left peck.

"Uh huh." She looked at him like Yeah, right as she swept a couple of the individual braids from out of her face. "I know what y'all was up in there doing." She exposed a toothy smile.

"Oh, yeah? What's that?" He smirked, rubbing his hand up and down his rock hard abs.

"Fucking!" She emphasized the F.

He laughed. "You something else, you know that?"

"So, I've been told." She twisted her finger in one of her braids as she went on talking. "Anyway, Tyson, good looking out, my girl needed some dick. Real spit." She lifted her hand for a high five. Smiling, he looked away shaking his head and letting her hand linger in the air. "Come on, Tyson, don't leave ya girl hanging now." He smacked her five and went to head down the hallway, shaking his head and smiling. She smacked him on his ass like a basketball player would his team mate after making a shot. "Keep up the good work, baby boy."

Damn, listening to all of that fucking done gotta bitch hornier than a jack rabbit. Shiiiid, I'm 'bout to break out this vibrator and call up my boo. Skylar retreated to her bedroom closing the door shut behind her. Moments later, the buzzing of her sex toy was heard as well as her talking nasty to her nigga.

Hearing a muffled voice coming up ahead, Tyson's forehead wrinkled and he slowed his walking once he heard Treasure mentioned. He quickly crept over, pressing his ear on the door and placing his hands against it.

"Treasure Gold getting it in with her bodyguard, boy, this is gonna be the biggest celebrity sex-tape since Ray J and Kim Kardashian." He overheard Preston, the butler, as he spoke into his cellular. "I'm talking big, I mean really big. I'm thinking, we should call it, uh, uh, Tyson's Treasure. I know we can't sell it without them signing off on it, but I know you know the right kind of people who wouldn't mind having this thing for their own personal collections. I was thinking maybe we could get a bidding war started and see what kind of dollars we can gross for this thing."

Hearing this infuriated Tyson. His scowled as his face flushed with redness and he felt his ears growing hot. His fingers curled inward and his thumb pressed up against them, creating fists. Wrinkles went across the bridge of his nose and veins pulsated on his temples.

"Grrrrr!" He growled like a ferocious lion and then kicked the mothafucking door off the hinges. Boom! That bitch flew inward and hung awkwardly off of the hinges. This startled Preston. His eyes went big and his cell flew out of his hand. He could have pissed his boxers when he saw the thug standing in the doorway; chest jumping up and down fast as he clenched and unclenched his fists.

"Wait! Wait!" he threw up his hands and walked backwards, in fear of what the raging man would do to him.

"That's yo' ass nigga! Come here!" he charged after him. In a flash, Preston pulled open the top dresser drawer and snatched out his expandable baton. With a flick of his wrist, he expanded its length just as Tyson went to swing at him. The butler stepped aside missing his attacker's fist, whacking him at the back of the knee and dropping him to a kneeling position. The thug hollered out and felt another blow to the back of his neck, then came one to his lower back. When he grabbed for this area, he was whacked in the throat.

"Arghhh!" he fell on his back, grabbing his neck and coughing; tears accumulated in his eyes.

Seeing that he was out of commission, Preston packed himself a duffle bag hastily. Smacking a blue dingy Nike baseball cap over his head, he kicked Tyson in his side and fled out of the door. A wincing Tyson scrambled to his bare feet, holding his side. Gritting, he darted out into the hallway where he found Treasure and Skylar who had just abandoned their bedrooms to see what was going on.

"Babe, what's the matter?" Treasure's forehead deepened with crevasses. She was standing right beside her bestie who also had the same expression.

"He was filming us having sex!" he called out over his shoulder as he hustled down the staircase, feet moving rapidly.

"Aww, hell naw!" Treasure took off to help her nigga with Skylar following closely behind.

Seeing Preston open the door, Tyson leaped over the staircase railing and landed on his feet with his hands touching the floor. He frowned when he felt the stinging in his feet from the fall when he met the Spanish tiled floor. When he heard hurried footsteps, he looked over his shoulder and saw his main thang and her right-hand coming down the staircase. Tyson focused his attention back on his fleeing suspect and went after his ass, running full speed ahead at the front door. Boom! As soon as he kicked open the front door he narrowed his eyes, throwing up his arms to shield his vision from the blinding, bright headlights of Showtime's Maybach as it drove through the gates. Tyson made it to the bottom of the step when a blur came whisking past him. Whack! Preston cracked him across the side of the head with his motorcycle helmet as he blew passed his line of vision on his lime green Kawasaki Ninja. Preston slid his helmet back over his head as he continued on leaving his victim down on his hands and knees, head throbbing like a sore thumb. Treasure and Skylar came down the steps and attended to Tyson.

"Are you alright, baby?" the crooner asked, concerned with her man's wellbeing. She and Skylar held his arms and helped him to his feet. The three of them looked up just in time to see Preston barely escaping through the narrow opening of the closing gates.

"What the hell's going on here?" Showtime asked, stepping out of his car along with Keith who had that steel at his side.

"Ya boy, sssss," Tyson hissed feeling the soreness in his head and a headache coming on. "He…he gotta away with a tape of…of me and Treas."

"Of you and Treas doing what?" he inquired with furrowed brows.

"What do you think?" A wincing Tyson asked, rubbing the side of his head. He looked at Showtime like he was a fucking imbecile for not knowing what kind of tape he was talking about.

"Shit!" Showtime ran his hand down his head and over his face, blowing hot air.

"I'ma see if I can catch up with 'em." Keith made to hop back inside of the Maybach but he stopped him.

"Don't bother, unc, that dick sucka is long gon' by now. Damn!" Showtime kicked the front passenger door of the luxury vehicle denting it.

***

Treasure, Skylar, Showtime and Keith all sat around inside of the living room. Showtime paced the floor swirling dark liquor around inside of his glass and occasionally taking sips, rubbing his hand down over his baldhead. He did this every time he was heated and in deep thought. Worry was plastered on Treasure's face as she thought about what would happen to her image if the tape was to go nationwide. Her eyes were pink and glassy and tears soaked her cheeks. Her bestie sat beside her. One hand was lying on her wrist while the other rubbed up and down her back soothingly. In the middle of the floor were the spy cams and mini surveillance cameras that Preston used to film everyone inside of the mansion. Included were several jeweled cased DVDs and loose wires and cords. Some of them were labeled while others had one or two letters but no one knew what they meant. Keith, Tyson, and Showtime had swept through the entire house to find this stuff after discovering a multi television display hidden at the back of his walk-in closet. When they turned on the monitors they saw that they were being watched in every room of the house, even outside of the mansion.

"What're we gonna do?" Treasure asked the CEO of her label. "If that tape goes viral…" she trailed off shutting her eyelids and biting down on her bottom lip, shaking her head. She sniffled and her shoulders shuddered. The platinum selling singer didn't want the world to view her getting it on with her man. More than once she'd seen the celebrities with sex-tapes be labeled as freaks or even worse, whores.

"Come here, baby," Tyson called out to his lady and opened his arms. Treasure stood to her feet and speed walked over to her love falling against him and throwing her arms around him. Her caressed her back and kissed the top of her head, listening to her cries as she shed tears behind the ordeal.

"Well, one thing's for sure, he can't sell the tape?" Tyson spoke up, garnering everyone's attention.

"How you figure?' Showtime questioned, taking a sip from his glass.

"I overheard him say that he can't put the tape out in stores unless Treasure and I sign off for it. The best he could do is load that shit up to the net."

"That's right." Showtime nodded. "That tape will never hit shelves without ya'll signatures. That's for damn sure."

"Do you think he'll put it out on the net?' Skylar sat up where she was perched.

"I doubt that. My man is looking for a pay day." Showtime told her. "He's not looking for no social media fame. Naw." He shook his head. "He's tryna get paid."

"True that." Tyson agreed. "I also heard him telling someone that he was going to auction off the tape. Something about getting a bidding war started for people that would want the tape for their personal collections."

Showtime swallowed the last of the liquor. He crunched on the ice and pointed to Tyson with the hand he held the glass in. "There you go. See, that's the only way he's gonna see some real paper off of it." He addressed Treasure who had the side of her face lying against Tyson's chest as she held onto him. Her face was wet from all of her crying. "Baby girl, you don't have to worry about that tape going viral. It's gon' end up in some wealthy crackas possession, for his own viewing pleasure."

Hearing this, the singer lifted her head up from her boo's chest. "That doesn't make me feel any better, I don't want nan' soul seeing that tape, I cannot and will not rest until its back in my possession."

"Yo, Show, you don't got any address on this fool?" Tyson's forehead wrinkled as he asked the question. "Family member, or girlfriend? I was thinking that if I could get a lead on 'em I could recover that tape before it reaches anyone else's hands."

"I don't but I gotta plug at the police station." He responded. "I'm sure my guy can pull up a file on this dick head. I'ma hit 'em up." He sat the glass down on coffee table and pulled his cell phone from the recess of his suit. "Gimmie a sec." The million dollar nigga stepped off to the side away from everyone's earshot. They all stared at his back as he spoke in whispers on his cellular. About three minutes later, he came walking back into their space, sliding the device back inside of his suit. "Okay, I got my man on it. We'll have that file in a couple of days."

"A couple of days?" Treasure's forehead dipped with worry lines. Within a couple of days she just knew that the tape would be in some pervert's hands.

"I know what you're thinking, baby girl, but be easy." He held up both of his hand like he was trying to tell her not to worry any further. "This mothafucka is thirsty. He's gonna wanna squeeze every dolla he can outta this thing. He'll be looking for enough dough to have him sitting high and pretty for a while."

"Don't wet it, baby," Tyson spoke, snapping her head in his direction. "Soon as I get them addresses, I'm up and on his ass like stink on shit." He caressed the side of her beautiful face, staring into her eyes. "Trust me, Beloved, yo' man got us." She closed her eyes for a time, enjoying his gentle touch. "You believe me, right?"

"Uh huh." She nodded, then laid her head against his chest and held him tightly.

"Show," Tyson called after his employer, garnering him to raise both of his eyebrows. "Soon as ya man give you that, holla at me, big dawg. I'm not letting my girl go out like that."

"No doubt, I'ma shoot that info straight at chu and let chu do yo' thang."

"Good looking out." He gave him a nod and took his boo by the hand, leading her up the staircase and heading for the bedroom. They stripped down naked and lay in bed, with her lying on top of him. He relayed to her that it was going to be alright as he stroked her back lovingly. She fell asleep listening to his soothing voice and the rhythm of his heart beat. Treasure believed Tyson whole heartily when he told her that he wasn't going to let that of them sexing get out. She didn't know what lengths he would go to insure that but with the way he claimed to love her, she knew without the shadow of a doubt that he was willing to go to the extremes to keep his world. When she drifted off, she had no clue of how truth this was.

Meanwhile in Showtime's study

"Baby girl is worried sick, man, you sure yo' connect can get that info on Preston?" Keith asked, sitting down before his boss's desk with a drink, swirling the liquor around in it.

"Yeah, I got it covered; he's a big wig up there." Showtime loosened his tie and kicked his expensive Italian leather shoes upon the desk, resting the fresh glass of liquor he'd just poured in his lap.

"If that footage was to ever get out lil' momma would be the talk of the world." He took a sip of his liquor. "I'm talking coverage of tabloids, radio stations, news channels, gossips sites, the whole shebang." He counted off the media outlets that were bound to have Treasure's name popping should her sex-tape ever drop.

Showtime's raised his eyebrows and his eyes bulged as he whistled. "That's some hell of a promotion; our songbird would fuck around and go diamond this go around with that kind of P.R." he took another casual sip from his glass and his eyes wandered off to the side as he thought about how big Treasure would blow up if her footage ever got out there. At first he was pissed that her privacy had been violated, but now with what Keith had said he was thinking that maybe it wasn't such a bad idea if her sex-tape was exposed on a national level.

"I see those wheels turning, nephew, but I can't let chu do that." Keith's serious eyes bored into those of the multimillionaire's. "You've already got cho foot on the poor girl's neck with that shitty deal you gave her, now you wanna expose her for all of the world to see?" he looked at him like Damn, you're one scandalous ass mothafucka if you willing to do that.

"Aww, come on now, unc, you know I ain't finna do no shit like that. I was just fucking with chu, OG." He cracked a smile, showcasing those gold fangs of his.

"Uh huh." Keith sat back in his seat, eying him suspiciously as he took a drink of the fine liquor.

He was surprised by his nephew, thinking that his shady dealings had limitations but clearly, he was wrong.

You're hands down the coldest mothafucka to have ever tied up a pair of gators, nephew, the killer thought as he listened to Showtime talk about his future business ventures.

***

Cody was in a wife beater and homemade du rag while down on his knees inside of his cell. He moved down the cold filthy floor wiping it down with a hot soapy rag, careful not to miss a spot. As he moved along, he could see his reflection on the floor. It was almost as if he was looking into a mirror. Hearing footfalls nearing his house he peered up to see Whispers and a host of niggaz. Cody stood up on his knees and felt his stomach drop below him. He was nervous but the scowl masking his face put up one hell of a front. He refused to buckle in the face of fear he was spawned from a different breed of gangstas.

"What's up witchu, C-Doggy Dog?" Whispers cracked an evil smile.

"What's brackin'?" Cody prepared himself for what may very well be the fight for his life. He knew that this day was coming and here it was.

"Oh, you know what's up?" the soft voice roughen grinned devilishly, stepping a foot inside of the cell with his goon squad on his heels.

Cody's heart pounded up against his ribcage feeling like an African drum being beaten by a pair of hands. In a flash, he yanked the T-shirt from his head that he was using as a homemade doo-rag. He whipped the shirt around his hand until it was secure around it. Snikt! He drew a shank from underneath the mattress, flipping it over in his palm. He jumped to his feet with his arms spread, stepping backwards until he bumped against the wall. His head snapped from left to right, watching the hard faces of the men that poured into his cell. His eyebrows were lowered and wrinkles went across the bridge of his nose. He squared his jaws and clenched his blade so tight that his hand turned white at the knuckles. He was ready to die. Ready to kill if need be; prepared to go down in a blaze of glory if it came down to it.

"Come on, mothafuckaz!" his wild, wide eyes darted around at the hostile faces of Whispers and his goons. "The first one of you bitches that steps up getting they shit slice the fuck up!"`Sweat beads oozed out of the pores of his forehead, dreads hanging loosely over his face, making him look creepy as his chest leaped up and down. His heart beating faster and faster, as the larcenous men stepped closer and closer. "Come on! Come on, goddamn it!"

Suddenly, Whispers and his goons froze in their tracks. Smiling fiendishly, the soft spoken man dipped his hand into his back pocket and pulled something out. The dips of Cody's forehead deepened as his eyes studied what his rival had in his hand, a contraband cell phone and a packet of heroine. This made the dread headed thug relax a bit and sigh with relief. Still, he kept his grip on his shank because shit could be a trick.

"Relax," Whispers kept his smile, tossing the cellular and the packet onto the mattress. "Your cousin wanted to make sure that chu got this. You're good for the H every three days. You come and see for your re-up."

Cody stood up straight mad dogging Whispers and his goons as he tucked his blade. He pulled the T-shirt loose from his hand and threw it on the mattress. He kept his eyes on the opposition as he picked up the packet of heroine, looking to it to them.

"What chu think, its poison?" Whispers asked, interlocking his hands at his waist. "We may have beef but I answer to a higher power. It is because of him and only him that you haven't been gang raped and thrown off of this tier to hang until you take yo' last breath. Don't chu ever forget that 'cause if ever that veil of protection is lifted, that'll be yo' ass boy. Keep that in mind. Alright crew, we on the move." He sounded off like a drill sergeant keeping his glaring eyes on the young nigga. With that command, the men surrounding him stood up straight like a couple of cadets and moved out of the cell, marching. His eyes lingered on the younger man for a minute longer before he headed out of the cell. As soon as Grief's lieutenant and his goons had dispersed, Cody ran to the bars. He looked up and down the tier to see if anyone would try to move on him. Seeing that the coast was clear, he ducked back off into his house and closed up. Drawing a sheet across the string hanging across his 6 x 9 space for privacy, he sat down on his bed and picked up the packet of heroin. Grabbing a XXL magazine and a playing card which he lay out on his lap; he dumped half of the contents of the packet out onto the magazine. Using his card he diced and smoothed out the drug as finely as he could before making a few thin lines of it. Carefully, he scooped some upon his card and snorted it up his nose, welcoming teary eyes as he blinked like he was just waking up. He pinched his nose shut to hold the effects of the drug and felt the drip at the back of his throat. After closing his eyes for a time, he did another line and lay back on his bed, slumped. He closed his eyes again and allowed his imagination to run wild. The heroine took him from the Hell he called home to a paradise you'd have to catch a plane to visit.

CHAPTER THREE

"Uh! Uh! Uh! Uh!" Yurika sounded with her eyes squeezed shut, her head bobbed up and down from Joseline's glistening pussy. Romadal was behind her Spider Monkey fucking her. His eyes were focused on her ass and he was licking his lips. Sweat trickled from his brow as he watched his rock hard dick pump in and out of her tightness, rapidly. He took his hands from her hips and pushed her head down into Joseline's coochie, letting her know to get back to eating her out while he fucked her from the back. Gripping her by her shoulders and getting down into a doggy style position, he rammed her like a mad man while staring a narrowed eyed Joseline in her eyes. The look he gave her communicated that he was going to be banging her ass out just like he was his current fuck-buddy, no doubt.

"Ah! Ah! Ah!" She raised her ass off of the bed and clenched the sheets having her Vajayjay eaten so well.

"Yeahhh, eat her pussy, just like…ahhhh." He threw his head back making his chin visible and gripping her meaty hips, burying his fingers into her flesh. "Uh! Uh! Uh!" he grunted as he stroked her fast and furious, his sweat dashing her back, further soaking it.

"Ah! Ah! Ah!" Joseline grew louder and louder.

"Uhh! Uhh! Uhh!" Yurika's hollered out in between eating her V. Romadal was behind her tearing that mothafucking ass up.

"Uhhh! Uhhh! Uhhh!" he grunted grew volumes higher. They were all making sensual noises, emerged in the hour of hot, passionate sex. "Shieetttt, ahhh, I'ma 'bout to bust Shit! Grrrr!" He was on the cusp of letting loose when the raid flow of automatic gunfire resonated outside and inside of the mansion. The threat of danger zapped the semen back inside of his dick and he hopped out of the bed, dashing across the bedroom. He ran out to the terrace butt naked, dick swinging from left to right. When he stuck his head out he saw two masked up niggaz running across his lawn, lighting shit up. The buffest out of the pair looked up at him and gave him the Death Sign, sliding his hand across his throat. This was his way of letting him know that he was a dead man.

Romadal's eyes bulged and his heart skipped a beat. He darted back inside where he found the girls slipping on their thongs and robes. Without a minute to waste, he put on his leopard print draws and stuffed his bare feet into a pair of sneakers.

"Daddy, what the fuck is going on?" Joseline asked with furrowed brows, tying her robe around her waist.

"Yeah, Daddy, what's happening?" Yuriko also inquired.

"We're under attack!" He pressed his ear against the wall and felt around it until he found a hollow space, knocking. Within the moment it took someone to snap their fingers the wall drew up into the ceiling, revealing a cache of rifles, handguns, grenades, magazines, and knives. He snatched two M-16 assault rifles off of the wall and slipped their straps over his head. After checking the ammo in both of his weapons, he racked them and let them hang at his sides. Next, he stuffed some extra magazines into the pockets of his robes.

"Daddy, what are we supposed to do?" Joseline asked, holding a sobbing Yuriko in her arms.

"Get in here." He ushered them both inside of the secret space where all of his artillery was hidden. He kissed them both in the mouth and on the forehead. "Stay here and don't come out until I tell you to. Do you two understand?"

They both nodded their understanding.

"Okay, be careful." Joseline gripped his arm. He gave her a nod and knocked on the side of the wall where he'd did before and the wall slid down, concealing the girls inside. They were left in darkness aside of the small holes inside of the wall. It was through them that they could see what was going on inside of the bedroom. All they could hear was their heavy breathing and Yuriko's sniffling from crying. They watched their Daddy flee the bedroom with both of his M-16s hoisted up at his shoulders. As soon as he retreated they heard a rush of gunfire and screams of men as they were chewed up by hot lead.

"Oh God, please, watch over him." Yuriko crossed herself in the sign of the crucifix.

"Ahh! Ahhh! Ahhh!" she broke down sobbing again once she heard the painful cries of their lover. Joseline pulled her close and held her tightly, rubbing her hand up and down her back soothingly. While doing this she still kept her eyes focused out of the small holes in the wall.

"He's still alive." Joseline reported, seeing Romadal retreat back to the bedroom and closed the door shut. Yuriko lifted her head from off of her girl's chest and peered out through one of the small holes in the wall. They observed their man look at his mangled and bleeding arm, grimacing. Right after there was a abrupt crash and glass raining. A muscular man masked and fatigued up swung in on a zip line and sent some hotshot through the kingpin's chest, opening him up.

Yuriko went to scream but Joseline smacking her hand over her mouth silenced her. She whispered something in her ear that calmed her a little. It didn't stop the tears from bursting out of her eyes, cascading down her cheeks and over her girl's hand. Once she had gathered her wits, they both pressed their faces against the walls to watch the happening through the openings. They both saw the muscular man pull the neoprene mask from the lower half of his face, revealing his identity. Both women committed the murderer of their man's face into their memory and were sure that they would never forget it.

Hearing a vehicle start up and leave the premises after the masked men cleared out the stash inside of the wall, the girls attempted to get out. They punched and kicked the wall but it wouldn't give to all of the punishment they inflicted upon it.

"Wait! Wait!" Joseline gasped. "It's become hard to breathe. All of this movement is sucking all of the oxygen from outta here."

"I know." Yuriko agreed panting. "I can hardly breathe, but what're we gonna do? We need to get outta here."

"Hold up." She felt around on the wall for one of the knives, pricking her finger on a sharp edge of one. "Ouch!"

"What? Are you, okay?"

"Yeah, I pricked my finger, but at least I know where the knives are now."

"Oh, right, now I get it. We can use the knives to dig are way out of the wall."

"Exactly." She drew two blades from off of the hooks on the wall. "Here." She passed one of the sharp weapons to her girl. Together, they picked away at one of the holes in wall until it grew wider and wider. One of them then snaked their arm out of the hole and knocked on space that Romadal had, sliding the wall up into the ceiling. The girls dropped the knives, falling to their hands and knees gasping for air. They quickly forgot about their erratic breathing when they looked up and saw their man laid out. Scrambling to their feet, they ran over to attend to them. Yuriko got down on her knees, pushing a lifeless Romadal over and pulling him into her.

She allowed his head to rest in her lap, bloodying her hands and body as she held his face. Tears dripped from her eyes and splashed onto his face as she leaned over, kissing his lips. Joseline kneeled down and took his hand into hers, caressing it. Her eyes welled up with tears and slicked her cheeks wet. She whimpered seeing the man that had been not only her lover but her father figure as well lying dead.

Yuriko sniffled and said, "He's dead isn't he?"

Joseline looked up at his bloody and mangled chest. Wiping her dripping nose with a curled finger, she nodded her confirmation of their lover's death. This caused the girls to breakdown sobbing louder. While Yuriko went on weeping, Joseline wiped her face damp and snorted the snot back up into her nose. She took two long, deep breaths and wiped the blood from her hands on her rope. She then got upon her bare feet.

"Joseline, what're we gonna do? Daddy's dead! He's dead!" she rocked back and forth, cradling the dead man's head in her lap.

"Get up!" Joseline ordered her. When Yuriko went on crying her eyes out and bawling, she yanked her up to her feet. She then shoved her up against the wall causing her to bump up against it hard.

Smack! Smack! Smack! Smack!

Her hands were like blurs going back and forth across Yuriko's face, leaving her cheeks red and stinging. The girl hung her head sniffling and wiping her nose with a curl finger, as her eyes trickled tears. They splashed on the floor.

"Snap out of it!" her nostrils flared, her chest heaved up and down. Her palms were stinging and throbbing having put hands on her girl but it had to be done. The bitch was screaming in hysterics. "All of that slobbering and crying ain't gon' do a goddamn thang to bring our man back, nothing!" she chastised. "Look at me!" She didn't lift her head up so Joseline stepped closer, clenching her jaws, she grumbled. "Look at me."

Finally, Yuriko lifted her head and looked her square in the eyes, her body rocking as she continued her sniffling. Her nose was red and her eyes were swollen and red around their rims.

"Yeah?" she asked timidly.

"Are you a lay down ho or a standup bitch?" she frowned and wiped her wet face with the back of her hand, not fully understanding the question posed. "I'm saying are you one of them hoes that's gon' lie down and take whatever or are you one of them bitches that's gon' stand up for hers? That's what the fuck I'm tryna find out."

Yuriko took the time to wipe her face damp with the sleeve of her robe. Closing her eyes, she took a deep breath and peeled them back open. "I'ma standup bitch."

"Good. Now that's what I wanna hear." She cracked a crooked, one sided smile. "Now, we ain't no killas, so obviously peeling this nigga'z cap is outta the question."

"Well…well, what do you suggest we do?"

Joseline hung her head and held her wrists at her back as she paced back and forth across the floor, thinking to herself for a time. Abruptly, she stopped and her head snapped up. She looked her girl dead in the eyes.

"We've gotta go to the cops, there's no other alternative."

"The police." She looked at her like You can't be serious.

Yuriko hated the police they'd killed her father in front of her when she was just seven years old. They pulled him over during a routine traffic stop and asked for his license.

"I know, I know." She held her by the shoulder, holding eye contact. "But this is as good as I can come up with. I need you to ride with me on this."

She stood their staring into her eyes like she was being hypnotized, turning her request in her head over and over again. Suddenly, she hung her head and took a deep breath, before throwing it back up. She closed her eyes and swallowed her spit. When she peeled them back open she nodded yes, willing to go along with what she had in mind.

"Okay, alright."

"Thank you, girl." Joseline hugged her closely and kissed her on the cheek. "Okay, you go and throw on something while I put in the call." She plopped down on the bed and snatched up the telephone, dialing 9-1-1. As of present day Joseline and Yuriko are holed up at her house under watch of two police officers which are stationed just outside of their door. This precautious was taken until the police could bring Malakai in for questioning and hopefully pin him for Romadal's murder. As long as he was free there was always a possibility that he could send someone at the girls to exterminate them.

The night after Preston evaded capture

"Hi! Ya!" Treasure bellowed as she playfully threw kicks and punches at Tyson. He blocked the attack and countered with one of his own. She backed up, smacking his fists to the side as they came. Swiftly, she ducked his leg as he brought the heel of his Air Force One around, punching him in the gut a little too hard and knocking the wind out of him.

"Ooof!" Tyson's face twisted in pain and he staggered back, holding his stomach.

"Are you okay?" she asked concerned, gripping his shoulder.

"Yeah, so where are we off to now, boss lady?" he smiled and rubbed his stomach. Right after, he draped his arm over her shoulder and they strolled down the sidewalk.

"I was thinking Big Momma Ann's café." Treasure hugged Tyson's arm around her neck lovingly. "I could go for a slice of apple pie with a scoop of French vanilla ice cream."

"Pie, huh? I can do that," Tyson said. She looked up at him and they kissed tenderly.

Tyson unlocked the Mercedes Benz that Showtime had won for him with the remote control attached to his car-key. He went to open the passenger door and Treasure grasped his arm

"Come on. It's a nice night out, let's walk," She told him.

"Really?"

"Why not? It's only down the block and around the corner." Treasure reasoned. "You can gimmie a horsey back ride over." She grinned widely.

Tyson smiled. "Come on." He crouched down and she climbed on his back. Tyson stalked up the sidewalk with Treasure hanging on to him.

"Weeeee! Getty up horsey," Treasure said like an excited little girl riding a pony for the first time. She patted Tyson on the ass and he sprinted up the strip. Treasure laughed and wrapped her arm around Tyson's neck. They moved up the block nearing a man in a cowboy hat, tight jeans and snake skin boots. Still in motion, about to pass the man by, Treasure snatched up the hat from off his head and placed it on hers.

Once they'd finally made it to the café Tyson let Treasure down to her feet. Breathing hard, Tyson held open the door for his lady to enter. Treasure removed the cowboy hat and slid into a booth toward the back. Tyson slid in on the opposite side of her.

"That was fun."

"Yeah, it was." Tyson agreed, picking up the menu that the waitress had just left given them.

"Oh, you can have this back. I already know what I want." Treasure handed the menu back to the waitress.

"What will it be, sweetheart?" the waitress smiled and pulled the ink-pen from behind her ear, ready to take Treasure's order.

"A slice of apple pie with a scoop of vanilla ice cream and whip cream on top," she told her. "Oh, and an ice cold glass of milk, please."

The waitress turned to Tyson. "And you, sir?"

"Oh, uh, I'll just have a chocolate and strawberry milk shake." He handed her the menu.

"I think it's safe to take your disguise off, it's ten o'clock at night. I don't think anyone will be coming through here at this hour," Tyson told Treasure once the waitress was out of earshot. Treasure had donned a wig of individual braids, some funny red glasses and a weird assemble to wear to the theater so she wouldn't be harassed by overzealous fans. She and Tyson had gone to see Street Fighter starring Sonny Chiba. It was a three movie showing: Street Fighter, Street Fighter 2 and Sister Street Fighter. Tyson had watched Treasure sulk around the mansion all that day. He could tell that she was worried about the footage of them being intimate being out there and he wanted to do something to cheer her up. So he decided to take her out to see the old Kung Fu movie, starring Sunny Chiba out in North Hollywood. The couple stuffed their faces with a big bucket of pop corn and filled their bladders until they felt like they were about to burst with extra large fountain drinks of Cola

Cola. The idea was to get Treasure's mind off of the sex-tape. And the way things were looking the R & B diva had gotten forgotten all about it, or at least pushed it to the back of her mind for the time being.

"Yeah, I guess the coast is clear," she replied, removing the funny glasses and the blonde braids wig and placing them on the side of the table.

"That was a bad ass movie," Treasure said.

"Sonny be putting hands on niggaz."

"I tell you I would have cringed if I had a dick when Sonny pulled off that guy's cock and balls in one tug. Ouch."

"One of the few moments where I wished I wasn't born a man."

The waitress came back and put their orders on the table. They thanked her and she left them to themselves.

"I'm glad you liked it. I could have bought it on DVD but there's nothing like watching it on the silver-screen. Plus, there's a different experience when you're watching a flick with an audience." He sipped his milk shake.

Treasure took a bite of her pie and ice cream. It was so delicious that it caused her to close her eyes and shake her head and say, "Umm-uh, this is like heaven, you've gotta taste this." She gathered some pie and ice cream on her fork and held it out to Tyson, while holding her hand under it. Tyson pulled the pie off of the fork. Munching it down, he nodded his head in approval. It was damn good.

"That's good, real good," he told Treasure.

"You got something on your mouth," she replied as she picked up a napkin, folded it and dabbed the ice cream residue from his chin. She'd gotten some on her finger and sucked it off.

"Why Treasure, are you trying to seduce me?" he asked with a smile.

"No," she smiled, looking at him sideways.

"Too bad, 'cause I was finna say it was working."

"You are too much, Mr. Tyson." She took a bite of pie.

"So I've been told." He took a sip from his milk shake. "That shit that happened earlier yesterday, was crazy, right? Showtime should have peeled homeboy. Shit, I should have done it myself. If that situation comes back around it could put you in a bad way, know what I'm saying?"

"You speak of murdering folks as if it's as easy as taking out the trash," Treasure told him. "Have you ever killed someone before?"

Tyson stared at Treasure for a moment. He leaned back in his seat and scratched the side of his face.

"My bad, I didn't mean to…"

"Nah, it's okay," he told her. "One day I was catching the bus home. I was in a red T-shirt, red Dickies, and red Chuck Taylors. You know, flamed up? The bus makes a stop and these two hard heads board, laughing and joking. I could tell from their attire and the way they said cuz they were from the other side. And this alarm starts blaring in my head, 'Enemies! Enemies! Enemies!' Now I'm already knowing it's about to go down so I prepare myself for it. It's two of them and there's one of me, but fuck it. I figure I'm pretty nice with my hands, I'll take those odds. It's not like I gotta choice, right? Anyway, they spot me and those jokes and laughs turn into mad dogs and snarls.

The tallest one steps up, bangs on me, 'what set chu from, cuz?' Real aggressive like. His fists are balled; his homie's fists are balled. They're ready for war. I am too.

So I jump to my feet, throw up my set and bang my hood, 'I'm Lil' T, from Eastside Outlaw Rolling 20s Bloods Gang!'

"Fuck slobs!" the shortest one hollers.

"Fuck crabs and all of their dead homies!" I holler back.

Boom! It pops off. We get it in and I'm giving it as good as I'm getting it. The bus driver comes to the back, some big bloated brother, shoves us off the bus. We hit pavement still squabbling. I catch the shortest one in the chin and drop him. Now me and the tallest one are going at it. He starts to tire and I go to town on his face and head. Next thing I know a large fist crashes into the side of my skull. I drop. Dazed and confused. I look up seeing double. There's this hulking image standing over me. My vision comes into focus and it registers to my brain that it's OG Paybacc from Gangstas; straight up killa nigga. I can't count how many of my homies he done put in the dirt. The three of them beat me unconscious. I thought I was dead until I woke up in the hospital. From that day forth I vowed to never go anywhere without being strapped. About a year later the same type of scenario occurs; only I'm coming outta the liquor store and I'll be damned if I let history repeat its self. I did what I had to do." He took a sip of his milk shake.

"Hey, you gotta do what you gotta do when your back is against the wall, right?"

"Two sho'," Tyson answered. "I'd rather their relatives get the call than mine."

Something bumped against the Café's window startling the couple. Tyson went to draw his .45, but when he saw pale ass cheeks pressed against the glass he let his hand fall. Outside there were a bunch of buck wild white kids who were drunk and high, spewing all kinds of shit. Tyson and Treasure laughed and shook their heads.

"What is it that you want outta life, Tyson?" Treasure asked. "What're your hopes and dreams?"

"That's a good question; no one has ever asked me that before," Tyson told her. "I never really thought about it. I mean, when I was growing up I couldn't see past the hood. Shit, I was so busy pulling licks that I never gave it any thought. I guess after I'm done out here, I'd like to see about opening my own restaurant. And run it like a family business, just me, my brother and my old man. It's always been a dream of his to be a chef at some big fancy restaurant. You know those classy five star joints where they give you those small plates of food that cost you an arm and a leg."

"That sounds more like your father's dream."

"They are one in the same."

"Well, when you're ready I'll be right here to help you in any way that I can. I got cha back."

"As I do yours," Tyson leaned over and kissed her. Treasure's cell rang. She looked at the screen. "Who's that?" Tyson asked her.

"It's Skylar."

"At this time of night?"

"Yep, something must have happened between her and her dude." Treasure pressed talk and before she could say 'Hello', Tyson snatched the cell from her.

"What's up, Skylar? This is Tyson. Treasure will have to call you back." He hung up, turned the cell off, and stuffed it into his pocket.

"Negro, no you didn't," Treasure said smiling, surprised he'd hung up on Skylar.

"Slim had you to herself for damn near two weeks, it's my time now," Tyson smiled. "Besides, she's back home. She's got her man to keep her company."

"A guy that takes charge; I like that characteristic in my man."

"Your man? I didn't know I was your guy."

"Boy, you better act like you know."

Tyson squeezed in the seat beside Treasure. "Gimmie another bite of that pie," he told her. Treasure took some pie onto her fork and fed it to Tyson.

"So?"

"So what?" he asked, taking the fork from her and helping himself to another bite.

Treasure nudged him. "You know what, us."

"Yeah." He nodded.

"Yeah, what? I wanna hear you say it."

"You're my lady."

Treasure turned his head toward her and kissed him. "You're not finna sit up here and eat all of my pie." She chuckled and took the fork for another bite. As she munched the piece of pie down he pecked her on the cheek. She looked to her right outside of the window and spotted a well lit store. In the windows were several male and female mannequins which were dressed up tuxedos and wedding dresses. The name of the place resided above, Cynthia's.

"Oh, oh, oh, we've gotta go there." Her eyes brighten and she patted his hand, pointing out of the window at the store.

"Alright, let's go." His dimples made a cameo appearance as he smiled again. He hunched over for her to climb upon his back again. Hurriedly, she wiped her mouth with a napkin, balled it up and dropped it on the table beside her saucer. Afterwards, she hopped up from out of her seat and climbed his back for a piggyback ride, he went running out of the café with her hooting, pumping her fist.

Three minutes later

Tyson and Treasure wandered inside of the store looking all around at the tuxedos and dresses, wearing expression of wow on their faces. They looked like a couple that was inside of a museum taking in all of the foreign artifacts. While Treasure was holding the arm of a see-through flower print wedding dress and observing it, Tyson was intrigued by the white tuxedo with a gold tie and vest.

"This mothafucka hard right here, babe," he said with a fist to his mouth, looking from the tuxedo to his lady. "What chu think?"

Still holding the sleeve of the see-through wedding dress, she turned around to her man. "Baby, that's you all day. I can see yo' sexy chocolate self in that thang."

"Really?" he smiled, not turning to her but still admiring the tuxedo.

"Most def'." She nodded. "Go try it on."

"Do you lovely people need any help?" the upbeat manager asked with a bright smile. He was dressed in a button-down, black tie and vest.

"Nah," Tyson said after stealing a glance at the man. He was holding up the tux and spinning it around, taking a good look at it. "We're straight, homie, you can point me into the direction of your dressing room though."

"Oh, sure." The manager turned around and pointed to the back of the store where the dressing rooms were. "Right at the back of the store, you can't miss it."

"G' looking out." Tyson dapped homeboy up. He looked like he didn't know what to do standing there with his fist held out. Old boy didn't know what to expect until the thug's fist met his.

"Oh." He cracked a smile of embarrassment, turning red in his cheeks.

"Hold up, babes, I'ma come with you." Treasure grabbed the dress she was so in love with and caught up with her dude. Together they went off to the dressing rooms.

Five minutes later

Tyson stood in the full-length body mirror looking over himself with a Colgate smile, satisfied with how he was looking in the white tuxedo. Seeing Treasure's reflection behind him in the mirror as she came out of the dressing room, a look of amazement came across his face. Stopping cold where he was, he watched her for a time as she seemed to glide across the floor. He turned around to her, eyes wide, mouth hanging open. She was smiling, appearing to step toward him in slow motion, all dramatic like in her favored wedding dress. The lights seemed to dim all around her allowing only her to be seen in the beautiful dress while the rest of her was surrounded by darkness. It was like she was performing on stage and being followed by a spotlight. The way she appeared to him didn't stop until she was standing right before him.

"Well, aren't chu gonna say something ,handsome?" She held up the ends of her dress and spun around in a 360-degree full circle.

"Trea…Trea…Treasure…" He looked to be in an in shock trance, taking in the full scope of her. "You're…you're the most beautiful woman I have ever seen in my life." He finally got it together enough to say, having previously been choked up.

Treasure smiled and giggled, holding a hand over her mouth. "You think so, babes?" She blushed.

He took her hand with both of his and brought it to his lips, looking directly into her eyes. "I know so, Queen." He placed a tender, loving, gentle kiss on her hand which made her blush further before he stood upright.

"I hope I don't run you off visiting a place like this so early into our relationship. It's just that I've always dreamed about getting married when I was a little girl. And when I seen this dress…" She held up the ends of her dress and looked herself over. "I just lost it."

"Nah, you not gon' run me off," he told her. "I kind of liked getting dressed up in their digs." He pulled on his collar and gave himself the once over. "Shidddd, a nigga don't look half bad."

"Model it for me, handsome. I wanna take in all of my man." she took a step back and eyed him like one of the judges at the American Idol auditions. Tyson crossed his legs and did a slow 360-degree turn, like he was standing on a rotator.

"What chu think, boo?" He smiled, showcasing the dimples in his chocolate cheeks. He adjusted the cufflinks on his tuxedo, stopping his turning so that she could get a good look at him in the perfect fitting ensemble. He looked just like what he was, a tatted up, thug ass nigga in a fly ass tuxedo.

"You look good, babe." Treasure smiled, boasting that billion-dollar smile of hers. Her eyes turned glassy, looking like Windex shined windows. She cupped her trembling hands to her face. "Oh my God, Tyson." She shut her eyes and tears jetted down her cheeks. Shaking her head from side to side, she whimpered. Her shoulders jerked a couple of time and then she broke down sobbing. His brows furrowed and he approached her, placing a hand on her shoulder. Abruptly, she whipped around and threw her arms around his neck, crying into the chest of his tuxedo. The manager of the store looked at him like he was questioning if everything is alright. He gave him a nod and placed his hands on his lady's waist.

"What's wrong, sweetheart?" He caressed her back, trying to sooth her troubles.

Treasure peeled her face from the breast of his tuxedo, where she left wetness in the imprint of her face. Tears were continuously rolling down her cheeks and her left nostril was threatening to drip snot. She wiped her wet cheeks with the back of her hand. “Its…it’s so surreal, baby.”

“What chu mean, Lover? Talk to yo’ nigga.” He pulled the handkerchief from his breast pocket and dabbed the moisture from around her eyelids and cheeks. Next, he wiped her lips and chin off, caressing the side of her face with his thumb.

She sniffled and he gave her the handkerchief, which she blew her nose with. Afterwards, she swallowed and looked back up into the eyes of her man. “We were right there, babe, in Jamaica. There was you and I. We’re wearing exactly what we were now. I was pregnant and there was a little boy. I think he was ours. It was our wedding. The sun was shining bright and the sand was warm underneath our feet. All of our friends and family were there; even my daddy was able to take leave from prison to be there. It felt so, so, so…” She looked off to the side trying to think of the word she was trying to say. “Real.” She looked back into his eyes. “I could feel the sun on my face, the sand underneath my feet, the cold platinum wedding band when you slide it on my finger.” She held up her manicured fingers and wiggled them, cracking a breathtaking smile. “The baby kicking inside of me,” Taking his hands, she placed them on the sides of her flat stomach. He looked down at her torso and smiled, revealing the gap between his perfect set of teeth.

“It will be real, baby, ‘cause I’m gonna make it a reality.” His tilted up her chin with his curled finger when she dropped her chin having felt embarrassed about what she’d experienced. “Trust and believe in me. All that you envisioned…I am gonna make a reality. You just watch and see.”

Twenty minutes later

Tyson came out of the store hunched over and carrying Treasure on his back like she was a child. She smiled and kissed him on the cheek. They both laughed as he traveled down the sidewalk, moving past pedestrians.

"Hahahahahahaha." Treasure laughed, going up and down on his back as he ran. The pedestrians looked like blurs with him running past them so swiftly. Her eyes went big and she hollered out. "Babe, wait, wait, slow down, ahhhh!"

"Haa! Haa! Haa! Haa!" Tyson trotted to a stop, breathing hard with a shiny forehead from perspiration. "Damn, Love, you gon' have to cut down on the chili cheese fries."

"You ass!" She smacked him on the back playfully.

He chuckled and let her down from his back, taking her hand as they walked down the sidewalk, taking in their surroundings.

"Where do you wanna go next?" He looked to her.

"Ummm." She held a finger to her lips while looking around. "How about that jewelry store?" she pointed to a mom and pop's jewelry store called Sergio's.

"Cool. Come on." He led the way to the jewelry store, pushing open the revolving glass door and crossing the threshold. As soon as they stepped inside they heard the soft music playing from the small speakers in the four corners of the room. Treasure didn't have a clue of who it was but Tyson did. He told her that it was the world famous singer, Frank Sinatra. The couple stepped to the glass display case and looked over all of the jewelry behind it. While the Bulletproof Love crooner was marveling a gold heart charm bracelet, her significant other undivided attention was on the diamond earrings.

"Oh, I'm most definitely getting this charm bracelet right here." She tapped her finger against the glass, pointing to the piece of jewelry that she had her eyes on.

"Yeah?" Tyson moved over and took a look at what she had her eyes on.

"Uh huh." She nodded.

"Heeeyy, how are you lovely people doing? Welcome to Sergio's, I'm Sergio." A tall dude in an ugly brown shirt and suspenders emerged from the back. He wore small diamond earrings and had a gold ring on every chubby, hairy finger. The portly man had hair on the sides and a thin mustache.

"Tyson." Tyson introduced himself as he shook the man's hand. He looked at Treasure. "And this is my girlfriend, Piper." He gave him the name he and Treasure had agreed on that night when she donned her disguise.

Sergio shook her hand as well. "Pleased to meet chu, Piper. You know, you resemble that singer. What's her name." he thought on it, massaging his chubby chin with his eyes staring out of their corners. "Treasure. Treasure Gold, that's her name."

Tyson and Treasure exchanged smiles. The jeweler hadn't a clue that the famous singer was her.

"I get that a lot and thank you. She is beautiful." Treasure grinned.

"Okaay," Sergio smacked his meaty palms together and rubbed them against one another like he was ready to get down to business. "Well, you got your sights set on anything?" he placed his hands on the glass and looked over the jewelry below them.

"Yeah." She showed him the heart charmed bracelet she had her eye on. He took it out and told her the price. What he wanted for it was peanuts to her. "Oh, and whatever my man wants." She casted that incredible smile at Tyson.

"Oh, I'm good." His eyebrows raised and he threw up his hands like he didn't want anything.

"No you not, you're getting them earrings I saw you eyeballing so show 'em." She smirked.

"Babe, I…"

"Nigga, we 'bout to be fighting up in this bitch if you don't take what I'm tryna give you." She gritted and threw up her fists, taking a fighting stance.

Tyson chuckled and threw up his arms to block her impending attack. "Alright, baby, damn."

"That's what I thought, punk." She told him while trying to conceal a smile on her lips and passing Sergio her Visa credit card.

"What is it that you would like, my good man?" He stood over the side of the glass display where all of the diamond earrings were.

"Those Princess cuts right there." Tyson pointed out to him, his finger tapping the glass.

"Alright." The jeweler unlocked and pulled open the sliding door, grabbing the set of gold and diamond earrings.

While the jeweler was busy getting the jewelry and cleaning it in the back, Tyson went to stand beside Treasure. At the moment she was staring down at the engagement rings with awe in her eyes. She looked like a kid at a candy store the way she was adorning the precious stones before her eyes. Tyson looked from where she was looking to her, smiling having seen the ring that her eyes were set on getting one day.

"Alright, I got cha pieces all cleaned up for you folks," Sergio informed them, standing before the cash register. "Will that be all for the day, or do you have your eyes on something else?"

Treasure didn't say a word; she was in a trance staring down at the engagement ring. Tyson frowned seeing this because he could tell that she really wanted it and one day he prayed that he was the guy to give it to her.

"Treas." He nudged her but she didn't budge. "Treas!" he spoke louder, nudging her again.

"Yeah?" she snapped out of it, turning around with her eyebrows raised and tilting her head back slightly.

"You want anything else outta here?"

"Uhhh." She glanced back at the engagement ring really wanting it, but knew that it would be some time before she'd gotten one. "No. That will be all thank you."

"Okaaay." Sergio punched in the keys of the cash register and gave them their total. He then swiped the card and had Treasure put in her code. Not long after the couple were walking out of the store hand and hand. The singer had her head leaned up against her man's shoulder, walking down the sidewalk. They stared up at the moon continuing their travel.

The night was serene and neither of them would change it for the world.

CHAPTER FOUR

The next day

Malakai rode the escalator holding a Macy's shopping bag as he stood side by side with Dakeemia inside of the Del Amo mall. Looking to her, he interlocked his fingers with hers and kissed her on the cheek affectionately. They locked eyes and exchanged smiles. Truthfully, she was the only other person in his life that he loved just as much as his grandmother. He couldn't get over how lucky he was to have met her, but he thanked God every chance that he got that he did.

Ten years ago while at a bachelor's party for a cousin's friend where Dakeemia was one of the girls there stripping, Malakai witnessed her about to be raped. He pistol whipped one of the bitch ass niggaz and blasted two of them in the ankle and kneecap, whisking the love of his life off and saving her from being violated. A month later the two of them went out to Las Vegas where they got hitched. Ever since that day the two of them had been inseparable.

"I love you." She spoke from the heart, her wedding banded hand gripping his tighter.

Still staring into her eyes he smiled harder. "I love you even more."

Again, they kissed lovingly and walked off the escalator. Malakai looked ahead and saw who he was looking for at the food court. Switching hands with the Macy's shopping bag, he pulled a wad off dead white men from out of his pocket and peeled off a few hundred-dollar bills. "I want chu to take this and buy you something nice from outta one of these stores while I go holla at this dude." He passed her the money. She folded it up and tucked it inside of her bra. She gave him a deep passionate kiss and pecked him on the lips twice before headed off. He smiled in appreciation of his sexy woman, watching her ass dance as she sauntered off into Nordstrom's. That song that Ludacris had a few years ago instantly came to mind.

My chick bad, my chick hood, my chick do stuff that ya chick wish she could.

Malakai smiled and nodded his head in approval of the Ride or Die chica he had on his arm. She was beautiful, loved his dirty draws and would bust her guns for him just as hastily as any of his niggaz would. He gave himself kudos for wifing her up. Hell, she had all of the qualities that a man wanted in a woman and more, so he would have been a fool not to. With his lady occupied, the hustler fell in step to handle his business.

Chief Sams and his wife sat at a table in the food court eating Panda Express. They'd just finished hitting up the last store looking for these specific pair of shoes, but unfortunately couldn't find them. The misses was ready to go to another store but the old man wasn't having it. He had to get some grub before he went any further. So here they were shooting the breeze over their meals and observing the people leaving and coming to the food court, when he made contact with the cat that he was suppose to be meeting that day. The man nodded ahead and he looked over his shoulder, spotting the men's rest room behind him. With that he knew that it was there that they would have their interaction. He gave his charge a nod as he passed him en route to the meeting place he'd suggested.

"Dear, I'm gonna go use the rest room. I'll be right back." He walked around the table and kissed his wife on the side of the head. Next, he adjusted his belt and made a beeline towards the men's restroom, toting a Macy's shopping bag. As soon as he crossed threshold inside he spotted the man he'd seen in the food court standing at the urinal. He'd just unzipped his jeans and pulled out his meat to his whizz, tilting his head back. A shopping bag was right beside his foot. The chief cleared his throat before stepping to one of the urinals, sitting the bag down. Unzipping, his pants he pulled out his shit and took a piss too. Only he stared ahead, focusing his eyes on the graffiti on the wall before him.

"Is that my money in that bag?" he kept his eyes ahead.

"Yep," Malakai replied, whistling and tapping his foot.

"Y'all left quite a mess up there at Romadal's place…fucking massacre." He shook his head like it was goddamn shame.

"Aye, we got the job done." He leveled his head and shook his meat. "You got cha cut too, a hunnit kay." He stashed his dick and flushed the urinal, moving to one of the porcelain sinks that was in a row of others. He turned on the faucet and lathered his hands with the soap from the dispenser. Sams took up space right beside him washing his hands.

"I expect the same every month." He reported, looking himself over in the mirror as he rinsed his hands. "Same time but different locations, I'll let chu know where. I'll keep my people off yo' back and give you the word on any drug crews looking to make a move. My people will bust who they can. You just keep the bodies to a minimum. With all that heat no one will be able to eat. Then you have a bunch of pissed off badges you've gotta deal with." He turned off the faucet and checked his teeth as he wiped his hands dry.

"Oh, I almost forgot." Sams unzipped his jacket and pulled out a manila envelope, passing it to him.

Malakai frowned as he opened the manila envelope and pulled out two 8 X 10 photographs. He looked from the photos back up to him.

"Fuck is this?" he inquired.

"Something you definitely wanna take care of, believe me." He gave him a serious look and gave him the rundown on the two women presented in the photos.

"Shit! Shit! Shit!" Malakai grimaced, holding the photographs to his forehead like he had a headache, pacing the floor. "How the hell did we miss them?" he stopped and took another look at the photos.

"I don't know but chu did. And they I.D'd you at the scene of the murders." Sam informed him. "With this many bodies them white folks will be looking to gas your ass." He shook his head shamefully, hating to see another black man get the death penalty.

"Damn, you don't have any intell' on 'em?" he pushed the photographs back inside of the envelope and closed it.

"Say no more. I've already got chu covered." He pulled a folded slip of paper out from his jacket pocket and passed it off to him. He took it and looked it over.

"Oh, thank God, you saved my ass, man." A smile curled the ends of his lips as he stared down at the address that he was given. Without warning he embraced the chief and patted him on the back. The older man cracked an amused smile, shocked by the hustler's sudden display of appreciation.

Malakai kissed the slip of paper and held it up to the ceiling, staring up at it.

"Get down to the 77th street division precinct as soon as possible. Homicide Detectives Flannerty and Freeman are working your case." He told him. "Knowing them they've already gotten a warrant for your arrest. If you want my advice call your lawyer and get him to go with you down there for questioning."

Malakai nodded. "Thanks again, I really appreciate this."

"Hey, that's what chu paying me for, son." He adjusted his belt and pulled his pants further up on him. "But take heed and get rid of those two, asap."

"You got it." The hustler replied, drying his hands off below the hot drier.

"Alright, kid, take it easy," Sams switched hands with the shopping bag and patted him on the shoulder on the way out of the door.

Having conducted his business, Malakai made his way out of the rest room and pulled out his cell phone. Looking over his shoulder he saw the chief and his wife emptying their trays before walking off hand and hand. He turned back around and speed dialed his right hand.

"Yo, Bizeal, we've gotta mess we need someone to clean up." Malakai gave his man the rundown on the situation Chief Sams had made him aware of discretely. Speaking in codes, he gave him specific instructions to contact a man who was known to make niggaz disappear for a substantial fee. Once he disconnected that call, he speed dialed his lawyer, Herman Gold. "Gold, what's up with it, fam? Yeah, I need to meet up with chu…"

Later that night

The night was at its darkest and coldest. A black Escalade sat parked beneath the freeway path where silence resided, save for the occasional car speeding past overhead.

Vroom! Vroom! Vroom!

The air sounded as vehicles whipped back and forth across the 105 freeway.

Holed up inside of the enormous truck were Bizeal and Crazy passing a smolder joint between them, smoke wafting around inside of the enclosed space, making the quarters resemble a sauna.

Crazy coughed hard as hell with a fist to his mouth having hit the joint too hard. His eyes had become red webbed and glassy, appearing to tear up. He couldn't even front that shit that Bizeal had on deck was official.

"Where you get that from?" he inquired curiously.

"The dread over at the Slauson that be slanging them bootleg DVDs," Bizeal replied, taking a couple of tokes. "I'm tryna get Malakai to switch connects and see about fucking with this fool's people. Shit we got now is okay but this shit is The Truth."

"Yeah, we most def' gots ta get that shit there on deck." His brows wrinkled as he pointed to the smoking J.

"Cough! Cough! Cough!" The husky man's body rocked as he went into a coughing fit after a couple of draws from the strong Kush.

"Puff, puff, give!" Crazy joked, patting him on the back, sounding like Smokey from the movie Friday. His eyes shifted down to the J pinched between his homie's thumb and pointer finger. "Let me hit that shit."

"Huh." He passed it off to him and gave a quick scan of their surroundings, a crease in his forehead. "Man, where the hell is this fool we 'pose to meet to twist this nigga'z cap back?"

"I think this him right here." Crazy spoke with smoke filled lungs, staring out of the passenger side window. When Bizeal looked, a Lincoln Town Car had just pulled up with pitch black tinted windows that made it impossible to see through. As a precaution, they gripped their head bussas for any impending drama. The driver side door opened and the chauffer stepped out, one leather dress shoe at a time. He was a tall dark skinned cat sporting a suit that was even darker. Once he adjusted his tie and cufflinks, he stepped to the back passenger door of the vehicle and pulled it open, his head on a swivel as he took in his surroundings. Emerging from the car was an old man that didn't stand a hair over 5 feet 7. He was draped in a hat, glasses and a suit which was under an overcoat. His cane was the first thing to hit the pavement followed by his ostrich skin shoes. The driver closed the door shut behind him and stood upright, his wrists crossed at his waist. He stared straight ahead with eyes shielded by round shades as he chewed on gum tight jawed. He stood by as the old man approached the Escalade, pulling open the back passenger door and sliding in onto the leather seats. As soon as his lungs met with the repugnant odor inside of the SUV his body rocked from coughing. He pulled his handkerchief from within the recess of his suit and held it to his mouth, gagging and coughing like he had lung cancer.

"You guys mind lettin' down a fuckin' winda in here?" he complained, trying to let the window down by holding down the switch that operated it. He pressed it harder and harder but it wouldn't work. Frustrated, he punched the window and the door panel with the back of his hand. "Goddamn thing doesn't even work. I'm gonna freakin' suffocate inside of here." He fumed, reeking of hostility like it was cologne.

"Chill out, pops, the child safety is on, but I got chu covered." Bizeal told him, cracking the windows on all of the doors with the control panel by his side. As soon as they were ajar the smoke went drifting out into the outside and bringing in the night's fresh air. The old man threw his head back and took a deep inhale, a crooked smirk forming on his thin lips as he breathed.

"Ahhhh, much betta." He tilted his head back down and coughed into the handkerchief. Once he'd wiped the extra spit from his mouth he folded it up and tucked it inside of his suit. “Now, let’s get down to business, who is it that you fellas need taken care of?”

“Show ‘em, C.” Bizeal nudged him and stole a peek at their passenger through the rear view mirror. He noticed that he had thick bags under his eyes and saggy cheeks. From his appearance he estimated that he was probably seventy-five to eighty years old. And judging from that cough he was more than likely fighting the flu or something even worse, cancer.

Crazy popped the glove-box and pulled out a manila envelope, passing it over his shoulder into the backseat. The old man’s wrinkled; liver spotted hand grasped it and opened it, removing two mug shots. One was of Joseline and the other Yuriko. He pulled out a pair of glasses and cleansed their lenses with his handkerchief, before slipping them onto his face. Quietly, he studied the faces of the women. When he flipped the photos over there was loads of information on both of them; old addresses, addresses of relatives, and even telephone numbers.

Having seen enough, he slid the photographs back into the envelope and closed it.

“Okay. The deal is twenty five grand a head. I’m sure my assistant has already made you aware of this.” The old man assumed, tucking the glasses away.

“We’ve got chu covered, pops.” Bizeal looked to Crazy. “Give ‘em that, fam.”

Crazy nodded and dipped his hand beneath the front passenger seat, pulling free a Ralph’s brown paper bag containing the money. He went to pass it into the backseat but their passenger wasn’t having it. He shook his head no.

“No, no, no,” he shook his head from side to side. “That’s not how we do business here. You will wire that money to an off shore account.” He passed them a folded piece of paper and they looked it over. “Are we good?”

"Yeah, we good." Bizeal nodded approvingly.

"Great. I'm sure you've got it from here. We've already gotten an address so I'll have my man on it tonight. " He knocked on the window and the chauffer opened the door, he stepped out just like he'd came, cane first.

Bizeal and Crazy watched as the chauffer of the Lincoln opened the backdoor of the vehicle for the old man. Once he closed the door shut, he hopped back behind the wheel and drove off. Now that the right people would be paid, all that was left was for Malakai to get the confirmation that his little problem had been taken care of.

***

"You get a line on Malakai Williams yet?" Detective Flannerty asked his partner as he sat on the edge of his desk and took a sip of coffee. He was a burly man with pink skin and brown hair that was thinning at the back of his head.

"Hell no, that black son of a bitch went M.I.A." Detective Freeman said from behind his desk where he scoffed down a hotdog wrapped in bacon with all of the works. The relish, ketch up and mustard mingled together and rained down on the napkin that he wore out of his collar. He wiped his mouth with a napkin and continued. "By now he's probably laid up in some Thailand whorehouse getting his knob polished by some tranny hooker." Freeman was a tall, slim dude that wore his sandy brown hair slicked back. His thick mustache hung slightly over his top lip. He resembled the 70s porn star John Holmes.

"Yeah, I guess you're right. I'm sure his mother blew the whistle on us. We probably just should have waited for our chance to pounce on the prick and brought him in." Flannerty shook his head. "I gotta bad feeling we've blown our load too soon." He took a sip of coffee.

"Don't speak so soon. Have some faith, my friend." Freeman told him before biting into a chip.

"Faith?" Flannerty raised an eyebrow. "I doubt this punk will just fall into our laps."

Someone clearing their throat drew the detectives' attention to their rear. They found an old Jewish man holding a briefcase accompanied by Malakai. The hustler wore a silly smirk on his face as he stood beside Herman Gold. One of the most widely respected attorneys in Southern California.

Herman cleared his throat with his fist to his mouth and said, "Detectives, I understand you'd like to interview my client."

Flannerty and Freeman exchanged surprised glances.

***

Yuriko lay across the purple lavender couch sipping a glass of white wine and reading a copy of His Dirty Little Secret. She wore a doo-rag, a big red T-shirt with the characters from The Flintstones cartoon on the front of it and big fluffy bunny slippers. She'd spent the past couple of days crying her eyes out over Romadal. Although she'd witnessed his murder with her own eyes she still couldn't believe that he was gone. His death shook her world to the core. He had been both father and lover to her and Joseline.

The bathroom door opened cutting a ray of light out into the dark hallway. A dark figure slithered out and made its way toward the living room drying her hair with a towel.

"Girl, it was hotter than a bitch in your bathroom. I thought I was gone faint in there. It felt like I was suffocating." Joseline complained. Her face was damp and her hair was wrinkled from the steamy hot water. She was in a white spaghetti strap shirt that boasted her hard nipples that poked out like baby toes underneath the thin cotton fabric. She had on sweatpants that were folded down a couple of times so they'd hold on her waistline. Her manicured feet were inside those see-through Chinese house shoes with the flower knitted pattern you could buy from the liquor store for $3 or $4 dollars. "I thought you would have a ventilation system or something in there."

"Yeah, I meant to tell you to keep the door cracked before you went in there." Yuriko told her, never taking her eyes off of the book.

Joseline plopped down on the couch beside Yuriko and took a deep breath. She welcomed the fresh air into her lungs. It was refreshing compared to the stuffy hot air of the bathroom. She looked over to Yuriko and could see the pain on her face as she read the novel.

"Are you all right, Riko?" Joseline asked concerned, brows furrowed.

Yuriko blew hard. She sat up on the couch and closed the book. "You think it was wrong for us to rat ol' boy out like that? You know how niggaz frown upon snitching in the hood."

"Girl, fuck these niggaz and these skunk scallywag ass bitches," Joseline told her, her head moved from side to side as she spat her contempt. "Ain't none of these gossiping mu'fuckaz gone pay your bills and make sure you got clothes on your back and a place to lay your head. So fuck them. Fuck them in their asses witta AIDS infected dick. We had to do what we had to do for us. Shit, ain't like we could have found the nigga and smoked our damn self. Dude is a real live killer. It ain't nothing for him to get it popping, you seen how he did Romadal." She said in the way of refreshing her memory.

"That was so fucked up how they did him, though. Why you think they wanted Romadal dead so bad?" her eyes turned glassy as she felt herself about to cry again just thinking about it.

"Who knows." Joseline shrugged. "It could be a number of reasons. Romadal had beef with a couple of crews that I know of. There's no telling who sent them niggaz to put that work in."

"You're right." She slid her hands down her face and blew hard. "I've just been stressing out over this whole ordeal. When I go out now, I'm constantly looking over my shoulders thinking some nigga with a motive is gonna appear outta nowhere and blow my brains out. I've become a nervous wreck." Her eyes welled with tears and spill down her cheeks.

Joseline took her hand into hers, rubbing it gently and comforting her. "All of this shit is going to blow over in a minute. The cops are gonna catch these niggaz, we're gonna testify in court and they're gonna lock all of their punk ass up and throw away the key. In the mean time you'll be okay. We got each other and two of L.A's finest outside your door." She reminded her of the two police officers parked outside of her house. They'd been there for the past few days watching Yuriko's home. Although the police were right outside the door she still had trouble sleeping.

"You're right. Thanks for having my back in all of this, Joseline." Yuriko wiped her tears from the corners of her eyes with her thumb and middle finger.

"Please." Joseline waved her off like the favor was nothing. "You know you're my bitch, now where the weed at?"

Yuriko laughed. "It's in the tray under the couch."

Joseline pulled a tray from under the couch that had Zig-Zag rolling papers and Kush already broken down upon it.

She sat the tray in Yuriko's lap and turned the flat-screen on. She looked to Yuriko, and she was staring at her.

"What chu waiting on, Skeeza? Roll up. I'ma guest here, shit." She flipped through the cable channels until she found Pineapple Express on Cinemax.

Yuriko reluctantly did as Joseline told her.

Joseline had just poured herself a glass of white wine and lay back on the couch when the doorbell chimed. "I got it." She told Yuriko heading for the door. Joseline took a quick glance through the curtains and found one of the cops that were assigned to watch the house on the doorstep.

"Who is it?" Yuriko asked.

"It's just one of the cops that's watching this place." Joseline told her. "Put that away, will you?" she said, referring to the tray of Zig-Zags and broken down Kush.

Joseline opened the door, but all she could see was a dark figure on the other side of the iron screen-door. She flipped on the light-switch and gave birth to a ray of light on the porch. The light filled out the officer's Haitian features. He had smooth dark skin and hair as thick as wool. His slender face boasted a friendly smile of cocaine white teeth as he chewed on Double Mint gum.

"Hi, how are you doing?" The Haitian officer greeted Joseline. "I'm sorry to bother you, but do you think I could use your bathroom? I had a Big Gulp and now it's wreaking havoc on my bladder."

"Uh huh." She smiled and nodded. "You sure it isn't number #2 that you have to do?"

"Scouts honor." He smiled, holding up his crossed fingers.

"All right." She gave a halfhearted smile, unlocking the door and let him in.

The officer smiled at Yuriko and gave her a nod. He looked the living room over, taking in its décor. "This is a nice place you girls have here." He commented.

"I thought you guys had to cut your hair once you joined the force." Joseline noticed his fluffy ponytail. "They are letting y'all rock ponytails now?"

"When it's part of your religion they can't make you cut it." He told her as he pulled on his length of ponytail.

"Ouch." Joseline frowned, staring at something on his shirt. The Haitian officer looked to her with a look of confusion. "The blood on your collar." She pointed to it.

He looked to the droplets of blood on his collar. "Oh, that's nothing. I cut my self shaving this morning."

Joseline's forehead wrinkled, seeing that he was wearing a 5 o'clock shadow. She looked to his name tag. "Well, the bathroom is down the hall and to the left, Officer…" she waited for him to fill in the blank.

There was a silence before he answered.

"Uhhh, Mills." He replied. "Officer Mills."

The name on the tag read: Jenkins.

"Yuriko, run," Joseline hollered to her best friend and kneed the officer in his balls, dropping him on his ass.

"Arghhh, you…fuckin' bitch." Kamal grimaced and pulled the police issued firearm from its holster. He staggered to his booted feet and drew a bead on Joseline as she ran for the hallway behind Yuriko.

Pop! Pop! Pop!

The gun recoiled as he cracked off triplet rounds, dropping her while she was in motion. She slowly crawled on her stomach toward the opening of the hallway, wincing with tears in her eyes.

"Uhhhh." Her face was a mask of pain as she crawled forward, using her manicured nails like they were claws pulling herself forward.

"Fuckin' whore!" Kamal limped toward her, holding his family jewels with one hand while the other gripped his head bussa. He stopped at her foot and mashed his boot against her ankle, immobilizing her. He leveled his steel at her skull, depositing three hot ones into the back of her cranium.

Pop! Pop! Pop!

Blood and pieces of brain bubbled from out of the holes and flowed out onto the floor.

Kamal pulled a second gun of his own from his waistline. Both guns held up at his shoulders, he cautiously moved down the corridor, taunting Yuriko as he went along. "Come out! Come out! Where ever you are!" He called out through the hallway. "You know, sweetheart, you could save me the trouble and kill yourself. How about it? Huh?" He asked, sliding across the wall and down the hallway. She didn't answer. "Fine then, have it your way!"

Kamal swung out into the doorway of the kitchen and met a roar of fire produced from a Zippo-lighter and a can of Raid bug spray.

"Rahhhh!" The hit man threw his head back and screamed at the top of his lungs as he was instantly set ablaze. He screamed like a banshee, spinning around and around in circles as he headed down the hall, dropping one of his guns. Yuriko dropped the bug spray and Zippo-lighter and took off toward the living room. She grabbed a firewood poker from beside the fireplace and repeatedly whacked the burning man as he spun around.

"Mothafucka!" Her face twisted with rage as she swung the poker, her arms looking like blurs while in motion.

Whack! Whaack! Whaaack! Whaaaack!

Bwap!

He cracked her in the jaw, which caused her to stagger backwards. She crashed to the floor and staggered bak up on her feet, massaging her aching jaw. After shaking off her daze, she lifted the firewood poker over her head and charged at him, only to be met with a copper laced bullet through the throat.

Blocka!

Yuriko fell back on the carpet kicking her right leg aimlessly and clutching her bleeding throat, reddish black blood seeping between her fingers. She gurgled up blood trying to say something and ran from both corners of her mouth, pooling at opposite ends of the floor.

Kamal wrapped himself in the curtains, suffocating the flames and extinguishing them. He emerged from the curtains smoking and with patches of hair missing. The skin of his face looked like a slab of barbecued ribs. The hit man clenched his jaws tightly trying to fight back the pain.

"Grrrr!" Gripping his banger, he straddled Yuriko and pressed his gun into her mouth causing her to gag.

"Gaggg." She tried to whip her head away from him, but the burner was too far into his grill.

He smiled wickedly and said to her, "Au revoir," which means goodbye in French before pulling the trigger and painting the floor with her blood and brain fragments. Specs of blood smacked him in the face as he closed his eyes. He climbed off of Yuriko's mutilated body and staggered down the hallway into the bathroom. Kamal looked himself over in the medicine cabinet mirror. Horrified and disgusted with the reflection he saw staring back at him, he slammed his fist into the mirror creating a spider's web. Afterwards, he then rummaged through the medicine cabinet gathering any medication for pain he could find. He threw back Aspirin,

Tylenol, Excedrin, and Motrin and washed them down with Nyquil. Angry, he slammed the bottle of Nyquil to the floor and walked out of the bathroom.

Stepping out onto Yuriko's porch, Kamal heard the sirens of approaching police cars. Across the street he saw one of the cops he'd shot slumped up against his squad car clutching a radio transceiver. The hit man knew that he was still alive because he could hear him groaning in pain. With that knowledge he moved to put him out of his misery, but when half a dozen of police cars came skidding to a halt before him, he changed his mind and made a run for it. As he ran along he occasionally stopped to let off a shot or two. He was able to lay down four cops in his wake, but once he reached the corner of the block he was quickly surrounded by police cars. He looked around as officers hopped out of their vehicles and drew down on him. With the way things were looking he knew that it was all over for him and he didn't give a fuck about dying. He was a killer so death came with the territory.

Kamal smiled and laughed maniacally. "Hahahahahaha! Fuck y'all niggaz, I'm out this bitch!"

He pressed his head bussa underneath his chin and pulled the trigger.

Blocka!

***

"Like I told you, Detective Freeman, I was at a party out in Westchester that night. It's a handful of people that can vouch for that." Malakai lied with a straight face. He was sitting beside Herman inside of the interrogation room. Detective Freeman had been hitting him with a barrage of questions trying to trip him up and get him to admit to something he hadn't meant to. His efforts went unrewarded though. The hustler was a veteran when it came to interrogations. He'd been under the scrutiny of the law before and it had only sharpened him.

"I used to be a matador, so I know bullshit when I smell it," The detective told him with a dead serious expression etched across his face.

The door opened and Detective Flannerty stuck his head inside. "Freeman, you wanna step out here for a sec?" he asked, adjusting his tie.

Freeman stepped out into the hallway. His partner said something to him that Malakai and Herman couldn't quite make out, but whatever it was it sent the detective flying off the handle. The door of the interrogation room rattled violently from the brute force of punches and kicks. The agitated detective came barging back into the interrogation room with madness in his eyes. Herman was on the edge but the boy Malakai wasn't moved. He wore a smirk on his lips. He already knew what had happened. Hell, he'd arranged everything.

"You think this is pretty fucking funny, don't chu?" Freeman fumed, turning red, nostrils flaring.

That bit of news stung the young hustler but he held his game face. "Yeah, it's a riot. I'd like to go now. Is that alright?"

Enraged, Freeman snatched Malakai up by the front of his shirt and cocked back his fist to punch him. He stared the young hustler in the eyes with wickedness only the devil could conjure up.

Herman cleared his throat. "Detective Freeman, if that will be all of the questions you wish to ask my client we'll be taking our leave now."

The detective released him and threw his head towards the door. "Get the fuck outta my sight!"

Herman headed out of the interrogation room with his client on his heels. He stopped in the doorway and turned back around to hotheaded law enforcer. “Have a nice day, Detective. Hahahahahaha!” He laughed heartily, closing the door behind him.

***

Boom!

The doors of the emergency room came flying open as Kamal was pushed on a gurney, hospital staff running along beside him. An oxygen mask was slipped over his head and placed over his nose and mouth. A doctor with latex gloved hands held open each of his eyes as he inspected them with a small flashlight. When the hit man pressed his gun under his chin and pulled the trigger it clicked empty, a police officer shot him in his elbow causing him to drop his weapon. He was then shot in his leg which dropped him to the sidewalk. The Boys quickly moved in and cuffed his burnt ass. Now here he was clinging onto life while doctors tried to save him death.

Three hours later

When Kamal’s eyes fluttered open he found himself wearing a hospital gown and handcuffed to the railing of his bed, an overhead light illuminating his face. His head moved around the room, but it was too dark for him to see anything. He looked to the door and there was a police officer guarding it. Having grown frustrated with the situation, he yanked and yanked on the railing causing it to make a clinking sound. The noise drew the police officer’s attention. Once he peeked inside and saw that the killer was awake, he turned to some people in the hall talking to them. A moment later Detective Flannerty and Freeman came through the door. The latter had a small tablet and a pen ready to jot down any information he could get. What the two dicks didn’t know was that killers bred like Kamal would rather face death than to rat. The hit man looked from left to right taking in the two badges before letting his head drop back down into the pillow. Closing his eyes, his mouth shot open and he laughed manically. He turned his head all of the way to the right and threw it to the left fast, snapping his own neck.

Snaaap!

The detectives frowned and looked at one another not believing what they'd just witnessed. They couldn't fathom a man breaking his own neck to escape prosecution. Cautiously, Detective Freeman leaned over him and checked the pulse in his neck. He was dead and wearing a smile on his face.

With Joseline and Yuriko out of the picture, Malakai had time to focus on the nigga at the top of his Shit List, Showtime.

CHAPTER FIVE

Mrs. Williams pulled up on 77th and Figueroa outside of a brown and tan colored home with a rusting fence and a dirt patched lawn. Once she killed the engine, she grabbed her cane and threw her the driver side door open. She made her way around her Benz and stepped upon the curb. As she approached the house she was seeking, she found a congregation of thugs down on their knees shooting dice. Cluttered around them were plastic cups of dark liquor, a Hennessy bottle, and cans of Olde English 800. The embers of cigarettes and blunts glowed and the smell of nicotine stunk up the air as smoke was expelled. Amongst these roughnecks was a man with a muscular upper body, sitting up in a wheelchair that resembled a fancy motorcycle. He was rocking a doo-rag with a flap and a tank top which a couple of thin gold necklaces lay over. The cat fidgeted with a toothpick at the corner of his mouth as he watched the crap game, occasionally taking sips of dark liquor from a plastic cup.

"Bet he don't six or eight, Tip Toe." The nigga in the wheelchair grabbed two wrinkled ten dollar bills from a stack of money he'd won that night lying on his lap.

"Nigga, bet," The man said like it wasn't nothing for him to bet that, throwing a twenty dollar bill near the challenger's chair. The two ten's were drover from the man black leather weight lifting gloved hand, landing on top of the other man's bills.

"Seven!" some of the thugs called out in unison.

"Shiieeet!" the man that had crapped out, stood up and kicked over his cup of liquor, spilling it. With his losing came the rest of his homies scrambling to gather their winnings, the cat in the fancy chair included. He scooped up his winnings and kissed them, smiling and showcasing his lone gold tooth. He dropped the bills on his lap onto of the other money. Scooping the dice up, he rattled them inside of his fist.

"Who got me faded?" he asked, grinning and ready to break a nigga for all he had.

"I got my back." Tip Toe threw down a twenty dollar bill.

Homeboy was about to roll the dice when Mrs. Williams called his name.

"Isaiah!" she called out to the stud in the wheelchair. Isaiah was his government name but on the streets he was called Gatz, because that's what he dealt in, guns. If you needed to get your hands on some iron, he was most definitely the man you needed to see. He had every firearm you could think of and he sold them all at a reasonable price.

Gatz and a couple of the thugs looked up. When they saw the old woman they focused back on the game. All of them accept the man in the wheelchair.

"Mrs. Williams, is that you?" he leaned forth, narrowing his eyes for a better look at her.

"Yes, young man, its Mrs. Williams." She gave him a warm smile. "I need to have a word with you."

"Oh yeah?"

"Yes. You gotta minute?"

"Sure." He passed the dotted white cubes to the dude beside him and snatched up his two ten's. After literally stuffing his winnings into his pocket, he rolled over to the fence and unlatched it. "Heeey, Mrs. Williams, what can I do for you?" he asked, adjusting the side view mirror on his fancy wheelchair.

The old lady took a cautious scan of her surroundings as if someone would over hear her discussion with the man sitting before her.

"I needa gun, Isaiah." She spoke in a hushed tone.

His forehead wrinkled. "Who messing witchu, moms? If it's a problem you ain't gotta lift no iron, me and mine will take care of that." He threw his gloved hand over his chest, meaning every word that came out of his mouth.

"No, no, no." she shook her head and cackled. "It's nothing like that, sugah." She patted his leg. "I just need something to protect my home. You know it's just me there now since Malakai is gone. I'd feel much safer knowing that I had a gun within arm's reach when I go to lay my head down at night, ya know?"

"I hear you." he nodded his understanding. "You sure you wouldn't feel more comfortable getting yo'self a registered piece, though? You know all of mine are off of the books so if you get caught with one of my babies you're looking at a felony."

"No. I'd much rather purchase it from you if that's fine."

"Well, I'm not 'bout ta convince you to spend ya money somewhere else. Follow me." He whipped around in his wheelchair and motioned for her to follow him, rolling toward the side of the house and heading to the garage. When he reached the door he lifted it and motioned her inside. She hunched over and made her way inside. He wheeled inside right behind her and closed the door shut.

"What chu looking for, moms?"

"A gun, any gun that holds at least ten shots." She nodded, holding her purse at her waist.

"Alright, I got just the thing." Gatz pulled open a dented up refrigerator and removed its door's panel, revealing several guns hanging on hooks. He outstretched his hand and unhooked a black compact handgun, passing it to her. The gun merchant lay back in his wheelchair, tapping his gold wedding band finger on the chrome rim of the chair causing it to make a cling sound. His attentive eyes watched the old lady close one eye and point the deadly weapon around the garage.

"What kind of gun is this?" she asked curiously.

"Taurus .9mm." Gatz stuck a toothpick into his mouth.

"How much?"

"Umm," he closed one eye and angled his head, massaging his chin thinking. "For you Mrs. Williams? Two fifty."

"Sold." She stuck the gun into her coat's pocket and taking her pocketbook out, pulling out three crisp one hundred dollars bills. After she passed him the money, she watched as he counted it, his toothpick dancing at the corner of his mouth as his lips slightly moved. "Are we good?"

"Yeah." He nodded, having finished counting the money.

"Goodnight." She made to turn around but he called her back. She looked at him with raised eyebrows, looking like she was saying What is it?

"Limmie see that piece, please." His hand grasped the barrel and he wiped the weapon down with a rag, passing it back to her. "There you go."

"Take it easy, young man." she said as she ducked her and went under the garage door as he held it open.

He plucked the toothpick from between his lips and said, "Yes, ma'am, you too, and please don't be a stranger." He smiled watching her back as she walked off, his only old tooth twinkled.

Mrs. Williams was off to make what she felt was wrong right.

The next day

Showtime and his crew rolled through the pillars of Inglewood cemetery three cars deep. He, Treasure, Skylar,Tyson, Dead Beat and Keith occupied the stretch

Mercedes, while the black on black Denali and H2 Hummer brought up the rear. Stashed inside was the rest of the Big Willies owner's entourage, which consisted of everyone from his personal assistant down to the street cats he came up with from his old neighborhood. Reporters, journalists, radio personalities and cameramen from just about every news station, news paper, radio station and hip-hop magazine littering the rich green lawn of the cemetery. The hordes of media moved in on the stretched Mercedes as it neared Blessyn's burial site, traveling down the paved path.

"Fuck they know we were coming?" Keith pulled to a stop, checking his surroundings through the black tinted windows. The media had swamped the Mercedes like a swarm of locusts, snapping pictures and tapping on the glass.

"I don't know, Keith. It seems like a brotha can't go anywhere without getting a camera, microphone, and/or pussy thrown in his face." Showtime shook his head shamefully, but he was fronting. See, he was the one that tipped the media outlets to them coming to visit Blessyn's gravestone that day. He figured the coverage would be good promotion for Treasure's upcoming album.

"I hear you, but I'm not complaining about the pussy, though." Keith cracked a smile.

"Shit. Me neither." Showtime showcased his gold fangs when he smiled, dapping him up.

"Y'all are some pigs." Skylar shook her head like Look at these mothafuckaz.

"I'm notta pig, I'ma mothafucking dog. Woof! Woof! Woof!" Keith barked and laughed.

"I don't get it," Dead Beat began, looking outside of the window. "We visit Blessyn's grave every year on his birthday and the media's never here. Now all of a sudden they pop up outta nowhere? Either somebody's gotta big mouth, or these reporters and journalists been doing their homework."

"Nah, it's some big mouth on our side, I'ma have to put a gag order on the nigga once I find out who he is," Showtime told Dead Beat as he looked himself over in the sun-visor mirror. He checked his nose for visible boogers and his teeth for pieces of food before spraying his mouth with banocka.

"I got the gag," Keith flashed his holstered .45. "You just give the order."

Showtime grinned and shook his head, closing the sun-visor.

"Fucking clown," Tyson said under his breath of Keith. He locked scowls with the killer through the rearview mirror. He had heard his insult. They mad dogged each other until a whimpering and sniffled brought Tyson's head around to Treasure. Her eyes were rimming with tears as she stared down at a picture of she and Blessyn from some time ago. In the photo she was smiling from ear to ear as he kissed her on the cheek in a brotherly way.

Tyson looked down at the picture and then back up at his girl. "You two had a thing?"

Treasure shook her head. "No. Blessyn was like my big brother. He was a genuinely good dude, you know? As cliché as it sounds, he was the type of brotha that would give you the shirt off of his back, which is why I don't understand how God could just up and take him like that. You got all of these rapists, pedophiles, serial killers and scumbags to choose from and you pick the realest nigga to have ever been squeezed out from between a woman's legs to call home? I mean…" frustrated, she blew hard and wiped her eyes with Kleenex from her handbag. "I don't know." She wiped her snotty with the tissues and balled it up.

Tyson took her hand and caressed it sweetly. "Don't try to understand how the Almighty moves, 'cause it will drive you crazy. Believe me I know. I done lost more loved ones than I can count on both hands. All we can ask of the Lord is that he give us the strength to overcome all of the hardships and struggles he sends our way 'cause like it or not, this is his show, we're all just on the center stage, you Griff me?" She nodded yes and with his pointer finger, he turned her to face him and kissed her lips.

Showtime put on his shades and turned to the backseat. "Y'all ready?"

Tyson made sure his twin .45s were secure in their holsters and grabbed Treasure's hand firmly. "Yeah, I'm ready," she told him and turned to his love. "You ready?" she nodded and gave him a halfhearted smile.

Showtime gave Keith a nod and he hopped out to open the door for his boss.

As soon as millionaire tycoon and his entourage stepped foot on cemetery grounds they were swarmed by the media. Treasure got everything from cameras to microphones to pens and paper shoved in her face for autographs. Showtime motioned the journalists and reporters in so that he could address them. He was hit with a barrage of questions to which he ignored and said into the microphones held before him, "Treasure will not be signing any autographs, taking any pictures, or answering any questions until after we've all paid our respects." The whole time he was talking camera phones and video cameras were flashing in his face. "That will be all." He moved forth with his entourage strong arming a path to Blessyn's gravestone.

When they finally made it to late rapper's black marble gravestone there were small stuffed animals, candles, balloons and a bouquet of dead brittle roses surrounding it.

Showtime removed the dead brittle roses from the gravestone and replaced it with fresh ones. Treasure came to his side and placed the picture beside Showtime's roses. Showtime gave everyone in his entourage wine glasses and filled them with red wine. They had a moment of silence in Blessyn's honor and sipped the alcohol. They then went around telling some of the funniest and memorable times they'd shared with the gangsta rapper. While everyone was sharing their stories video cameras were rolling and camera phones were flashing. Once they were finished paying respects, Treasure answered all of the questions from the media and signed what seemed like a million autographs being that her fingers and wrists were aching.

"Unfortunately ladies and gentlemen we have to be going," Showtime told all of the media outlets present.

"Don't forget Treasure's newest album 'Forever me' will be in stores September 26th. Also, be on the lookout for her second single Immortal featuring Blessyn; we're dropping the video for it next month." Showtime threw up the peace sign and made way for the limo with his entourage clearing a path.

Moving through the mass of bodies with Treasure by his side, Tyson took a brief glance over his shoulder and saw a blue van in the distance. The van seemed out of place sitting there, but he paid it no mind reasoning that it was probably one of the news stations vans. With that thought pushed to the back of his mental, he continued on his way back to the Mercedes limousine.

***

From the passenger seat of a blue van, Malakai watched Showtime and his entourage head back to their rides through binoculars. "There they go."

"Yo, B, hurry up and pull off. We can cut them off at the gates." Crazy said from the back of the van, where he was crouched down between Malakai and Bizeal. He was in a black T-shirt with a ski-mask resting on top of his head. His gloved hands gripped an M-16 assault rifle with a drum. He tapped his steel-toe boot on the floor, anxious to send Showtime and his entourage to that big recording label in the sky.

Bizeal sat behind the wheel smoking a cigarette. He was clad in all black as well. Only he donned a black beanie and sweatshirt. He flicked his cigarette out of the window, sending embers flying along with it before resurrecting the engine. Right then, Malakai grabbed his hand.

"Nah, hold up," he told him.

"Fuck you mean? We gotta burn this nigga before he gets away." Bizeal frowned.

"You got us up here strapped up, locked and loaded. I'm ready to send these mothafuckaz on their way." Crazy spat.

"Yo' lil' hot ass is always ready to jump outta the window, why don't chu take the time out to carefully observe yo' surroundings." Malakai nodded to the side view mirror. When Crazy took a glance, he was surprised. He was so excited to kill something that he didn't even scan the area before he made his move.

"For real? I didn't even see them crackas, man." Bizeal forehead wrinkled when he glanced in the side view mirror. At the gates of the cemetery, he spotted several police cruisers.

"Fuck!" Crazy bellowed punching the wall of the van. He was pissed off that he wasn't going to be adding a couple more bodies to his resume.

"Fuck is wrong with you? Throwing a tantrum like a fucking three-year-old," Bizeal snarled, nostrils flaring.

"Y'all niggaz relax, you'll get cho chance for some action. You've just gotta be patient," Malakai told them as he watched Showtime and his entourage drove off through the binoculars.

Yeahhh, rest assure you gon' most definitely get what chu got coming to you, best believe that, he thought, nodding his head with an evil grin on his lips.

That night

Tyson lay submerged in soapy hot water with Treasure lying against him. Their faces and upper half of their bodies were shiny from perspiration and the steam rising from the water. Along the edge of porcelain tub were vanilla scented candles burning with flames. The light from the candles flickered off of the egg shell white walls and casted shadows. Treasure's cellular lay beside the tub on the tiled floor. Keith Sweat's Make it last forever blared from the device, serenading them. Their eyes were shut, and their faces formed jovial expressions.

"Tyson."

"Hmmm?"

"What did you get locked up for?"

Tyson peeled his eyelids open and took a deep breath; he sat up inside of the tub. "Well, I knew this was coming sooner or later."

"You don't have to tell me if you don't want to, babe. Your past is your past, I'm only concerned about our future together."

"Nah, you my boo, so you should know. I don't want any secrets between us." He interlocked his fingers with hers and brought it to his mouth, kissing it tenderly. He then turned toward her, kissing her mouth with just a little tongue. They pecked lips and went back into their positions. "Alright…" Tyson began to tell the story.

***

With the help of a private investigator Tyson was able to track down his mother. She was living with her husband in Calabasas, a suburb of Los Angeles County. He wanted to sit down with her and see why she had left her family for another man. No matter how hard he tried he couldn't understand how a woman could walk out on her children and her husband of eleven years. Tyson had tried to get Moon to roll up out there with him, but he chose to stay behind. So, he went out there alone on Christmas night, thinking that she'd be happy to see him. He knocked on the door, but he didn't get an answer. Figuring that they probably couldn't hear him because of the holiday music playing, he went around the front of the house where he saw a window when he'd first driven up.

Tyson peered through the window with his hands cupped around his face, trying to get a good look through the dirt smudged glass. His eyes looked around until they landed on his mother and her new husband who were sitting on the couch watching their kids tear open the last of their gifts which were sitting beneath a well-lit Christmas tree. Seeing this enraged him being that these kinds of moments were stolen from him and his older brother because their mother had left them for another man. He could feel his skin growing hot as his blood boiled to a scorching temperature. His ears warmed and he could literally feel steam rising off the back of his neck.

"Fredrick, you mind pouring the kids some eggnog before you take out the trash?" he heard his mother, Belinda, ask of her husband.

"Alright. Y'all come on." He waved the children along. A couple of minutes later the kids came running back inside of the living room with cups of eggnog with their father trailing behind. He walked across Tyson's line of vision with a garbage bag. Seeing this, he pulled his .45 off of his waistline. Careful not to be seen, he crept alongside of the house and stooped low in the bushes, his tool held up at his shoulder. With his head turned toward the door, he listened closely as the door was unchained and unlocked. There was a screech as it was pulled open. He peeked from where he was kneeled in the bushes, seeing Fredrick's silhouette with the garbage bag, pushing open the door. The old man pushed the glasses back upon his face and stepped out onto the porch.

Listening to Fredrick shuffling about, Tyson wiped his tear streaked face with the back of his fist. Seeing that he was nearing, he raised his gun and pulled the trigger. His strap jerked violently as it spat heat, striking his victim's kneecap and leg. He dropped to the porch losing the garbage bag in the process and howling in pain.

"Oh my God!" Belinda hollered out, seeing what had happened from the doorway.

Soon as she said that, Tyson emerged from out of the bushes with twigs and loose leaves on him. He smacked the remnants from the bushes off of his shoulder and took his time coming up the steps, gun gripped in his hand. His vindictive eyes watched as Fredrick attempted to crawl away wincing. He constantly looked over his shoulder as he pulled his weight toward the front door, leaving blood smears in his wake.

"You take my momma away from me and my brotha, break my father's heart? And expect to live happily ever after? Uh uh," he shook his head like You despicable mothafucka. "You gotta 'notha thang coming, homeboy. You got the right one in this one here." He smacked his hand against his left breast where his heart resided, pumping the blood into the body of one of the thuggest niggaz there ever was.

Tyson came up the steps casually, his accusing eyes focused on Fredrick. The old man looked like he saw water being turned into wine.

"Oh, please, please, please, I've haven't done anything." He bitched up like he slipped on a thong instead of boxers that morning. "She's a grown woman; I didn't force her to do anything."

"You didn't stop her either, mothafucka!" he gritted, tears cascaded down on the cheeks. Hearing police cars hurrying to his location, he figured he should hurry and push this nigga'z wig back. Fredrick squeezed his eyes shut and mouthed a silent prayer, waiting for a bullet to send him where everybody and their momma had wings. Tyson applied pressure to the trigger. It made a slight squeak as he began to pull it back and that's when it happened.

"Tyson, nooooooo!" a voice bellowed from the doorway.

Tyson's head snapped up and his eyes met the tear streaked face of his mother. Her hands trembled uncontrollably as she was fearful of what her youngest son may do to her husband. Standing beside her were their children that they had together. Tyson's face tightened with anger and he swung his banger up, pointing it at her. Her and her children were startled, they moved backwards, afraid of getting blasted on.

"Bitch, I should shoot chu dead in yo' mouth for even flapping yo' tongue at me," He growled, nostrils flaring up and his eyelids narrowing. "You left both of yo' sons and yo' muthafucking husband over some dick?" He angled his head and tightened his eyes at her, like Bitch I can't believe you.

"Baby, I…"

"Shut up! Shut up! You shut. The. Fuck. Up," He demanded, spit jumping off of his lips, they all cried out afraid that they were going to catch some hot fire from the end of his gun. The thug settled his finger on the trigger. He was about to set it off but the thought of being haunted for the rest of his life knowing that he'd murdered his own mother stopped him. How could he lay down the woman that gave birth to him and his brother? No matter how foul she was, she was still untouchable in his eyes. Not only by others but his hands as well. He lowered his gun and darted out towards the streets. As soon as his Chuck Taylor Converse graced the black top, he was swarmed by police cruisers. He spun around looking for some place to run but he was surrounded. Seeing that they had him by the balls, he tossed his burner and lifted his hands in the air surrendering.

Present

"I acted off of my emotions like a female and when I think about that now…" Tyson trailed off shaking his head as he balled his fist tight, biting down on his bottom lip. He shut his eyes and then peeled them back open. "…When I think about that now, I wish I could go back in time and stop myself from doing that shit. Homeboy didn't deserve them bullets that came outta my gun. That nigga didn't owe my father shit, they weren't family or homies. As far as my mom's goes, she lost a great man in my father. We're talking about a cat that bent over backwards to provide for his family, and what did he get from her in return? Her ass to kiss!"he shook his head, like it was a goddamn shame. "As much as I hear that niggaz ain't shit, these hoes ain't shit either."

"I can contest to that," Treasure conceded. "Well, where are they now?"

"Who? My mom's and her old man?"

"Uh huh." She nodded.

"Last I heard they moved out to Hartford, Connecticut."

"You haven't heard from your mother?"

"Nah, I don't care to either. Fuck her."

Treasure nodded her understanding.

Knock! Knock! Knock!

"Who is it?" Tyson hollered over his shoulder.

"It's Show. Y'all throw on something when you come out. I'm taking everyone out to get fresh and fly for my big bash, on me." His voice boomed from the opposite side of the door.

"Alright."

"You wanna get out now, Ty?" she looked up at him, seeing his nostrils and underneath his chin. "I was thinking that we could sit here just a little while longer."

"That's what chu wanna do?" his eyes lowered, and he smirked.

"Uh huh." Her eyes lowered and she smirked too.

They kissed slow and sensually. She turned around and he wrapped his arms around her. He leaned his head back and she rested her head back against his chest. They shut their eyes enjoying the warmth of one another's bodies and the rhythms of their heart beats.

***

When Showtime and his clan entered through the doors of Leon's the employees broke their necks trying to attend to their every beck and call. They knew when he came to spend, he came to spend big, real big. The employees made him, and his crew felt like royalty while they were shopping. They were served flutes of Moet and horderves; this was the kind of treatment all of the ballers received when they came through the store.

Tyson lay back in a black suede sofa chair sipping champagne and watching Treasure as she modeled various ensembles for him. Ten outfits later she ended up with a beautiful strapless white dress with a thick gold belt, gold heels with a small buckle at the feet, and a matching handbag. She also copped the other nine dresses she'd tried on before they left the store.

While Treasure, Showtime, and Keith bought their gear from the Leon's, Tyson opted to go across the street to the Louie Vuitton store. He tried on two fits before he settled on what he was going to hit the club wearing. He stuck with a LV beanie, shades, a black and gray checkered print scarf, an LV sweat shirt, with matching belt and sneakers.

Dead Beat was the only one out of the clique that didn't hit a high end department store. He opted to get his garbs from a second hand thrift shop. He had a style all of his own. He picked up a tall hat, a blazer, a Donald Duck T-shirt; stone washed jeans which had tears at the knees and a pair of Vans. He also picked up a pair of cheap shades. With that last item accounted for, his outfit for the night was complete.

Once all of the shopping was wrapped up, everyone went to grub up at Treasure's favorite place to eat, McDonald's. The ride back to Showtime's mansion was fairly quiet, save for the scoffing of food and the sound of straws vacuuming up the last of the beverage in their cups.

"You know, Tyson, I've been talking things over with the team and we've all agreed that we'd like to continue to have you on board after your time is up here, if you'd have us of course." Showtime said before taking a sip of his Strawberry milkshake.

Tyson looked from Dead Beat to Treasure who were both wearing smiles. He looked to Keith, and he had a plain expression. He couldn't tell if his eyes were on him though, they were shielded behind tinted shades, and he was eating Chicken McNuggets.

"You mean you don't have anything to say?" Tyson asked him, raising an eyebrow.

"Nope," Keith answered, dipping a chicken nugget into sweet & sour sauce and biting into it.

"You aren't pissed that I'm being extended this offer?" he looked at him like Nigga, I know you've got something to say. Tyson leaned forward, clasping his hands together trying to read Keith. He couldn't believe he wasn't bitching and complaining. The throwback gangsta made it known when Tyson first met him that he didn't want him riding with Big Willie records.

"Nah, you're all right with me, kid," Keith wiped his mouth and hands with a napkin before balling it up. "You've made your bones. It would be an honor to have you on the team." He extended his hand to Tyson, and he gave him the side eyes, twisting his lips. No one could tell him that something wasn't up.

"Is this nigga serious?" Tyson looked to Showtime and pointed a finger to Keith.

"Are you kidding?" Showtime asked, looking at him like he should know better. "My uncle doesn't have a sense of humor. He's the most serious cat I know."

Tyson blew hot hard and said, "All right," shaking Keith's hand.

"So, you'll stay?" Showtime asked Tyson as he rubbed his hands together.

"Yeah." He smiled and nodded. "I'll stay."

"Welcome aboard. Here's to the family," Big Willie's CEO raised his cup up.

Treasure kissed Tyson on the cheek and raised her cup along with everyone else.

“To the family,” They all said in unison touching their cups.

CHAPTER SIX

Snikt! Snikt! Snikt!

The katana blade sounded as it sliced through the melons hanging from the branches of an apricot tree in the backyard of Dartanian's mansion. The melons were still for a time then their bottom halves came loose and fell to the ground, one by one. The bear of a man stood surrounded by the large green ripe fruits. He was clad in a wife beater, sweatpants and oriental, thick wood bottom sandals. His head, face, and body, all glistened with beads of sweat. His hairy chest heaved up and down as he breathed heavily. His meaty hands clutched the handle of his katana, holding it out stretched with his left knee bending forth.

He paused in his pose for a moment, and then suddenly, he spun on his heels swinging the blade like the master swordsman he was. It whistled through the air and the other halves of the melons hit the ground at his feet. While in the motion of swinging the katana, he swung around and sliced off one of the twins' mane of curly hair. The mane of curly hair floated in the air like a lone leaf before settling on the ground. The twin's face was frozen with bug eyes and an open mouth. She stood as still as a mannequin in a department store window. She thought that at any minute blood would come running down her face and the top of her skull would fall to the ground at her feet.

"Am I…am I, okay?" Eliza managed to get out. She was the oldest of the twins by four minutes.

"You're fine," Dartanian told her. "I only got your mane."

"Are you sure?" she asked, touching her forehead for blood.

"Positive. Your talking is confirmation enough," he assured her, sheathing his katana. "I told you and your sister about wondering so close when I'm out here practicing, I could have taken that pretty lil' head of yours off. This blade is sharp enough to pierce stone." He claimed, wiping his face with a white towel, and then throwing it over his shoulder. "Where's your sister?"

"She's inside of the gym," she replied.

Dartanian sat his cane down on the table and cut the end off of a Cuban cigar, sparking it up, taking the time to blow smoke up into the air.

"Do the two of you have any plans tonight?"

"No. We were just gonna kick it at home and watch Netflix and eat Napoleon ice cream." She sat down at the table. "Why? You've got any place in mind you'd like to go tonight?"

"Indeed I do." He pushed a flyer before her and she picked it up, looking it over.

"I heard about this, daddy. This is the big birthday bash at Nocturnal for Showtime, the CEO of Big Willie records," she said excitedly, a big ass smile on her cute baby face.

"Sure is. He's an old acquaintance of mine. We've been invited," he informed her. "Think you and your sister are up to roll out tonight?"

"Hell yeah!"

"Great." He smiled, mashing out his cigar and pulling out his wallet. "I want chu two to take my black card and go shopping. Buy yourselves something real nice, okay?" he slid his black American Express card before her and her eyes lit up like a winning slot machine in Vegas.

"Okay, thank you, baby." Eliza hopped out of the chair and ran over to him, planting kisses all over his face. "Rashidaaaaaa!" she ran back toward the mansion screaming her sister's name, anxious to go shopping for the night's big shindig.

***

"Yo, we need to be there if you wanna get this nigga," Bizeal said from the couch, having just finished sprinkling weed into a swisher. He was now in the process of licking it closed.

"Oh, we're most def' gon' be in that thang, best believe that." Malakai spoke from the love seat where Dakeemia was perched on his lap, running her hand up the back of his neck and head. One hand had a firm grip on her thick chocolate thigh while the other held the flyer to a gentlemen's club called Nocturnal. This was the same club Showtime was having his big birthday bash. "If that scandalous ass nigga gon' be up in the spot, then we are too. I'ma gon' avenge my brotha." He stared ahead at nothing, scowling and nostrils flaring. He balled up the club flyer and let it drop at his feet.

"How the hell are we gon' get them thangs in there? You know security gon' be extra tight," Crazy said, never taking his eyes off the flat screen TV which he was holding a remote control to.

"Wait, D, didn't you use to work there?" Bizeal sat up on the couch.

"Yeah, the owner keeps trying to get me to come back. That midget mothafucka has been ringing my phone off the hook."

The wheels of Malakai's mind began turning and he massaged his chin, thinking on it.

"Baby, you think he'll let chu work that bash tonight?" he asked his lady.

"Oh, most def'," she answered, tracing his face with a manicured nail as she placed soft kisses on his cheek.

"Boo, you sure?" he looked to her for reassurance.

"Uh huh." She tilted his chin up so that he would be looking up into her eyes. Her bottom lip swept up against his and her tongue slithered inside of his mouth. They kissed passionately, angling their heads and murmuring.

Briiiing! Briiiing! Briiiing!

Dakeemia placed her Bluetooth on her ear and picked up her cell phone to see who it was calling her. Shorty was on the screen accompanied by a picture of a midget with long dreads dressed up like a rapper.

"Babe, this him right here," she informed her man. When she said this everyone gave her their undivided attention.

"Crazy, turn that shit down." Once the volume was lowered, Malakai looked to his boo. "You think you can sneak us some straps up in there?"

"I can do that. They don't check any of the girls that work there."

"Alright, answer it." He nodded.

Dakeemia pressed the button on her Bluetooth and answered the call.

"Boss man, what's up? Oh, of course I can work tonight. I could use the extra money."

Malakai, Bizeal and Crazy all exchanged glances, smiling sinisterly. Tonight was the night that Blessyn's murder would be avenged.

Later that night

Celebrities, ghetto stars, and underworld players came out to celebrate with Showtime for his 37th birthday. DJ Felli Fel announced the CEO of Big Willie records arrival as soon as his Mauri Italian leather shoes crossed the threshold of Club Nocturnal. He was razor blade sharp in a charcoal gray apple jack, a black silk shirt that was unbuttoned to boast his chiseled chest and hug his bulging biceps and charcoal gray slacks. He accessorized with his gold crucifix necklace and a gold black face presidential Rolex watch. Colorful balloons, glitter, and ribbons fell from the ceiling along with dollar bills. Entourage at his back, Showtime made his way through the club kissing the cheeks of his female guests and slapping hands with his male ones. He wore a bright radiant smile fit for one of those posters in a dentist office, his gold fangs twinkling under the lights.

Showtime and his crew were led to the VIP section where they littered the furniture and were served buckets of Belaire Rose on ice along with some of the finest weed you'll ever breathe. The scent from the bright green, purple crystal buds was so strong that you could catch a high off contact. Showtime popped black bottles and got as high as giraffe pussy. He got so faded that he found himself on the stage dancing with the strippers. Tyson, Treasure, Keith, Dead Beat as well as the rest of the crew applauded and cheered him on, even going so far as to throw tips on the stage.

The scantily clad foxes occupying the stage with Showtime, pushed him down into the chair blindfolded him and bonded his hands to his back with pink furry handcuffs. The lights of the club went out leaving a neon blue light illuminating over them at the center of the stage. They took turns seducing Showtime with lap dances, nibbling on his earlobe, and sucking on his bottom lip. All of the foreplay left him with a tent in his slacks. His hardness was as stiff as a statue chiseled out of stone.

One of the strippers unzipped his slacks and pulled his thick, veined dick from its imprisonment. She wrapped her warm, juicy mouth around his love muscle and deep throated his full potential. The sensation caused him to tilt the chair back on its hind legs with the tips of his shoes. While she went to work slobbering down his meat, the other stripper sucked on his balls. The dynamic duo switched roles every five minutes until eventually Showtime exploded into one of their mouths. Right after, the stripper with the semen in her jaws spat it into the other stripper's mouth and she swallowed it like an Aspirin. She then sucked her fingers clean as if Showtime had the most delicious cum, she'd ever tasted.

The lights came back on in the club and everyone applauded the performance. The strippers lead Showtime to one of the private booths in the back of the club, where they sucked and fucked him of every drop of semen he had left. Thirty minutes later, he emerged from the back with a half empty bottle of champagne, dangling at his side. A 10-foot chocolate cake with strawberry ice cream filling with an airbrushed photo of Showtime in a king's garb awaited him. The heading read Happy Birthday Showtime, and the bottom read The King of Cali. The lights were turned out and all that was left were the tiny flames of candles in the cake. Everyone sung Happy Birthday to Showtime, and he blew the candles out. They all applauded and cheered. He grabbed a hunk of the cake and crammed it into his mouth. He sucked the frosting from his fingers, grabbed another hunk and mashed it into Treasure's face. She was surprised at first but quickly retaliated, smashing a hunk of cake into his face. Tyson spun her around and smashed a hunk of cake into her face.

"Oh, you're gonna get it now!" Treasure laughed and wiped the cake off of her face.

"Aye, new booty!" Keith called out. As soon as a laughing Tyson turned around, he mashed the cake into his face. The killer laughed hard and loud, holding his stomach with both hands. "Hahahahahahaha!" The entire club grew quiet and still; no one had ever heard the hard face; quiet man laugh let alone crack a smile. His laughter was quickly silenced by a handful of cake to the face, thrown by Showtime. A big food fight broke out with everyone laughing and slinging chocolate cake.

Later that night Showtime opened up all of the gifts he'd received for his birthday. He'd gotten everything from luxury cars to cash. But it was Dartanian's gift that really stood out to him; he had gotten him the same watch Arnold Schwarzenegger had worn in Terminator 3. It was designed by Audemar. When Big Willie records CEO cracked open the black box it came in, he found the watch as well as a small pamphlet with information on the watch as well as the film.

"Same Audemar Arnold wore in T3," Dartanian informed him. "I know it's everyone's least favorite Terminator, but still I know a collector, such as yourself could appreciate a fine watch."

Showtime put the watch on and marveled the piece that adorned his wrist. Seeing a thumb smudge on the face of the watch, he fogged the face of it with his hot breath and shined it on his shirt. Taking another look at the watch, he smiled. "Yeah, man, I like this. This is a nice joint right here. Thanks, fam." He slapped hands with Dartanian and embraced him.

"Happy birthday, my nigga." Dartanian smiled.

Sometime later

The lights slowly dimmed as Felli Fel announced the next dancer coming out to perform. "Everyone get cha pocketbooks and wallets out and show some love for the beauty witta booty, Ms. Chocolate Ty." Rounds of applause erupted in Nocturnal but quickly subsided once Dakeemia walked out dressed in a white wig, cat eye contacts, a snug fitting white blazer and matching patterned leather boots that reached her thighs. A black leather bag, dangled at her side as she made her way up the stage, all eyes on her.

Dakeemia pulled her blazer off and threw it into the audience. This left her perky balloon like breasts exposed as well as her shaven snatch. She sat on the stage with her legs spread apart for all to see. She parted the lips of her love tunnel with one hand and fished around in her bag with the other until she produced a funnel. She placed the funnel in between her pussy lips and pulled out a can of lighter fluid from the bag. She poured the lighter fluid into the funnel and down into her womb. She set the lighter fluid to the side and took out a Zippo lighter. She produced a flame with it and held it outstretched before her snatch. Using her pussy muscles, she sprayed the lighter fluid from her vagina, which mingled with the flame, and gave birth to a big roar of fire.

Froooooosh!

Oh's and Awe's were heard amongst the audience and then a round of thunderous applause. Dakeemia was putting on one hell of a show. Bills of all dominations were thrown into the air, and they all came raining down on her and the stage. The chocolate beauty ignored the money and continued on with her performance.

Meanwhile

Showtime chilled on the sofa taking pulls from a bleezy and blowing smoke rings into the air as he watched the show. A thick cinnamon complexion fox was perched in his lap with her arms wrapped around his neck, nibbling on his earlobe and whispering sweet nothings into his ear. She was sex playing him, trying to convince him to take her home for a night he'd never forget, which would cost him five stacks. While the enticing young lady kept Showtime busy, Keith was taking in the scenery watching the scantily clad strippers as they moved back and forth across the floor. He'd been fighting the urge to smack the booty of a tall, slender caramel chick with a tear drop ass and a twisty hairstyle. This was her fourth time walking past him in that black thong that her ass swallowed. Those meaty dark cheeks seemed to be calling his name. Keeeeith! Oh, Keeeeith!

Smack!

Keith's palm went across the caramel chick's right butt cheek, causing it to jiggle. It stung and startled her all at the same time. She swung around on her stiletto heels in one swift motion. Her face twisted in a scowl. Her ghetto sexy ass had a drink in one hand and her stinging cheek in the other.

"That's gotta be jelly 'cause jam don't shake like that, uhhhuhhh." Keith narrowed his eyelids and bit down on his bottom lip, referring to caramel's ass, biting on his curled finger.

"Keep your hands to yourself, you thirsty ass trick!" She growled and sashayed off. Keith watched her as she went along, groping the bulge in his pants and smiling the entire time. That big old ass of hers had him under her hypnosis. He could tell from the irregular size of it that she'd gotten it from a series of butt injections. But he didn't give two shits because he still wanted to run up in that.

"I'm leaving here with something to fuck on tonight," he said to no one in particular, taking a sip of his Hennessy and Coke. Just then a thick Ethiopian girl with straight jet black hair and almond eyes had just strutted past him, booty dancing. She was in her own little world, throwing her ass and taking sips of her Daiquiri en route to a nigga she believed she could get to trick a few dollars on her.

"What's up, ma?" Keith asked, eying her seductively.

"The rent and car note," she replied not even bothering to look his way. "You've gotta pay to play, sweetheart."

"Shiieeet, money ain't a thang, ya ain't know?" He held up a thick knot secured with a rubber band.

"Oh, so it's like that?" she smiled excitedly as she stepped to him, sitting her drink down and straddling his lap.

"Yeahhhh, that's what I'm talking about." He shut his eyelids and grinned. He leaned his head back and switched hands with the drink. "Mmmmm." He enjoyed her warm, wet tongue placing a hickey on his neck. A smile spread across his lips as Little Miss Thickness proceeded to give him an experience he'd never forget.

"Mmmmm," Keith moaned, entering the doors of utopia.

***

"Look at these niggaz slipping, they don't even know he got it coming," Bizeal was focused on Showtime and Keith when he spoke to Malakai out the corner of his mouth, taking a sip of his Vodka and cranberry.

"Once Dakeemia gives the signal we airing both of these faggots out," Malakai replied, watching his lady perform on stage as he twisted a toothpick at the corner of his mouth. While Bizeal and Crazy indulged in alcohol, he opted for a glass of ice water with a slice of lemon. He knew from experience that he wasn't any good while under the influence when it came to gunplay. So, he wanted to be sober and able to concentrate when it came time to twist his intended victims' caps back.

Yeah, niggaz, live it up 'cause tonight will be your last night on this earth.

It was only a matter of time before Malakai filled his brother's murderers with some hot shit. All he was waiting on was the signal from his wife that she'd secured their weapons and they were going to sneak off to get them so they could lay Showtime and punk ass bodyguard the fuck down.

"Come on, my nigga, let's burn these mothafuckaz before the lights come back on," Crazy said, tapping his foot and drumming his fingers on the table top impatiently. He was antsy and couldn't wait to slump Showtime, Keith, and anyone else that got in their way.

"Hold it down, fam," Malakai told him, gripping his shoulder trying to calm him down. "We can't stink these niggaz without the straps."

"Fuck the straps, homie, all we need are a couple of these babies," he held up one of the empty bottles of Moet that was on their table. "I say we break the bottoms of these bitches and rush VIP."

"And get gatted the fuck down in the process?" Bizeal's brows furrowed, looking at his man like he wasn't crazy but a complete fucking imbecile. "This is their function, dick. You think those mothafuckaz aren't packing? You better wise up. I swear to God, C, you don't think." He shook his head pitifully and took a sip of his drink.

"Yo, man, I'm getting tired of you telling me that I don't think and that I'm fucking up." The young nigga scowled.

"Well, start thinking and stop fucking up," Bizeal scolded him, squaring his jaws.

He and Crazy's bickering continued, but Malakai couldn't hear them because he was fixated on Dakeemia. She jumped on the pole and slowly slid down upside down. For the first time that night she made eye contact with him and winked.

"We on." Malakai shot to his feet and headed for the men's room with his boys on his heels. Dakeemia winking at him let him know that the weapons she'd snuck into the club were duct-taped underneath the sink inside the men's room. She'd brought them in when she came in for her swift that night. He knew they had about a snowball's chance in hell of getting into the exclusive event with guns on them.

***

Dartanian was perched between Rashida and Eliza smoking a Cuban cigar while they sipped flutes of champagne and watched the show.

"Daddy, do you think we can bring a new girl home to play with, pleeeease?" Rashida begged, giving him puppy dog eyes and pouty lips. She looked like a child asking her father could she keep a stray dog.

"We'll see, baby," he replied, patting her leg with one meaty hand and taking a drag off his cigar with the other, blowing smoke into the air. Eliza walked over to him and he removed the Cuban from his mouth. He put the cigar between her full pink lipstick covered lips and she took a pull, drawing the smoke into her lungs. She held the smoke hostage in her lungs for a while and then blew a gust of smoke.

"Jesus, that thing tastes awful." Eliza's face balled up. She took a swallow of champagne to wash the foul taste out of her mouth.

"It's an acquired taste, baby," Dartanian said smoothly and took another pull of his illegal tobacco. "Fuck are these niggaz going?" he sat up in his seat seeing a trio of men wearing scarves over their mouths and big brimmed hats coming out of the men's room. The men were headed to the VIP section where Showtime and his crew were. Before he knew it the trio of men was drawing down on the hulking bouncers that were guarding the velvet rope of the VIP section.

Dartanian jumped to his feet and spat out the Cuban.

"The shit is about to hit the fan," he announced, unsheathing his katana from his cane. Snikttt!

"What's the matter, daddy?" Rashida asked concerned, looking from him to the VIP section.

"Is everything okay, baby?" Eliza questioned, worried.

Treasure sat on Tyson's lap. They both sipped flutes of expensive champagne laughing, smiling and sharing the occasional kiss. Skylar sat on the side of them, smacking a stripper on her ass as she grinding into her crotch. In between the fingers of her right hand were several folded singles that she planned on tricking off on the exotic dancers that night.

"You like pussy too, huh?" Tyson cracked a grin at his lady's best friend, seeing how she was so engrossed with the assets of the stripper's curvaceous body.

"Hell yeah." Skylar smiled and glanced at him. She focused her attention back on the delicious piece of ass blessing her lap. The girl giving the sensual dance stood up, turned around and straddled her waist. She stared deep into her Skylar's eyes as she danced sensually on her, allowing her to inhale the smell of her sweet perfume. The nude goddess's long, wet looking hair tickled her nose as she leaned over into her face, kissing her lips. When she pulled back, all Skylar could taste was cherry. This was because she was wearing flavored lip gloss.

Tyson and Treasure chuckled watching the show. They then focused on each other, staring into the depths of one another's souls through their eyes.

"You know how lucky I am to have met you?" he said seriously with a straight ass face. She dropped her head, shutting her eyelids and blushing. A smile graced her lips. With a curled finger, he tilted her chin up so that she'd be looking up at his face. "I'm serious," he told her, rubbing her chin lovingly with his thumb. "I'm the luckiest man in the entire world." His eyes bleed the truth and she knew he meant it.

Treasure wiped away the tear that peeked over her eyelid with a curled finger. She then sniffled.

"I'm the lucky one," she told him what she truly felt.

"What I just say?" He faked anger, a line forming a forming across his forehead.

"What I say?" Her lips formed an easy smile.

"Gimmie a kiss." Placing his hand behind her neck, he pulled her closer. Their lips mashed together as their heads turned at an angle, their tongues invaded one another mouths. Their lips massaged one another in a wonderfully, deep, emotional kiss that you could just barely hear the saliva moving around in their mouths. When they pulled back, they wiped the shiny corners of one another's mouths.

"This champagne has gotten to my bladder." Tyson tilted his flute and looked inside at the slightly yellow alcohol. "I'ma have to drain the one-eyed snake, boo."

"Okay." She rose from off his lap.

"I'll be back." He kissed her before heading off. Right as he was leaving, the stripper broad that was giving Skylar a lap dance, come saunter by him with George Washingtons' hanging out of her G-string. He stole a peek at her ass but kept it moving. Soon after, a succession of gunshots went off sending the entire club into pandemonium. He ran and took cover behind a nearby couch, drawing one of his .45 automatics. When he looked up, he saw Treasure and Skylar taking refuge behind the couch they were perched in. That's when it set in that shit was about to get real and he was going to do everything he could to keep the woman he loved out of harm's way.

***

Malakai barged into the men's room with Bizeal and Crazy on his heels. They retrieved the guns that his wife had duct-taped underneath the sink. After checking the magazines of their weapons to make sure they were fully loaded, they smacked them into the butts of them. Next, they removed big-brimmed hats and scarves from the trash can, putting them on as a disguise. Wearing the large hats and the scarves over their nose and mouths made them look like Alec Baldwin when he starred in The Shadow. The threesome started towards the door and a slender Puerto Rican man in a tie and button-down came in.

"Holy shit!" His eyes bugged when he saw them and he ran right back out of the men's room. Malakai and his niggaz were right behind him. The hustler winked at Dakeemia who had just blew lighter fluid out of her mouth onto a torch she held and created a roar of fire.

Froooooosh!

The flames blew out near the audience's faces, and they leaned back in their seats, golden illumination shone on their faces.

"Whoooaaaa!" Their eyes bulged and their mouths formed O's.

Dakeemia smiled proudly, giving Malakai a slight nod and continuing with her performance.

Malakai and his boys moved in on the hulking bouncers guarding the velvet rope of the VIP section. When the bouncers saw their guns, their eyes went as wide as saucers and their stomachs twisted into knots. The raised their palms in surrender but before they could utter a plea for their lives their bulky frames were riddled with smoldering hot slugs. The bouncers fell awkwardly to the floor with spaced out looks in their eyes. They were dead. The loud clapping of gunfire caused the club goers to scream in a panic and scramble for the nearest exits, trampling others in the process.

Malakai and his boys quickly ran up the steps that lead to the VIP lounge. Showtime saw the trio and their guns he sobered up quick mouthing the words Oh, shit. He shoved the stripper from his lap and dove to the floor, knocking over a table in the process. Tyson kicked off the floor flipping over the sofa he and Treasure were seated on and spilled them onto the floor. The rest of Showtime's entourage had shot to their feet and went to pull their heaters. They were all already dead but didn't know it.

Bop! Bop! Bop! Pop! Pop! Pop! Blocka! Blocka! Blocka!

Malakai and his niggaz squeezed their triggers, their guns sounded like firecrackers going off. The hot shit they unleashed tore through the muscles and arteries of the entourage causing their blood to mist the air. They all wore looks of agony and death as they fell to the floor.

Malakai reloaded his gun and cocked one into its chamber, looking around cautiously. He stepped in between the bloody bodies that lay sprawled on the floor, looking for his main targets: Showtime and Keith.

When he spotted them the two stripper bitches that were entertaining them were fleeing as fast as they could in their high heels, screaming in hysterics. Showtime tried to make a run for it but ended up tripping over the dead body of one of his entourage members, falling on his face. Keith was bout his though. Fuck running, that nigga pulled out his .45, but before he could end Malakai's movie, the hustler was rolling the credits on his.

Blocka! Blocka! Blocka! Blocka!

The killer wore a face of agony as his shoulders danced, with each shot that he absorbed. When he hit the floor breathing sporadically and blood bubbled out of his mouth, Crazy rushed over and crushed that ass.

Pop! Pop! Pop! Pop!

Once the young nigga finished him, he looked up and saw Showtime crawling away. All he saw was his wagging ass as he hurried away. He went to put the smash on him, but Malakai calling his name stalled him. When he looked at him he shook his head no and told him that he was his. He nodded his understanding and set his sights on Dead Beat who was running away. Pointing that head bussa at him, and walked forward, firing away.

Pop! Pop! Pop! Pop!

Malakai saw the producer fall down at the corner of his eye, but he didn't pay his any mind. He reloaded his heater and sped walked over to Showtime, evil eyes peering over his scarf.

"Where you think you going, mothafucka?" He spat with contempt.

"Ugh!" Showtime grimaced as he kicked him in the ass causing him to fall forward and carpet burn his forehead. He kicked him in his side and he turned over grimacing, holding his ribs. Malakai pulled his scarf down so that he could see the face of his executioner. He wore a scowl and a hatred of burning fire in his pupils.

"This is from my brother, through me, straight to you." He applied pressure to the trigger.

Poc! Poc! Poc!

Malakai stumbled backwards and crashed to the floor, still holding his gun. From where he lay behind the cover of the couch, Tyson relieved the trigger of his .45. Bizeal kneeled to attend to Malakai's injuries. He'd taken all three rounds in the chest before toppling over. Seeing his homeboy go down pissed Crazy off and he took his anger out in the form of bullets, reducing the couch Tyson was stashed behind into rummage. He had ejected the spent magazine from his gun and smacked in a fresh one when he felt a sting and then fire across his arm.

Once Showtime realized that Crazy and Malakai were occupied, he ducked off behind the couch alongside Treasure and Skylar. Crazy spun around after being attacked, finding Dartanian standing behind him with a katana dripping with blood, staining the carpet red. The youngster went to blast on him and he struck again. Dartanian's movements were so swift that Crazy wasn't sure if he had budged at all. His only confirmation was his hand coming loose from his wrist bone and falling to the floor, firing the weapon in his palm. Dartanian drew back his katana preparing to strike Crazy's beating heart when he got an elbow to the gut and a kick to the chest that flipped him over the guardrail and sent him crashing down on two tables, toppling them.

***

Bizeal was creeping upon Tyson where he was stashed behind the couch until he heard Crazy's blood curdling scream. His head snapped in his direction to see Dartanian lashing at him with his katana. Seeing this he ran over to him, elbowing him in his gut and kicking him in the chest. Once he flipped over the guardrail and landed on a table, breaking it in half, Bizeal darted over in a hurry to finish him off.

Bop! Bop! Bop! Bop!

The dread head dusted his old ass off like it wasn't shit.

"Noooooooo!"

"Noooooooo!"

Bizeal's head snapped around hearing the screams of two women. His eyes bulged and his mouth formed an O when he met twin nickel plated .380s.

***

From where he was behind the mangled couch, Tyson whipped out his second .45 automatic. Using the hand that held one of his guns, he wiped the sweat from his forehead. His heart was beating uncontrollably inside of his chest. He had to make sure Treasure lived through this thing because if not his cousin Cody would be getting whacked out along with her. The last thing he wanted to happen was to lose two loved ones in one night. That's why he was going to do everything in his power to protect her. Not only was it his duty, it was his obligation being that she was his woman.

Tyson looked across from him where he saw Treasure, Skylar and Showtime hiding behind a couch similar to the one he was stashed behind. They all had fear in their eyes, especially Showtime. The thug was surprised at how the women seemed to be holding it together the best.

"Babe, are y'all alright?" he questioned with concern. She nodded yes. "Good, listen, there's a backdoor exit right behind y'all. I'ma create a diversion so y'all can hop over the guardrail and get outta here, okay?"

"No, no, no, I'm not going anywhere without my man," Treasure spoke defiantly, looking at him like he was crazy if he thought she was leaving him.

"You gon' have to, sweetheart, I told you that if something happens to you then that's my cousin's life gon' too. My hands are tied here. My only mission is to protect you, so if you don't make it tonight that it for my family. There isn't any telling what yo' old man and his people would do to him behind them walls."

Treasure looked like she was thinking about it, so he pressed her some more. "Baby, I need you to do this for me, okay? No questions ask."

She took a deep breath and nodded. "Okay."

"Okay, then, on the count of three."

She nodded, accepting his terms. With that, he began the countdown.

"One, two…"

"Noooooooo!"

"Noooooooo!"

The twin screams caused Tyson's brows to furrow. He peered over the couch to see Bizeal looking shook with Rashid and Eliza pointing their nickel plated .380 at him. Tears streamed down their faces having seen Dartanian get blazed up. They went to pull the triggers of their weapons.

Splocka! Splocka! Splocka!

Dakeemia came over the guardrail, wearing a black hood and even blacker sunglasses, her gloved hand firing a compact gun. She nailed both of the twins causing them to hollering out, dropping their straps. Bizeal gathered his wits and joined the firefight along Malakai, their hands slightly twitching as their thangs bucked in their grips.

Blocka! Blocka! Blocka! Bop! Bop! Bop!

Bullets went in and out of Rashida and Eliza's bodies causing them to do the Harlem Shake on their feet even after their deaths. Once the shooting stopped smoke wafted in the air and the girls went crashing to the carpet, blood pooling around them. Seeing Crazy lying on the floor moaning in pain and his severed hand beside him, Bizeal ran over to him in a panic. He picked up his homeboy's hand and stuffed it into the pocket of his blazer. He pulled him to his feet and threw his good arm over his shoulder. He then picked up his banger and tucked it on his waistline.

"You okay, bae?" Dakeemia's gloved hand caressed the side of Malakai's face.

He nodded and said, "I'm good, help Bizeal with Crazy. I'ma go after Showtime."

"Alright." She headed off to assist his right-hand man.

Malakai's head snapped up when he saw Treasure, Skylar and Showtime making a break for the guardrail at the opposite end of the V.I.P section.

"Nah, that ass ain't getting away tonight, homeboy!" he said to himself, dropping the magazine out of the bottom of his gun and reloading it quickly. When he lifted his head bussa in Treasure, Skylar and Showtime's direction, Tyson scrambled to his feet and ran toward her. He ran as fast as he could, adrenaline pumping and heart racing. His eyes were zeroed in on his pointer finger which was closing around the trigger. His head snapped from the gun to an unsuspecting Treasure, Skylar and Showtime. He gritted and seemed to get a burst of energy, picking up speed, his legs looking like blurs while in motion. All he could hear was his heavy breathing inside his ears and his pounding heart. "Haa! Haa! Haa! Haa!" He whipped his head back and forth between the gun and the woman of his dreams, rapidly. The gunman's finger curled around the trigger and applied pressure to it. Tyson thought he could hear the chamber of the gun opening up and the pin slamming into the butt of the copper bullet inside of it.

"Treasuuuuure!" he screamed at the top of his lungs, veins rolling up his neck and his temples. The sound of his voice brought her around just in time to see fire shoot out the barrel of the gun as a single shot was launched. Her eyelids peeled open wide, and her jaw dropped. She and Skylar were frozen, but Showtime wasn't. He dove to the floor out of the way of the line of fire. A bullet came out of the gun along with smoke. It appeared to be moving in slow motion to them all, especially the thug and his lady.

Seeing the table in front of him, Tyson jumped off of it and leaped into the air like he was diving into a pool. Time sped up again when he slammed into his girl, tackling her to the floor and shoving her friend down. "Ughhh!" they hit the floor hard, knocking the wind out of his lungs. When he peeled his head up from the surface, he saw people running back and forth across him screaming. The entire club was chaos, broken glass, blood and dead bodies were lying out flat everywhere. When he locked eyes with the shooter there was something familiar about his eyes. He'd seen the man before, but he couldn't quite place him. That's when he had a flashback of an inmate tackling him in the yard back in prison, saving his life. He remembered lying down on the ground thanking him. This gunman was Malakai.

Malakai looked to be surprised that he'd shot the R & B singer. His eyes showed compassion and sympathy, but he knew he couldn't stand there in a stupor he and his niggaz had to get the fuck from up out of there.

"Come on!" he motioned for his clan to follow him as he retreated toward the back door exit of the establishment. They were right on his tail, swinging their guns around to pop anyone that dared to follow them.

Tyson wanted to go after them, but he knew that without a strap he didn't stand a chance against them. He'd be slaughtered without a doubt.

"Oh shit!" Showtime's voice came from his left and he looked to him. The head honcho of Big Willie records nodded to Treasure. When he looked down, he saw the red dot at the center of her chest quickly expanding.

"Oh, oh my God," Tyson eyes welled with tears and his lips quivered, he felt like someone was squeezing his heart. "Not chu…not my Treasure. Awww, baby, you can't do this to me, sweetheart! Not now, honey, you can't leave me now." he scooped her into his arms, lying her head down in his lap. He interlocked his fingers with hers and stroked her hair continuously with his other hand. He sniffled and big tears fell from his eyes splashing on her beautiful face. Her eyelids were shut, and her lips were a straight line. Her body slight shock as he sobbed.

Showtime was climbing over the guardrail when he spotted all of the dead bodies sprawled out on the floor, saturated in their own blood. When he saw Tyson with a bleeding Treasure in his arms wailing it fucked him up, but seeing Keith and Dead Beat lying out full of holes caused him great grief. He climbed back over the guardrail feeling like the buster ass nigga that he was. People still running back and forth across him screaming and yelling from the panic of the shootings. The C.E.O of Big Willie records was in a world of his own as he walked upon the two men. One he loved like family while the other was family. Tears rolled down his face rapidly as he kneeled to Keith, checking the pulse in his neck. He'd expired. He looked to Dead Beat, but miraculously he was still alive.

"Oh, God, whyyyy? Whyyyyyy, my Treasuuuure!"

Showtime's head snapped over his shoulder and he saw Tyson still holding the singer in his arms. Skylar was standing beside him punching a number into her cellular. He figured it was 9-1-1 being that she'd only pressed three buttons. He turned his attention back around to Dead Beat. His form was littered with black holes that ran with crimson streams. Tears flowed freely from the corners of his eyes and he gargled on blood. Looking up at Showtime, he tried to say something but only ended up spitting up more blood.

"Don't…don't try to say anything, my nigga. Just…just hold on, help is on the way," he assured him, gripping his bloody hand with both of his. Tears constantly slid down his face seeing Dead Beats life slip from him. He could tell from the look in his eyes that he was almost gone. The producer's grip started to loosen, and his eyes rolled to their whites. He let unleashed his last breath and lie still, lifeless. Showtime shut his eyelids with a brush of his palm. Next, he bowed his head and crossed his himself in the sign of the crucifix.

Once the media got a hold of the shooting at the gentlemen's club they dubbed it, The Nocturnal Massacre. A total of ten were left dead while another two were seriously injured. The incident was on every news channel and radio station worldwide. Rap magazines and news papers covered the story with interviews from people that were there. Showtime got exactly what he wanted, promotion, not only for Treasure, but for the late, great rhyme spitter, Blessyn, as well.

Keith and Dead Beat were buried on a Tuesday at 11 o'clock in the morning. They had a beautiful ceremony where their bodies were brought into the cemetery by horses and carriages and doves were released into the sky. Showtime wore a solemn face throughout the entire funeral. No one had a clue that since the men's deaths he'd been fucking like a porn star and partying like a rock star. Every night he'd get drunk and coked out of his mind and have unprotected sex with random women. It was like he was headed for self-destruction the way he was behaving. No one caught on to what he was doing because they were all busy grieving themselves.

CHAPTER SEVEN

Two weeks ago the doctors had successfully removed the bullet from Treasure's chest. Though the wound would heal over time, she'd most likely live the rest of her life as a quadriplegic. When the doctor that had performed her surgery relayed the information to Tyson he went blind with rage, tearing up everything in the waiting room. It took six security guards to restrain him until he calmed down. The police were going to haul him off to jail but the doctor convinced them to do otherwise. He felt the young man's pain and he didn't want him to spend the day in lock up.

"Are you okay, son?" Henry asked Tyson as he sat beside him with a cup of black coffee. Vapors rose from the dark liquid and disappeared into the air. Henry had popped up at Moon's house to see if he'd heard from Tyson since he hadn't been returning his phone calls. Initially, his oldest son wasn't going to tell him that his brother had called him because he had some trouble on his hands, but after the old man convinced him to do otherwise. Once he was given the rundown, Henry and Moon strapped up and moved out to check on his baby boy. His youngest had gotten himself waist deep into some shit and he'd be damned if he was going to allow him to face it alone.

"Pop, I'm pretty far from okay, and I won't be until I have that nigga Malakai's body at my feet and his blood on my hands." He held his hands before his eyes and balled them into fists, causing veins to form in his forehead and neck. His jaws pulsated he clenched them so hard.

"I don't know Treasure from a can of paint," Moon started, turning from the waiting room window where he was staring down at the streets below. "But them niggaz hurting her in turn hurt chu and any pain brought to my brother is a pain that will be given to his enemies a hundred-fold, you Griff me?" he slapped hands with Tyson and embraced him.

"That's love." he said to him from over his shoulder.

"Straight up."

"But look, before we give this nigga a closed casket, I wanna get Treasure settled in the house and take some time to gather my thoughts."

"Take all of the time you need, son." Henry patted him on the back.

"Ty," Moon called for his younger brother's attention. When he looked to him, he nodded to the doorway of the waiting room. Tyson turned around and found Skylar and Treasure. His boo was in an electric wheelchair that she operated by maneuvering a curved black steel rod with her mouth.

Tyson smiled at Treasure, and she smiled back. He leaned over and kissed her.

"You ready to get outta here?" he asked her pleasantly.

"Yeah, let's blow this joint." She smiled, glowing like a pregnant woman.

Moon and Henry exchanged glances. Treasure was acting way different than they had expected. They thought she'd be depressed and withdrawn, but to their surprise she was more upbeat and jollier due to the circumstances.

"You must be Ty's father and brother, Henry and Moon. I've heard so much about the two of you." Skylar looked between the two of them. They nodded in agreement. "I'm Treasure's B.F.F, Skylar." She extended her hand and Henry took it, kissing the back of it while staring into her eyes.

"Pleasure to meet chu." He cracked a smile and patted her hand.

"Tyson, I see where you get your good looks from now." She smiled causing the old man to smirk. Next, she shook Moon's hand.

Tyson grinned and shrugged like Hey, what can I say?

"Well, let's gon' and get outta here, my love," Tyson bowed and outstretched his hand toward the doorway.

"Nice to see there's one last gentleman in the world." Treasure smiled and rolled out the door.

"Moon, pop, Sky, let's roll," he motioned for them to follow him.

Suddenly, he cellular rang and vibrated. He dipped his hand inside of his pocket and pulled it out. Seeing Grief on the screen caused him to take a deep breath. That's when he remembered the shot-caller telling him in prison that whatever happened to his daughter would happen to his cousin behind the wall, maybe even worse. The device slightly shook inside of Tyson palm, and he constipated on not answering it again like he had the past couple of days, but he knew that if he didn't see what was up with the old man that it could be the end of Cody.

"Ty, aren't chu gonna answer it?" Henry asked. He, Skylar and Moon were looking over his shoulder at the screen of his cell phone. They knew all about Grief and the agreement that was made.

"Babe, it's daddy, isn't it?" Treasure asked concerned. He nodded yes.

The cell stopped ringing, but picked right back up, shaking and vibrating in his hand. With its ringing all of their hearts seemed to beat slow and hard, consuming their ears with their sounds.

Thump! Thump! Thump! Thump!

Tyson swallowed hard. Sweat masked his forehead and he rubbed the screen of the cellular with his thumb, staring down at Grief's name. Feeling like a pussy for not answering it, he decided to drop his nuts.

"Alright, fuck it!" He pressed answer and brought the device to his ear. "Yoooooooo!"

"Don't fucking yo' me, lil' young ass nigga!" Grief growled into the phone. "What the fuck did I tell you would happen if baby girl was harmed, huh? What the fuck did I tell you?"

"Look, man, I…"

The call disconnected and sent Tyson into a panic. His hearted raged inside of his chest like it was trying to leap out of it.

"What he say?" Moon inquired.

"Is everything good, baby?" Treasure worried, rolling over to him in her wheelchair.

"No, sweetheart, yo' father is going to go after Cody. I've gotta reach 'em before his goons do." He scrolled through his call log looking for his cousin's name.

***

When Treasure had gotten shot, Tyson hit Cody up to let him know the deal. The next morning at chow the young thug started a fight and got sent straight to the hole. He was only let out once a day to shower. Right after, he was heading right back to segregation. Cody hated being alone but understood that his being there meant that he'd stay alive. See, he knew that he didn't stand a snowball's chance in hell going up against Grief's goons by himself. Those niggaz would have put the smash on him on sight. Now, the nigga was tough, but he wasn't no goddamn fool. That's for damn sure.

Cody planned on riding out the rest of his bid in solitary confinement. So, when it came time for him to be released, he was going to start another altercation that would send him back to the hole. His only hang up about being locked up within the small space was his limited access to heroin. He thanked God that he grabbed a couple of packets of heroin from his stash before he set it off up in the mess-hall. Because had he not he would have been as sick as a goddamn dog.

Cody stood with his back to the spraying showerhead lathering his body with soap on a rope. He closed his eyes, leaned his head back, and washed the shampoo from his nappy dreads. Bringing his head back down, he peeled his eyelids open and found a naked Whispers standing before him smiling wickedly, boasting his beige teeth. He looked around and there were two naked men standing on each side of him wearing scowls and gripping ice pick like shanks.

Shit, how the fuck these niggaz get in here? A wide-eyed Cody looked around in a panic, heart pumping furiously inside of his left breast. Punk ass, C.Os, would sell they own mommas out for a payday. Fuck it, if it goes down then it goes down, but I ain't 'bout to shut my eyes forever without giving these bitch ass niggaz a fight.

"Yeah, what I tell yo' bony ass? I was gon' settle up witcha, right? Well, today's the day," Whispers laughed sinisterly, but the young thug quickly shut him up with a hard right to the mouth that drew blood and dropped him, holding his bleeding grill. Feeling another one of the goons at his side, Cody swung the soap on the rope around and cracked him in the face with it. The impact broke his nose and bloodied his mouth causing him to stagger backwards. Once the rest of the goons started closing in on him, Cody started swinging on them, hitting some but missing others. Eventually he grew exhausted and collapsed where he stood, eyes narrowed with his chest jumping violently.

"Haa! Haa! Haa! Haa!" His breaths were loud and husky as he watched the goons closing in on him, too exhausted to do anything but lay there as they had their way with him. Before he knew it he was surrounded by bare, wet feet which were standing on the shallow covered surface of the shower floor. He grabbed one of the goon's ankles and made to pull himself up, but a swift kick in the jaw left him lying on the side of his face. Eyes rolled to the back of his head, his open mouth leaked blood, turning orange as it swirled down the drain of the enormous shower.

Grief appeared in the shower doorway tossing back peanuts from his fist. He wore a plain expression as he watched a bleeding, Cody. From his reactions and the look on his face it would have appeared that he was watching a movie at a theater.

Slowly getting upon his feet, Whispers spat blood on the floor and wiped his bleeding mouth with the back of his hand. Grasping a fistful of Cody's dreads, he yanked his head all of the way back, showcasing his Adam's apple. Cody groaned in pain, but the sight of his being hurt only excited Whispers. Grief's second in charge's face twisted with a scowl and he squared his jaws, displaying his discolored teeth. He snaked the fist that held the shank around his neck and pressed the tip of it into his flesh behind his ear, blood trickled. Still smiling sinisterly, Whispers looked up at Grief and the Oakland shot-caller gave him a nod. This was the signal for him to handle his business. He went to slice Cody's jugular when a cell phone vibrated and rang, stealing his attention. When he looked up he saw the OG holding up a finger for him to wait a minute as he stared at the screen of his cell phone. Tyson was on the display. He started not to answer it, but decided to let the nigga hear his cousin gasping for air once his throat was slit.

"What's up?" Grief spoke into the cellular, tucking the wrinkled pack of peanuts.

"Don't kill 'em, daddy, it's me, Treasure!" she shouted into the phone as soon as his voice greeted her.

"Baby girl?" Grief frowned. He found his eyes tearing so he turned his back on his goons, not wanting them to see him like that.

"Yes, daddy, it's me. I'm fine."

"Thank God." He shut his eyes and took a deep breath.

"Daddy, you can't hurt or kill Cody, okay? I love Tyson with all of my heart and he's, his cousin. I know his death will drive a wedge in between us and he'll not only hate chu but myself as well."

For a time, Grief was silent thinking on it as he bit down on his bottom lip and clenched his fist. He really wanted to have his guys off Cody to keep good on the threat he made to Tyson, but the love and affection of his baby girl meant so much more to him. Opening his eyes and unclenching his fist, he peeled his eyelids back open and replied to daughter.

"Alright, baby, I'll leave 'em be." He listened as Treasure sighed with relief.

"Thank you, daddy, thank you, thank you, thank you."

"You're welcome, pumpkin, anything for my baby, I love you."

"I love you, too. Speak to you later."

"Okay, baby girl." He kissed her through the phone and she returned the gesture. Grief disconnected the call and turned around, sliding the cellular inside of his jean jacket. Whispers was in the same position he was before with the shank to a barely conscious Cody's jugular. His raised eyebrows asking, Yay or Nay? When it came to killing his victim. Grief shook his head no. Disappointed, Whispers shut his eyes and silently cursed, fuck. He then released

Cody's dreads, and his face smacked down onto the wet floor. He and the other goons went to dry off and get dress. Once they were done, they let out of the shower room, leaving Grief watching their victim. Cody's back rose and fell as he breathed hard on the surface of the shower room's tiled floor. The old school gangsta allowed his eyes to linger on him just a little while longer before turning around to catch up with his crew.

***

After they left the hospital, everyone went their separate ways. Henry and Moon took it back home while Skylar, Tyson, and Treasure rode out to the townhouse out in Lawndale. They took refuge there being that they didn't feel safe at the mansion. Now that they had a place, they felt comfortable laying their heads, Tyson planned to be at Treasure's every beck and call. He was going to cook for her, feed her, bathe her, dress her and comb her hair. There was a lot of hard work in caring for the singer, and he was positive that a lot of nights he'd be left exhausted and mentally drained. The job was a heavy load to carry but he knew his love for her would egg him on.

That night, while Skylar opted to go to bed early, Tyson prepared a scrumptious Italian dish for him and Treasure. He made lasagna, a Caesar salad, garlic bread and Brunello red wine. The couple sat before the "50 flat-screen in the living room watching Donnie Brasco. After the movie Tyson bathed Treasure and attended to her hygiene. Once he was done he laid her down in bed and crawled in beside her. He arranged her arms and legs so they'd be interlocked with his own, with him holding her in his embrace. They lay there talking for hours.

"Babe, when Smokey got outta that yard Moon took off down Adams. This nigga was running so hard that his heels were kicking him in his ass." Tyson relayed a story to his love. She laughed so hard that tears formed in the corners of her eyes. "Francis 'Moon' Williams, the Fastest Man in the World. Forest Gump, eat your heart out." The couple laughed harder. He wiped the tears of laughter from her face and then his own. "Yeah, those were the good old days." He wiped the tears that threatened to spill over his eyelids.

"Boy, you guys were a trip growing up." Treasure said, coming down from her laughter. She quieted down having found Tyson gazing into her eyes lovingly. The look on his face said it all; he didn't have to utter a word. He was madly in love with her. She looked away blushing, but he tilted her chin up so that she'd be looking him square in his eyes.

"You know I' m crazy about chu, right?" Tyson put it out there, his eyes still locked on hers as he traced her face with his pointer finger. She giggled, smiled, and nodded. Right after, he kissed her long and deep, pecking her on the lips before pulling away. There was a long silence between them as they looked into one another's eyes.

Treasure broke their gaze. She cleared her throat and said, "So, ummm, you love me, huh?"

"Without a shadow of a doubt," he replied with seriously intense eyes. He was sure of two things in life. And that was he was going to do whatever it took to eat and that he loved her with every inch of his heart. For him the sun rose and set with Treasure Jones.

"Good, then you'll have no problem doing me this favor." Her eyes stung with hotness and the rims of her eyes outlined with tears, threatening to trickle.

"Whatever it is, you got that, T. That goes without saying." His forehead wrinkled, wondering why his Next Breath, which he affectionately called her was on the verge of slicking her cheeks with wetness. Sitting there beside her in bed he meant every word, squeezing her hand passionately. His soft brown eyes bleeding all of the adoration he felt for the woman lying beside him. He lifted her delicate hand and brought it to his lips, kissing it gently, his eyes never breaking from hers.

Treasure stared into his eyes. She swallowed, taking her time before speaking again. "I want chu to let me go."

"Oh, you wanna travel? I thought you were gonna drop something serious on me with the tears in yo' eyes and…"

"No!" she interjected with her blurting. "I mean…I mean, I meant…let me go from this life, release me." Her eyes wandered down, ashamed to look into his eyes. Timidly, her eyes crept up and met his face. She could read the devastation etched across his face.

Tyson's heart sunk and his stomach flipped. He sat up in bed. "I don't understand," he began, running his hands down his face and taking a deep breath. "Why would you want me to do something like that? You're not happy here with me?"

"No." Treasure shook her head rapidly, tears cascading down her cheeks. "Not happy living this life like this." She gave her body the once over and sniffled, being in her current condition was a real mind fuck for her. "I can't live like this any longer. This body has become my prison and this world has become my cell. I can't do something as simple as scratch my nose when it itches, or caress your face how I so desperately want to do now." She stared into his eyes regretfully, wanting to hold him and tell him how much she loved him. The last thing she wanted to do was offend him and make him think otherwise about their relationship. She just didn't have the willpower to live the rest of her like how she was.

"So, that's it?" Tyson looked at her with tears rolling from the corners of his eyes. "You get me to open myself up to you? Get a nigga to fall in love with your ass, and then you eighty-six me?"

"No, baby, it's not like that." she shook her head, assuring him.

"Yes, it is!" he snapped, wiping his face with his shirt as he paced the floor. "Nah, fuck that, Blood! I'm not killing you!" When he said that she sobbed and cried loudly, "You said you were my rider, right? Well, you're gonna ride with me then, right here on this earth. You're gon' hold me down just like I hold you down. That's what love is about, sticking by your man or woman, no matter what; through their ups and downs. Well, this is a down, Ms. Gold. Me and you are gon' ride for each other until the wheels fall off. And I don't wanna hear any more about this dying bullshit, do I make myself clear?" Treasure nodded yes. He stormed out of the bedroom, slamming the door behind him causing portraits on the wall to rattle.

An hour later

Tyson lay in the dark on the living room couch staring up at the rotating ceiling fan. Tears welled up in his eyes as he thought about what the love of his life had asked him to do. He loved her too much to let her go. Although he tried to, he couldn't imagine a life without her. Before her he never knew what true love was, and now that he had experienced it he wasn't willing to let it go. Closing his eyes, he thought about what he would do if he were in Treasure's condition. Could he live out the remainder of his life as a quadriplegic? Could he spend his last days as helpless as a new born baby allowing people to take care of him? Or would he be like her, asking to be put out of his misery? He thought long and hard about her situation and decided to grant the songstress her wish, but it would definitely come at a cost.

Tyson pulled one of his .45s from under the couch pillow and walked up the steps to his boo's bedroom. When he peeked inside he found her staring up at the ceiling with a tear soaked face. Once he shut the door behind him it made a click that alerted her to his presence. A smile emerged on her face upon seeing the gun in his hand. To some it may have meant death, but to her it meant freedom. A freedom she yearned for and would do anything to obtain.

Finally, salvation, she thought.

"All right," Tyson said, sitting down beside her in bed, his .45 dangling between his legs. "I'ma do this, but after I do you, I'ma do myself." His glassy pink eyes made contact with hers and held them hostage.

"No, Tyson…" she took the time to swallow spit before proceeding. "Baby, this is about me. This has absolutely nothing to do with you." Her misting eyes pleaded with his, begging him to change his mind.

"I love you, Treas, so your decision has everything to do with me. Besides, I know a life without you is a life that I don't want any part of." He spoke from the heart, hoping that she'd change her mind and stick it out with him. Although even if she didn't, he had it in mind to go all of the way with his plan. He meant every word he'd just laid on her then. He really didn't want to be alive if she wasn't going to be by his side.

"It's just fucked up that Cody has to be involved in this shit." The expression that Treasure gave him was confirmation enough to let him know that she'd forgotten about his cousin. "What, you forgot that whatever happens to you will happen to him that fast? Your father made that plain the day I left The Beast. That was our agreement. You die and Cody dies. So, that's two lives you'll be taking with you. I can deal with it. With all the dirt that lil' nigga done did he knew karma would be coming around some day anyway." He cocked his head bussa, chambering a copper bullet into the head. "I love you, Treasure. I'd do anything for you." Taking a deep breath, he pressed the gun at the center of her forehead and brought his index to the trigger. She started breathing hard, chest jumping up and down. Her eyes pooling with tears as she thought about what was about to happen whichever option she chose she wasn't going to be happy with. If she allowed him to go along with her wish he'd kill himself and his cousin would follow soon after. If she decided to live, then she'd spend the rest of her days a cripple depending on others.

Oh, God, please tell me what to do? Treasure thought to herself, I love him so, so, so much. I can't allow him to do this. Me is one thing, but the nigga I love and his people, no!

She looked to Tyson's trigger finger as it was applying pressure to the trigger. "Wait! You win!" Tears ran down her cheeks. "You win, okay? Happy now?"

Tyson snatched the banger from her forehead and looked away. He bowed his head and massaged the bridge of his nose, breathing heavily. "Haa! Haa! Haa! Haa!" his cheeks swelled and deflated with each breath. He couldn't believe what he'd come so close to doing. Suddenly, his head snapped up and he looked to her, sniffing back snot. Tears flowed down his cheeks in abundance. His voice cracked with heavy emotion once he spoke again. "Baby, I'm sorry. I'm so, so, so…sorry, boo."

"Haa! Haa! Haa! Haa!" She breathed just as heavily as him. That moment was intense, very intense. She hadn't come that close to death since the shooting at the club. "It's…it's okay, baby. Gimmie a hug." She whimpered and sniffled, throwing her head back as her bottom lip trembled.

Her eyes pooled with tears again and broke free down her face. “Gimmie a great, big fucking hug.”

Tyson dove on the bed and hugged her tightly. That night they both sobbed long and loudly before eventually falling asleep in those very positions.

CHAPTER EIGHT

The next night

Tyson was dressed in all black from head to toe standing over the dining room table, screwing silencers on the ends of his .45 automatics. Scattered upon the table top was a box of bullets, a couple of grenades, and a blueprint of The Sheridan complex that he procured himself the night before. Malakai was a hot boy in them streets, so it was easy for him to get the information he required on his whereabouts. He paid the right people, and they gave him exactly what he wanted. He took what he was given and decided to make a move. Tyson had gotten dressed up like a crack head and made it down inside of the basement of The Sheridan where he stole the blueprint of the building. He was surprised at how easy he was able to slip in and slip out undetected. Not only was he able to take the layout of the place, but he was also able to take note of how many hitters the hustler had on deck. Malakai had plenty of gunners in his organization, but he was sure that he and his father would be able to take them down, seeing as how they had the element of surprise on their side.

Knocks at the door drew Tyson's attention; he took one of his guns before he went to go see who it was. He glanced through the peephole and when he saw who it was he relaxed, his shoulders slumped. He unchained and unlocked the door before pulling it open. On the opposite side of the door he found both his father and brother, who were also dressed in all black like he was. They wore serious expressions as they dapped him up and stepped inside of the unit. Once he shut the door behind them, he joined them at the table.

"What chu got there, pop?" Tyson patted his old man on the shoulder as he came to take up space beside him. He noticed the long, bulky case in his gloved hand.

"Yvette," he replied, sitting the case on the table top and popping its locks. He lifted the lid and revealed the disassembled parts of an M-16 with a scope, an infrared sighting and a knife attachment at its barrel. The old head went about his business of assembling the assault rifle while his sons chopped it up.

"So, what's the plan?" Moon asked Tyson.

"The plan is for you to go after this nigga Preston, while pop and I go raise the stocks in coffins," he told him as he rolled up his blueprint of the infamous apartment complex.

"What chu want me to do to the nigga?" Moon's eyes held seriousness as he folded his arms across his chest.

"I don't care what chu do to that faggot, just make sure you get that tape back." Tyson gave him a look like Do whatever the fuck you want to that bitch ass nigga when you catch up with him.

"I got chu faded." He slapped hands with his brother and embraced him.

"G' looking."

Tyson passed him a file containing information on Preston. Showtime's man had finally gotten the information. He slid it to him and the C.E.O of Big Willie made sure that he got it in his hands. Inside there was a number of addresses that the butler could possibly be found. Highlighted was Preston's boyfriend's address which he was urged to try looking for him first. Moon glanced through the file before closing it.

"Hey y'all." Skylar gave them a wave as she descended the steps. Moon and Henry looked up at her, their eyes following her as she approached.

"How ya doing, young lady?" Henry smiled and kissed her hand, causing her to blush.

"'Sup wit it?" Moon dapped her up.

"Ain't shit, Moon," she answered, then looked to the bangers in Tyson's possession. "Soooo, uhhh, Ty, what chu plan on doing with those guns?" Skylar placed her hands on her hips and shifted the weight of her body from one foot to the other.

"There's only two thangs you can do with guns, Skylar." Tyson stashed the twin bangers on his waistline.

"What's that?" She frowned curiously.

"God's will or the Devil's work." He threw his thermal over his guns.

"So, where's the woman that stole my baby boy's heart?" Henry inquired.

"Oh, she's upstairs asleep." Skylar threw a thumb over her shoulder.

"How long has she been asleep?" Tyson wondered.

"About twenty, twenty-five minutes now."

"I'll be right back." Tyson said to his brother and father, before descending the staircase two steps at a time in a hurry. He slowed to a stroll as he made his way down the hallway, nearing the door of his lady's bedroom and turning the corner inside. When he found Treasure, she was lying face up with her eyes shut, chest rising and falling peacefully. She looked like a Ghetto Snow White to him at that moment. A smirk infiltrated his face but when he thought about what had happened to her it vanished. He took a knee beside her bed, caressing her hand with his as he stared up at her face.

"I'm on my way outta the door, Queen," he spoke with a hushed tone so he wouldn't wake her up. "When I come back, I'm sure I would have earned my place in hell, but I don't mind. This nigga touched what was mine so he's gotta feel it. Ain't no way I could let this violation go unpunished. I'd spend night's tossing and turning in my sleep. Anyway, I just came up here to get me a good luck kiss before I head out into the field for battle." He paused for a time as he caressed her hand with his thumb. Abruptly, he leaned over her person and kissed her tenderly on the lips. Next, he stood erect staring down at her.

"I love you, Treasure." He waited a moment and then left; face scowling as ventured off to raise the murder rate in Los Angeles.

***

Mrs. Williams got dressed in black fatigues and combat boots which she laced up tightly. She then slipped on a coat and pulled a beanie down low over her brows. Next, she pulled black gloves over her hands, flexing and extending her fingers in them. Walking over to the mirror of her dresser, she looked herself over and was pleased with her appearance. Mrs. Williams pulled open her top nightstand drawer and removed the Bible inside, sitting it on top of it. She opened the Holy Book at its center and revealed a square that was cut out of it. Inside of the square there was her Taurus .9mm. After she took out the gun and checked to make sure that it was loaded, she closed the Bible shut. She then tucked the burner on her hip and headed over to a portrait of a white Jesus Christ. Standing before it, she hung her head and spoke as if he could hear what she was saying.

"...Heavenly Father, forgive me for what I feel I must do. Amen." She crossed herself in the sign of the crucifix and lifted her head. Afterwards, she made way for the door but stopped herself short when she saw the portrait of herself, a young Blessyn and Malakai. A smile stretched across her face as she turned to walk toward the portrait. Picking it, she brought it closer and admired the pleasant faces on the photo. The thought of Blessyn being shot down in cold blood made her pupils grow hot and tears shot down her cheeks. She wiped her face with the back of her hand and remembered a time when both boys were little.

Mrs. Williams was lying on her side asleep in her bed wearing a sleeping mask. Hearing weeping at her bedroom door, her chubby fingers twitched, and she stirred awake. She sat up and turned over in bed, flipping the mask up from over her eyes. Looking over shoulder, she found her oldest grandson at the door. Her forehead crinkled and she turned around in bed, planting her swollen bare feet on the carpet. Once she pulled the sleeping mask from over her head, she tossed it upon the dresser and turned her eyes on her grandson.

"What's wrong, grandma's baby?" Mrs. Williams asked an eight-year-old Blessyn.

"My mom and my dad."

"What about them, sweetness?"

"Did God take 'em away 'cause he hates me?" He broke down sobbing, teardrops dripping to the carpet.

This question made her look alive, wincing. "Oh, Blessyn, what makes you think that the Lord hates you?"

"'Cause he's punishing me for being bad."

"The Lord is kind and merciful. He loves all children; he would never punish a child."

"He does hate me, big ma, he does." He sniffled and wiped his crying eyes with the back of his hand. "He took my parents away, 'cause I be actin' up in school."

"Awww, don't say that, come here, son." She hugged him tightly and kissed him on top of the head. "God took your mother and father 'cause he wanted them to be angels and serve him in his kingdom."

"Yeah?" He looked up at her with pink, moist eyes that bled tears.

"Yes, baby boy." She managed a smile, eyes tearing up. Using her thumbs, she swiped the tears from his cheeks, and dried his face with the sleeve of her gown.

"Are you sure?"

"Uh huh." She smirked and nodded. "Your mother and father are in a better place, a place far greater than this world that we live in."

"Big ma, you promise?"

"Yes, baby, I promise." She wrapped him in her chunky arms and rocked him back and forth, humming a calming, soothing tune that put him at ease. When she peeled her eyelids open, tears went running down her cheeks. In the doorway she saw a small silhouette of a person that appeared to be wiping their eye.

"Big ma, I can't sleep," five-year-old Malakai told her.

"It's okay, Mal, you can sleep in here with me and your brother." She opened her arm, and he came running as fast as his feet allowed. Her arm pulled him a group hug along with his older brother. Smiling, she kissed him on top of the head.

After sitting the portrait back down, Mrs. Williams shut her eyes and took a deep breath. She then exhaled and continued out of the bedroom, flipping off the light switch as she crossed the threshold. She was on her way out of the door to break one of The Ten Commandments.

***

Bizeal and Crazy sat on the sofa eating Chinese food and watching 300 on the 70-inch 3D LG flat-screen. They stuffed their faces while Crazy gave commentary on the scenes that played out on the widescreen before them.

"Here we go, he's about to kick this nigga down that big ass hole," Crazy said, stuffing his mouth with Chow Mein, but never taking his eyes off of the screen. He now wore a prosthetic limb with a knife attachment having gotten his hand severed at Nocturnal that night by Dartanian. Malakai put in a call to this young doctor that he'd put through medical school back in the day, but it was too late for his hand to be saved. The crazy part about it was that he didn't even stress over the loss of his hand because he felt that the plastic arm with the knife attached added to his name.

Malakai peered out of the window of his 13th floor apartment taking sips of Cognac. A half smoked blunt rested behind his ear. He was wearing a black sweatshirt with Watts across the chest; Levi's which hung off his ass and Nike Cortez'. Although his eyes were focused out at the streets below, his mind was somewhere else altogether.

Damn, how the fuck we get that close and miss this nigga? I had my chance to get Showtime and the slimy mothafucka slipped right between my fingers, he shook his head. That's alright though 'cause in the end he's gon' get his. That's on my brother.

Malakai pulled out his cellular and called up Dakeemia who was at home. When he was locked up, it was their conversations, working out and reading that got him though his stretch. His girl always knew what to say to make him feel better about things, just like his grandmother. He loved those two women the most in the world.

The phone rang and rang until Dakeemia's voicemail picked up.

She must have fallen asleep, Malakai thought, exhaling his hot breath frustrated. He waited for the voicemail recording to finish so that he could leave her a message.

"What's up, babe? I was just thinking about chu, bang my line once you get up. I love you, deuces." He disconnected the call and slipped the cell phone back inside the pocket of his jeans. After letting the curtain fall back over the window, he walked over to the sofa and sat down. He wore a mask of concentration as he took a sip of his drink. Seeing the expression on his homeboy's face, Bizeal punched the mute button on the remote control, silencing the flat-screen.

"What's up, Mal? What's on your mind?" he asked concerned.

"Showtime." He stared ahead at nothing, looking like he was in a trance. "We gotta get this fool."

"We will homeboy, I promise you that." He gave him a stern look.

"We promised you that." Crazy gripped Bizeal's shoulder from over the couch.

***

Tyson and Henry sat in the tree across the street from The Sheridan apartment complex which was the tenement that Malakai had drugs pumping out of. The darkness and wild leaves of the tree helped to camouflage the father and son pairing from the armed men patrolling the grounds of the building. Henry took in the complex and its surroundings with his night vision binoculars. He took mental notes of how many men there were in all guarding the place. Henry lowered the binoculars from his eyes and said, "Okay, we got about four on the ground there and two on the roof. God knows how many are inside. From what I've gathered, Malakai stays on the 13th floor and his lieutenants round out the rest of the floors. All of them will be holding, no doubt. But after I knock these cats over out here I'll be right behind you."

Henry hung the night vision binoculars on one of the tree branches, leaving them dangling. He removed his M-16 from his duffle bag and laid it across his lap.

"You ready, son?" Henry asked his son. Tyson nodded but his old man could see that he was worried. "Tense, huh? This ought to take the edge off." He pulled a bottle of Hennessy from his bag, twisted off the cap, and passed it to his youngest son. The thug took the bottle of dark liquor to the head, spilling droplets onto his fatigues. He passed the bottle back to his father who took a long guzzle. He brought the bottle down from his mouth and wiped his chin with a gloved hand. He then screwed the cap back on the bottle and stashed it in the duffle bag.

Tyson jumped down from the tree and landed on his legs like a cat. Gripping a .45 in each of his hands, he hunched over and ran towards the apartment complex. As he neared the entrance, he heard the soft whispers of Moon's silenced M-16 and before his eyes the men guarding the grounds of the complex collapsed where they stood, dead. To the untrained eye it would have appeared that the men were being picked off by murderous phantoms, but the thug knew exactly who it was handing down their death sentences, his father. The Marines had trained him in the art o f murder. Killing for him was as easy as tying his shoes. He did the deed with precision and without remorse and that's what made him so good at it.

Choot!

The last body had collapsed by the time Tyson reached the entrance. He placed his back against the complex and poked his head inside, seeing crack heads shuffling around like zombies. They were all oblivious to the men that had been laid out just outside the door. Seeing that no one was focusing on the door, Tyson threw the damn thing open and stormed down the corridor.

***

"What do y'all think?" Malakai asked Bizeal and Crazy of the plan he'd brainstormed.

"Solid." Bizeal slapped hands with him.

"That's what's up." Crazy answered, holding smoke in his lungs from the blunt he was smoking. He leaned forward and slapped hands with his brethren also.

"So, when you tryna get at homie?" Bizeal asked.

"Shit, the sooner the better," Malakai taking the bleezy from Crazy and hitting. "I'm thinking about tucking that nigga in tomorrow night."

"Smooth," he nodded, recovering the L from his man and taking a pull, drawing smoke into his chest.

"What up with that bitch, Treasure?" Crazy frowned and threw his head back.

"She's paralyzed from the neck down, sentenced to live a life worse than death." Malakai shook his head shamefully, hating that he'd shot Treasure by accident. His sights were set on Showtime, but she'd gotten in the way. My bad, lil' momma, if I could take that shit back would, but my hands are tied here, he felt remorseful for the horrible act he'd committed. Once he found out that Showtime and Keith were involved in his brother's murder it had been fuck Big Willie records and everybody associated with them, straight like that. But Treasure was different. They'd always been cordial and gotten along, so it was torturing his soul knowing that he was to blame for her being laid up in her condition.

The sudden eruption of rapid gunfire brought Crazy and Bizeal to their feet, guns at the ready. Malakai rushed into the bedroom and returned with a Glock .40. Bizeal opened the door and the hustler's henchmen poured in, automatic weapons in hand.

"Fuck is going on down there?" Malakai frowned, checking the magazine of his assault rifle.

"Some gung-ho nigga stormed the building. He laid a couple of us out." One of the henchmen reported.

"Wait a minute, you mean to tell me there's one mothafucka in here kicking up this shit storm?" Bizeal inquired, feeling like one man shouldn't be a problem for them. He should have been executed on sight leaving them to go along about their day.

"Don't sleep, B, if a nigga run up in our spot like that, best believe he ain't by himself." Crazy told him. "That would be a suicide mission."

"I'm with Crazy, homie ain't here alone." Malakai spoke up. "Y'all take six men apiece and split up. I'ma hold it down here."

"Alright." Bizeal replied, picking out his six and motioning for them to follow him. Crazy picked his six and gave them orders to follow his lead.

Once his henchmen had left, the Top Dawg set on the arm of his couch and rested his Glock on his thigh, watching the door attentively. Whoever came through it was going to wish that they wouldn't have.

Who the hell could this be running up in the spot? And how in the fuck did they get passed them head bussa's downstairs. His brows furrowed and he picked up his walkie talkie, he contacted everyone stationed outside on the grounds of the tenement. When he didn't get an answer from any of them, he raced to the window and peered out, seeing all the bodies strewn out dead.

"Oh, shit!" His eyes went wide, and his jaw dropped.

***

"Yo, Damon, Joe!" a stocky henchman called out as he came through the roof's door. He had come to warn the guards upon the roof that they had an intruder in the building seeing how they weren't answering their walkie-talkies.

Gripping his burner, he walked around the entrance and found the guards strewn on the graveled rooftop, bleeding out dead. Upon further inspection, he spotted a zip-line cable that led from the corner of the roof to across the street to a tree. He made to turn around to report to the others his discovery, when his right-eye socket exploded in a spray of blood and gore. "Ugh!" The stocky henchman fell into a heap, head pooling on the rooftop. Henry stood behind him with his smoking and silenced M-16 assault rifle held firmly in his gloved hands. Henry swung his weapon around and disappeared through the doorway of the roof.

***

As soon as Tyson crossed the threshold, he dipped off into a dark recess of the lobby where he couldn't be seen. He made note of the henchmen toting weapons and the crack heads moving about. If he was going to take out Malakai then he needed to get passed them. Tyson understood he had to kill them all. There wasn't any way around it. It had to be done because as soon as they saw him, they were going to try and fill him with some hot shit. Seeing something red out of the corner of his eye, he turned his head and spotted the fire alarm. A light bulb came on inside of his head. He tucked one of the silenced .45s into his waist and pulled the lever down, sounding off the alarm. As soon as eerie siren wailed, he took a peek around the corner and found the smokers staggering around like nothing had occurred. Right after he made one of the henchmen heading in his direction to shut off the alarm. Now was the perfect time. He swung out from his hiding place and sent one through his forehead, sending blood and brain fragment flying out of the back of his dome. The splatter hit both some nearby fiends and henchmen.

"What the fuck?" one of the men frowned, touching his shoulder and coming away with blood. His eyes bulged when he saw his man collapsed to the floor.

"Oh, Jesus!" a crack head hollered seeing the man laid out of the floor along with the others. This sent them into a panic, and they went running in the direction of the entrance. Once the other junkies overheard them screaming about someone being shot and then seeing the fresh corpse, they went hauling ass after them. A stampede was quickly formed as fiends came pouring into the hallway terrified. Tyson ran against the rush of smokers, taking in some God-awful scents as he went along. The henchmen couldn't see him through the surge of bodies within all the chaos which was perfect for him. Clutching both of his .45 automatics, he handled his business like a marksman executing headshots with precision and leaving niggaz lying at funny angles, dead.

Choot! Choot! Choot! Choot!

He'd dropped a nigga like a fly and move on to the next. He'd just cleared the 2nd floor and had opened the staircase door when bullets slammed into it, creating small indentions. Tyson peeked through the small square window in the staircase door and saw a man clutching a pistol advancing on him. He stuck one of his .45s out just far enough so the barrel would be visible and pulled the trigger. The gun bucked three times propelling the man backwards before he fell to his demise.

Tyson was jogging up the steps to the 3rd floor when another man appeared on the landing with a MAC-10 spraying at him. The thug dived over the guardrail with bullets that were meant for him ricocheting off the guardrail, sparks flying. Hearing his intended target hollering in agony, the man smiled wickedly and hurried down the steps anxious to finish off his kill. He cautiously poked his head out over the guardrail and frowned when he didn't see anyone. But once he felt the barrel of a gun press against his gut, his eyes bugged and his mouth dropped. That when the son of a bitch's back erupted and sent fragments of spine and shredded flesh flying everywhere. The henchman hung himself on the guardrail and Tyson climbed over the joining guardrails of the 1st and 2nd floor. Heading up the steps lines emerged on his forehead when he heard a child crying for his momma. He slowly crept up the stairs and tucked his weapon on his waist. When he peeked over the upper guardrail he saw a dope fiend laid out with a belt around her arm and a needle hanging out of a vein. Her eyes were stretched open and her mouth was ajar. A bronze skinned boy with cornrows, about five years old, was on his knees beside her trying to shake her awake, tears trickling from his eyes. It broke Tyson's heart to see this. His crossed himself in the sign of crucifix. Feeling someone's presence as they stepped near, the little boy looked up to find the thug. His eyes pooled with a fresh set of tears and his bottom lip quivered.

Tyson took a cautious look around before taking a knee and opening one of his arms. "Come here, lil' man, it's all right."

The boy ran over to him and threw his arms around his neck, sniffling as tears rolled, staining the shoulder of his thermal. He scooped the little dude up into his arm and continued on his mission.

***

Henry kicked a henchman in his stomach, and he doubled over. Next, he swung the butt of his M-16 across his jaw, breaking it. Brackkk! The man hit the landing, and the old man kicked his pistol aside, sending it sliding across the floor, tumbling down the steps. Henry pressed his boot against the dude's chest and stabbed him through his left peck with the knife that was attached to his M-16 assault rifle.

"Yuckkkk!" The man sounded when Henry yanked the knife from out of his chest, the blade was soaked with blood. Blat! Blat! He staggered forward grimacing when two bullets slammed into his bulletproof vest. Diving to the side, he swung his M-16 around and pulled the trigger, unleashing a barrage of missile shaped rounds that splattered his assailant's blood all over the walls and steps he was running up. The bullet riddled man fell backwards and went tumbling down the steps from which he came.

Henry lowered his assault rifle and let his head dropped to the landing, breathing hard. "Haa! Haa! Haa! Haa!"

***

Crazy jogged down the hallway of the 13th floor with half a dozen armed men bringing up the rear. He barked into his walkie talkie as he moved along.

"Bird, you and your crew get cha asses to the 13th floor, the mu'fuckaz are up here!"

"All right, I'm finna..." the voice was cut short by gunfire and the tortured screams of men.

"Fuck!" Crazy cursed. He threw his walkie talkie aside and pulled his P-89 from his waistline. He pulled the 13th floor staircase door open, and a bloodied henchman rolled out before him, eyes staring into space. He ignored the body and motioned for his men to flood the staircase with a sweep of the hand he held his gun in. The henchmen poured in through the door and he went in behind them. Hearing the stampede of trigger-happy men coming up the steps, Henry fished around in his gym bag until he produced two grenades. He pulled the pins out of them with his teeth. Tink!

Zink! He tossed them down the staircase and they went dancing down the steps where they met the next landing and the henchmen. They froze in their tracks and looked down at the explosives.

"Ooh, shiii…" One of them hollered out before they all hurriedly retreated.

Ka-Boom!

***

A Colt .45 recoiled as it got off two rounds; its welder was a slim light-skinned cat rocking a Mohawk. He had snuck up behind Tyson when he came through the door of the second floor holding the little boy, ignorant to his presence. The sneaky mothafucka was about to blow his brain from out of his skull when the building had suddenly quaked, disturbing his equilibrium and sending the twin shots into the ceiling. Tyson spun around and kicked the Colt loose from Mohawk's palm. Next, he kicked his kneecap inward, breaking it and dropping him to his good knee.

"Arghhhh!" Mohawk screamed out in excruciation.

"Look away, lil' man." The little boy did as he was told and Tyson pressed his strap to Mohawk's forehead, pulling the trigger. Blood splattered everywhere and the man's head bent at a funny angle, his forehead open and smoking. When his body hit the floor and his eyes were staring up at the ceiling, the thug went about his business. His running down the corridor caused the child to pounce up and down in his arm.

"What's your name, soldier?" Tyson asked him with a smile.

"Trenton."

"I'm Tyson, Trenton, nice to meet chu."

"Nice to meet chu too."

He managed a dimpled smirk and he rescuer gave him one back.

Tyson looked away and continued his run down the hallway, tucking his head bussa on his waist. Next, he pulled a grenade from off of his hip, caressing it with his thumb as he ran forth. He was so closed to getting his revenge that he could taste it on the tip of his tongue.

***

Henry stepped through the ruined 13th floor staircase door holding his ribcage where the bullets had struck him in his bulletproof vest. Although his side was sore, he was grateful to be alive. He looked around the hallway and it was littered with fried dead bodies. There were small fires scattered throughout the hallway. The walls and floor was scorched black and splattered with blood. He looked over the bodies as he stepped between them, making his way down the hallway. Suddenly a sharp pain shot through his hip causing him to roar out in agony and drop his M-16 rifle. Crazy forced him up against the wall with his forearm pressed against his windpipe. He smiled wickedly as he stared into him eyes. He unsheathed a bowie knife and dug it into his hip. The left side of Crazy's face was fried black to a crisp and his eye was discolored. The wild ass nigga pushed his forearm further into the old man's windpipe causing him to grimace. He yanked his blade from out of his hip and put it in his left nostril, pulling until it looked like its tip was about to puncture the skin.

"Ooof!" Crazy doubled over after being kneed in his balls. He grabbed his family jewels, and his cheeks puffed up from the pain he was experiencing. Henry turned his palm up and slammed it upwards, driving his aggressor's nose bone into his brain, using it as a dagger. The force behind the assault sent him stumbled backwards with cross eyes. Henry took the time to admire his handiwork, Crazy lay dead with blood running from his eyes and nostrils.

Henry picked up his M-16 and jogged down the corridor. Bending the corner at the end of the hallway, he ran right into the deadly end of Malakai's Glock. "Drop it like it's hot, nigga!" He snarled his demand. The old man did as he was told and raised his hands in surrender.

Damn, youngin' caught me slipping, Henry felt defeated.

***

"Fuck you think these niggaz are that ran up in the spot?" a henchman asked Bizeal as he rode the elevator with him and five others. They all held tight to machineguns, their trigger fingers itching to catch a few bodies.

"I don't know, fam," Bizeal admitted, tapping his foot impatiently as he waiting for the elevator to stop on their designated floor. "Could be some of Romadal's people coming to get some get back."

"If it is they're gonna wish they never came in our house, 'cause it's about to be a wet T-shirt contest out this bitch." One of the henchmen claimed as he held an AK-47 with a banana clip the shape of a capital Jay. He kissed the assault rifle and threw its strap over his shoulder. It had been quiet as of late and he had been dying for some action.

"Damn, Marlo, don't chu think that's a overkill?" the cat standing on the opposite side of Bizeal asked, taking in the AK-47 with the huge banana clip his comrade grasped. He held tight to a Mossberg pump.

"Man, ain't no telling how many of them fools done got into the building." The man with the AK-47 answered. "Besides, I've been dying to see what she can do to some flesh. I bet she tear a mothafucka to shreds." He referred to the assault rifle in his clutches.

Ding!

The elevator doors had just begun to open when something fell from above and landed between them, rocking back and forth. The threesome looked to the floor and saw a live grenade at their feet.

"Ah, fuck!" Bizeal was the first out of the elevator with the henchmen falling in behind him, hauling ass up from out of there. The grenade exploded flipping the henchmen and slamming Bizeal face first into the hallway wall, busting his mouth. When he fell back from the wall he left a length of blood trailing from his lip. Thud!

The husky man lifted his head up from the floor, grimacing. His mouth was bloody, and he was missing four front teeth. Hawk! He harped up some blood and a missing tooth that had settled inside of his mouth, spitting them to the carpet. Once he wiped his dripping lips with the back of his fist, he looked to his horribly mutilated leg. The bone of it was visible as well as its muscle and nerves. The flesh surrounding it resembled bloody pastrami meat.

"Ah, shiiet." Bizeal winced, touching his disfigured limb. He then looked over the henchmen who were all scattered about dead and burning, limbs and shit missing. There were two lying nearby. The first one's eyes were bugged, and half of his head was missing. The other was alive but groaning in agony. He was left with bloody stumps for legs and his right arm was mangled.

"Uhhhhh!" he sounded like a walking dead man, eyes rolled to their whites.

Thud! Thud!

The noises came from the ruined elevator simultaneously, causing Bizeal to whip his head around. For a moment everything was still then Tyson came strolling out without a scratch on him. He picked up the Mossberg pump that lay beside one of Malakai's dead men. When Bizeal saw him blast the only breathing henchman in the chest he knew he was next so he scrambled over to the AK-47 with the huge banana clip. He swung it around ready to cut Tyson in halves and met a hard kick to the face that broke his nose and caused snot and blood to fly. The impact of the assault made his dreads lift from off his shoulders. Bizeal lay on his back teary eyed from the pain. The excruciation was so great that it was blinding to him, making him blink consistently. Tyson pressed the barrel of his Mossberg to the dreads skull. He was about to turn his lights out when he heard a voice coming from a nearby walkie talkie.

"My man, Tyson, we meet again. It's just too bad it's under these circumstances. Check it out, my nigga, I got cha pops up on the 13th floor, room #1300. I suggest you come say your goodbyes before I put him in a permanent retirement home, ya feel me?"

"Hahahahahahaha!" Bizeal laughed hardily, but when Tyson mashed him boot onto his ruined leg, he drew tears and caused him to whine like a bitch getting back shots. The thug cocking the slide on his Mossberg pump shut that ass up real quick. "Go ahead and kill me, cock sucka! I won't be the only soldier to have died in war!"

Shut the fuck up." Tyson mashed his boot harder onto his leg and he bawled. Next, he looked over his shoulder to the door of the staircase, whistling sharply. The knob turned, the door clicked unlocked, and the kid he'd rescued pushed it open. "You alright, Trent."

"Yeah, I'm okay."

"Listen, I got something I've gotten handle, but I'll be back for you, alright?"

"Okay." He nodded.

"Alright then, you wait for me right behind that door."

"Alright."

Tyson smiled and he smiled back. Once he closed the door back a scowl veiled his face and looked down at Bizeal.

"Kill me, mothafucka, gone and get it over with!" he snarled.

"I'm not gonna spill you yet, Goldie Lox, you're coming with me." He pulled the heavier man up to his good leg by the front of his shirt. He let the shotgun fall at his boots and whipped the .45 out from his waist, pressing it against Bizeal's back. "Move yo' ass, nigga." He gritted.

Together they headed for the #13 floor where all of the carnage would come to a head.

***

Showtime came through the door of his mansion high out of his mind. He'd been invited to a wild ass party out in Malibu by one of his business partners, Dick Sterling. Dick was an old white man that loved money and pussy just as much as he did. Every month the wealthy bastard would throw these swinger parties where the participants pick their partners by grabbing random car keys out of a bowl. Whoever keys you ended up with would be who you would be fucking. That night the head honcho fucked about ten different wives and snorted heroin off their asses and tits. He had spent four hours straight fucking in which he never busted a nut, but that was because he had that Dope Dick from shoveling all that H up his nose. After finally having enough, he got dressed, grabbed his keys, stepped over the sprawled bodies on the floor and made his way to his car. Now here he was, back at home, with a full bladder begging to be relieved. Staggering down the hallway, he turned the corner and made his way inside of the bathroom. Feeling on the wall in the dark, he eventually found the light switch and flipped it on. His eyes stretched wide open, and he nearly had a heart attack when he saw Mrs. Williams standing before him. He gasped and clutched his left peck.

"Mrs. Williams, what're you..." The rest of the words died in his throat when his eyes wandered down along the right side of her where he found her meaty hand gripping a .9mm Taurus. His eyes looked back at her face, and it was scrunched up. Her eyes were unforgiving and her trigger finger twitching.

Showtime's eyes bulged and his mouth formed an O. He spun around and dashed out into the hallway. He ran out to the left and had almost cleared her line of vision when the first shot rang out.

Bloc!

"Arghhhh!" he hollered out and grimaced, grabbing his shoulder. He ran along as fast as he could, occasionally looking over his shoulder in fear of the old lady. He could see her shadow on the carpet and the wall inside of the hallway as she was emerging from the bathroom. "What the fuck...what the fuck did I do?" Showtime had just bent the corner of the hallway when a second shot resonated, flying over his head. He'd almost made it out of her sight when a third ripped through his calf, tearing through bone and tissue. "Rahhhh!" he fell to the floor and looked down at his wounded leg. Grimacing, he crawled away hurriedly, glancing over his shoulder, terror filling his mind and heart. The shadow of the old woman showed on the carpet as she strolled through the corridor en route to him.

"Why...why are you doing this, Mrs. Williams?"

"Blessyn, you killed my grandchild, my baby boy. He was so precious, and you took him away from me." She sniffled and tears pooled in her eyes, bottom lip quivering. The passing of her oldest grandson was a few years ago but it was fresh to her like it had happened yesterday.

"No, Mrs. Williams, listen to me, I…Ahh! Ahhh! Ahhh!" His eyes nearly leaped out of his head, and he clutched his bloody kneecap with both hands, trying to add pressure to it. "Grrrr!" He threw his head back and gritted, eyes squeezed shut. Feeling the heavy-set woman footsteps as she walked upon him, he peeled his eyelids open and found himself being eclipse by her shadow. When he looked up, she was mad dogging him and locking her jaws, making them pulsate. She leveled the .9mm at his dome, pressing it against his forehead. "Please, Mrs. Williams, please…" he held up his trembling hands in surrender, staring up at the gold crucifix she wore around her neck. "Thou shall not kill! Thou shall not kill!" he squeezed his eyelids shut and interlocked his fingers together, begging. "Oh, God, please, spare me! Please, have mercy on my soul, Father!" tears outlined his eyelids and wet his lashed before jetting down his cheeks, meeting at his chin dripping.

The gun slightly shook in Mrs. Williams' old, wrinkled hand. With a squeeze of the trigger, she could end his life, but there was only one problem; what she wanted to do went against all that she believed in. Not to mention she kept hearing her intended victim repeating repeatedly, thou shall not kill.

"Thou shall not kill! Thou shall not kill! Thou shall not kill!" Showtime's old buster ass recited trembling, like a lone leaf on a branch in the winter. He swallowed hard and waited for the bullet that would cut his life short. But when nothing happened, he peeled open one eyelid and then the other, looking all around in awe. Mrs. Williams was nowhere in sight. It was as if she had vanished.

Showtime let his head drop down to the carpet, wincing from his wounds. He pulled his cell phone from out of his pocket and punched in a number 9-1-1, pressing the cellular to his ear. Someone picked right up.

"Hello?" he gritted. "Yeah, I need an ambulance."

CHAPTER NINE

Malakai stood with his back to the window, one hand gripping Henry's shoulder and the other pressing that thang to the left side of his back. He planned on using the old dude as a human shield and flat-lining his son before he finally murking him out.

"Malakai!" a voice boomed from the doorway.

The hustler's head snapped up and he found Bizeal there with his hands up, pouncing up and down on his good leg. Tyson was hidden behind him with a Mossberg pump pressed against his spine. Seeing his man with his leg mangled angered Malakai. His eyes darkened and his nose scrunched up.

"Fuck is up with chu, nigga? I saved yo' life in the pen, looked out for you, and you come gunning for my head? You disloyal, fool ass, bitch made, punk!" Malakai spat heatedly sounding like Denzel when he played Alonzo in Training Day.

"My girl!" Tyson replied sharply.

"Your girl?" He frowned and his eyes darted to the left, thinking. He flashed back to what had happened back at the club, accidently shooting Treasure and seeing her bleeding in his arms. "That was an accident, lil' momma got caught up in the crossfire. I apologize, homie, real shit."

"Fuck yo' apology, nigga! She's never gonna walk 'cause of you!" Tyson roared, tears dancing in his eyes.

"Fuck you want me to do, huh? I said I was sorry but that's as far as it goes." He roared back. "Hell else do you want?"

"Your life." His eyebrows arched and wrinkles went across the beginning of his nose.

"Nah," he bit down on his bottom lip, shaking his head. "You can't have that, homeboy, but chu and ya old man can share what's in this Glock. 50/50."

"Let my pop go and me and you can get busy we these toys."

"I ain't letting shit go, nigga, fuck you in yo' mothafucking ass with Magic Johnson's dick!"

"Fuck this nigga, Mal, you know how I'm built. I ain't afraid to die! Smoke this faggot!"

"Shut up!" Tyson shook him violently by the back of his shirt, disturbing his dreads.

Briiiing! Briiiing! Briiiing!

A ringing cell phone silenced the room and had everyone looking around wondering where it came from. Tyson and Bizeal's eyes settled on Malakai who was wearing a Bluetooth. He pressed the button on the metallic blue device and spoke like he wasn't in the middle of a standoff.

"Sams, what's cracking?"

"What the fuck do you have going on up there, man? We're getting reports that it's a fucking war zone up there!"

"Just a lil' sitch ain't nothing to worry about."

"Bullshit! There's about four cars headed that way. You need to get the fuck from out of there and fast too, you and your people!"

Malakai went back and forth with Chief Sams like he wasn't in a serious ass situation where he could end up dead within the time it took to pull a trigger. Tyson locked eyes with his pop. His old man gave him a nod, giving him the signal. With that, the thug shoved Bizeal to the floor at the exact same time his father threw his head back, busting the hustler's grill. Henry dove out of the way and Malakai staggered back, smacking a hand over his bloody mouth, eyes narrowed into slits. When he peeled them back open

Tyson was drawing his second .45 from his waist, extending it alongside the other. Malakai's stretched wide open and his jaw dropped. Tyson mad dogged him and clenched his jaws so tight that they pulsated. His hands did a little dance when he squeezed the triggers of his duo handguns. They spat embers with rapid succession, propelling the hustler back toward the window. He crashed through the window's glass entangled in the curtains.

"Ahhhhhhhh!" He fell towards the surface below bringing glass shards along with him. It seemed as if he was plummeting in slow motion, going through a tree and snapping a couple of its branches as he fell. Coming down through the branches delayed his fall and he hit the ground, slowly getting up moaning in pain.

"Are you all right, pop?" Tyson tucked one of his bangers and pulled his father to his feet, examining him for any wounds.

"I'll be okay, son, go get 'em." He patted his shoulder.

"Take this." He whipped out his other banger and passed it to him. "There's a lil' boy on the 10th floor. His name is Trenton. He's on the landing at the staircase door. Tell him I sent chu and get 'em outta here."

"Got cha." Henry turned around and saw Bizeal pulling himself up from the floor with the support of his last leg. He'd just stood up right when the old man came advancing in his direction. The ex-Marine didn't even look his way when he pointed the gun at his head and pulled the trigger. His head snapped to the right and his dreads went up in the air like they were being blown by a powerful wind. The husky man fell off to the side, hitting the carpet. His blood pooled at his head. Henry thumbed his nose as he speed walked down the corridor.

Tyson looked down out of the shattered window. He thought his mind was playing tricks on him when he saw Malakai running off into the night. With as many slugs that he sent at him he thought for sure that he would have been dead. Hearing police cars sirens approaching, he looked ahead and saw the flashing lights of several vehicles far off in the distance. They were speeding in his direction. Determined to avenge his lady, Tyson tucked his head bussa and took a couple of deep breaths. He leaped out of the window and grabbed one of its strongest branches. Next, he climbed halfway down the tree and jumped down to the ground. Whipping out his steel again, he looked up at Malakai and went after him.

***

Moon parked his Buick Regal in the alley two houses down from the place his victim was supposed to be holing up. Once he murdered the engine, he placed a neoprene on the lower half of his face and pulled the drawstrings of his hood, enclosing it around his head. With a gloved hand, he popped open the glove box and took out some fishing wire, wrapping it around his fist. Next, he hopped out of the hooptie and crept up the driveway of the house. He hopped the back gate of the house and landed its backyard. He moved as stealthy as a thief, tip toeing up the steps of the back porch.

Taking a cautious look around, he pulled out the pins he'd need to pick the lock of the back door. Having gotten the door open, he snuck into the house. When he emerged into the kitchen's doorway, he could see that the house was pitch black save for the light over the stove. He made his way towards the staircase and froze in his tracks when he heard grunting and moaning.

"Ugh!" he heard a deep, masculine voice.

Next, he heard shuffling around and two men conversing. Then he heard a door opening and closing shut. Footsteps followed shortly thereafter, and they were heading in his direction. Acknowledging this, he hid beside the refrigerator with his back up against it. A minute later, the refrigerator door was being pulled opened and a light casted from the opening. He inched his head out and saw the face of a pitch-black man with a shaved head and a graying goatee. His was leaning over inside and his eyes were scanning the items on the racks hastily.

"Baby, hurry up, the whip cream is drying." A gay man's voice cried out.

"I'll be right there!" he called out over his shoulder, then focused his attention back on the refrigerator's contents. Massaging his goatee, he said, "Now where is that extra bottle of Kool Whip? I know I had it in here somewhere. Ahha." A jovial expression went across his lips when he spotted the bottle at the back of the frig, hidden behind over items. He grabbed it and shook up the can. Tilting his head back and opening his mouth, he went to spray some inside of his mouth.

"Yuckkkkk!"

Moon yanked a length of fishing line back against his neck and tightening it around his throat, cutting off his oxygen. Preston's eyes shot open, and his jaw dropped. He dropped the can of Kool Whip, and it made a ping when it hit the floor at his bare feet, rolling up against the refrigerator. Gagging, he tried to slip his fingers beneath the fishing line, but it was too tight around his neck. In fact, it was pressed so hard against his flesh that small streams of blood ran.

"Aaagggagggg!" His eyes bugged, turning glassy and red webbed as saliva pooled in his mouth, dripping from his big bottom lip. Quickly, tears welled up in his eyes and spilled down his cheeks. Moon pulled back further, curling his spine and lifting his victim to the tips of his toes. "Arghhhh!" Preston grunted and choked, his legs thrashed around, and he tried to claw his attacker's hands but they were gloved. Moon pulled the fishing line even tighter around his neck, adding the pressure of all of his weight. Beads of sweat formed on his forehead and rolled down his face. The armpits of his T-shirt darkened from perspiration. His face twisted and he clenched his teeth, straining. Preston's struggling grew weaker by the minutes until he finally went as limp as a noodle. His eyes stared out of their corners and his tongue hung out the side of his mouth. He was dead.

Having accomplished his mission, Moon still holding the fishing line around Preston's neck, dragged his body backwards inside of the living room where he sat him up on the couch. The way he left him slumped it looked like he had fallen asleep there. Moon tilted his head back breathing hard, his chest heaving up and down. Pulling the mask down from the lower half of his face, he wiped the sweat from his forehead with the back of his gloved hand, then wiped the perspiration from his mouth.

"Baybeee, what's keeping youuuu?" the gay man called out once again.

"I'll be…" Moon started off groggily, so he cleared his throat and tried again, mimicking Preston's voice. "Here I come, uh, uh, lover boy." He pulled the mask back over his face and wrapped the line around his fist. Next, he pulled 357. Desert Eagle Cross Draw from off his waistline, cocking a round into the head of that big son of a bitch before creeping up the staircase like a teenager coming home passed curfew. Once he met the top of the staircase, he crept down the hall with his shadow bigger than his person on the way. His sights were set on a door who's light casted from the inside out into the corridor's wall. He believed the gay nigga that was calling out to Preston was in there. Pressing his back up against the wall, he slide forward holding his gun up to his shoulder, his head turned toward the door. Once he reached the door, he heard the gay dude whining and moaning. Gripping his banger with both hands, he swung out into the doorway of the bedroom with his tool aimed. He found a skinny ass Puerto Rican cat with a hair cut like Ricky Martin's under the covers, eyes closed as he played with his nipples, making sensual noises.

"Play time is over, Fruit Cake!" he muffled voice woofed from behind the neoprene mask. His deep masculine voice startled the gay guy, making him cower under the covers and scream like a broad. "Shut cho goddamn mouth for a put a hot one through it!"

"Okay, just don't rape or hurt me." He pleaded.

"Oh, trust me, the last thang I'ma do is rape you. But I will hurt chu if you don't gimmie what I want."

"Well, what's that?"

"The tape Preston has of Treasure. Ante up and you live to do some mo' fruity booty gay shit, alright?"

"Wait a minute, where Preston?"

"Preston's downstairs taking a nap, and yo' ass gon' go to sleep too, if you don't…Ahhhhh!" He shrilled with eyes as big as saucers. He looked down and found a midget in a diaper biting the shit out of his leg. Moon spun around in circles screaming and shaking his limb like the leg of his jeans were on fire, but the little fucka kept gnawing at his leg. "Arrrrrr, fuck!" he through his head back consumed by the antagonizing pain. Once he realized that his shaking wasn't getting the midget off, he cracked him on the top of his skull with the butt of his Desert Eagle, furiously and repeatedly. Whack! Whack! Crack! Thrwack! His head opened to the white like a baked potato and blood oozed out of his scalp. The midget fell back on his ass wincing and showcasing red stained teeth.

Moon looked down at his wounded leg and grew hot, his face balling up in a rage. He gritted and pointed his tool at the little man, curling his finger around the trigger. Crash! A lamp exploded against his head causing him to drop his gun and stagger aside, clutching his dome. He saw stars and half-moons, but when he saw the gay dude hurrying to pick up his piece, he snapped out of it almost instantly. Moon ran to recover his weapon before homeboy did but they both ended up grabbing it at the exact same time. He tussled over the banger, trying to rip it from one another's hands. While Moon's hand was wrapped around the handle, his foe's hands were on top of his and his finger was settled on the trigger.

"Grrrrrr!" the husky jack boy growled.

"Ahh! Ahhh! Ahhhh!" the homo cried like a sissy, trying not to lose the quarrel.

"Ahhhhhhh!" Moon threw his head back screaming as the four foot man sunk his teeth into his calf. This gave the homosexual enough time to point the lethal end of the gun at his face. Seeing him pull back on the trigger, he snapped his head to the left just as it recoiled upon fire. The bullet passed his ear and set off an eerie siren in his head. He released his hold on the Desert Eagle and stumbled backwards, tripping over a lone dress shoe. He fell on his back, blinking like crazy hearing the strange sound blare inside of his ears, a look of confusion plastered on his face.

Looking up, he saw the gay nigga lifting up his gun. This was at the same time that the midget was getting upon his feet. Moon looked to his right and found a pair of sneakers lying strewn about. He snatched one of the sneakers just as the gay dude was pointing his Desert Eagle. Right when he was about to pull the trigger, Moon launched the sneaker in his direction. It struck him in the face causing him to holler and wince, seeing white. Dropping his banger, he staggered backwards with his hands cupping his face.

"Grahhhhh!" the little man growled, blood running over his face in small streams as he charged forward, his hands posed like a bear's claws. Moon launched the last sneaker at the little fella, striking his face and dropping him to the floor. He laid on his side cupping his face as well, blood seeping between his fingers. Seeing both men at his mercy, Moon snatched up the Desert Eagle and got to his feet. He put one in the midget's tiny heart. The thunderous roar of the big gun made the gay dude looked alive, eyes enlarged, mouth hanging open.

"Oh, please, oh, please, don't kill me!" he said with his hands together in prayer, begging and moving his legs like he had to pee bad.

"Where the fuck is the sex tape? I'm only gonna ask that once." He spoke with dangerous eyes, his weapon pointed dead at old boy's thinking cap.

"It's in the safe inside of the closet." He panicked.

"Open it up 'fore I open up yo' forehead!"

"Okay." He timidly opened the closet and pulled the drawstring that triggered the light bulb, giving light to the small space. He pushed the clothes hanging up apart and exposed a shiny, black digital safe. With shaky hands, he pressed in the digital code. He got it wrong the first two times, until he felt that cold steel against the back of his cranium.

"Test my gangsta if you want to." Moon grumbled; finger settled on the trigger ready to let something go if homeboy didn't stop fucking around.

"Okay, alright." He shut his eyes and took a deep breath before presuming with the code. Beep! A green light flashed on and the door popped open with a thunk noise. When he pulled the door ajar there was a few stacks of them dead white guys and a DVD inside of a violet case.

"There you go, take it." The homo cried, hoping he'd just take what was inside and leave.

"Nah, you can have it." Blam! He put one below his right eye and blood splattered against the inside of the closet door. The gay dude hit the carpet, lying awkwardly on his side with his leg twisted under him. Moon tucked that thang-thang at the small of his back, snatched a pillowcase off of a pillow on the bed and raked all of the goods into it, tying it up. Looking to the dead midget, he realized that his DNA was inside of his mouth so he searched the closet for something he could stash his little ass in. Coming across a Puma duffle bag, he snatched it up and unzipped it. He set the pillowcase aside, stashed the little man in it and zipped it closed. With a grunt, he hoisted up the bag and the pillowcase, taking them both in one hand. As he headed down the staircase he pulled out his cellular to text his father.

Mission complete.

***

Malakai half staggered and ran away from The Sheridan complex. Wincing, he pulled up his sweatshirt and saw several mashed bullets stuck to his Kevlar bulletproof vest. He stuck his hand underneath the vest and massaged his tender wounds. "Grrrr!" he fault back the pain in body which felt like it was on fire. Looking over his shoulder he found Tyson running toward him, gun at his side.

"Haa! Haa! Haa! Haa!" Tyson breathed heavily chasing after Malakai, trading shots with him along the way.

"Haa! Haa! Haa! Haa!" Malakai stopped by a nearby tree, leaning up against it as he reloaded his strap. After cocking one into the weapon's chamber, he brought it up and busted back, making his enemy stoop low behind a parked car. By this time the police sirens were dangerously close.

Tyson peeked over the trunk of the whip he was hiding behind and saw his target fleeing. He ran out from behind the vehicle and went after that ass, determined to put a body on his gun. He was exhausted and could barely keep up with the faster man. Seeing that he made it into the middle of the street, he pointed his head bussa and let one loose. Malakai fell awkwardly to the ground with his arm tucked underneath him. Gripping his gun with both hands, Tyson ran towards his kill. He glanced up and saw twin florescent orbs heading in his direction. Paying the approaching vehicle no mind, he kicked Malakai. When he didn't move, he examined his form for a gunshot wound. Once he didn't see one his forehead crinkled. And just that quick, the man that was thought to be dead rolled over and sent one through his gut. Tyson's eyes bulged. He gritted feeling fire rip through his side, falling over as headlights shined on his face. Malakai pushed up from off the ground, coming up gripping his gun. He glanced over his shoulder at the Crown Victoria which had just stopped beside him. The driver side door open and Chief Sam's hopped out. He ran to the trunk of his car and popped it, lifting it.

"Come on, man, I've gotta get chu outta here before my people arrive."

While he was talking Malakai's eyes were casted down on a squirming Tyson, holding his side as blood seeped between his fingers.

"I'll be right with chu, Sams, just let me tie up this loose end." He spoke as if murder wasn't a mothafucking thang. And truthfully, it wasn't for niggaz like him. Tyson scowled at his would-be killer, clenching his teeth. He wasn't scared of dying, he was prepared for it. "This is the end of the road, homeboy." He leveled his Glock at the thug's dome and his finger went to squeeze the trigger.

Briiiing! Briiiing! Briiiing!

Keeping his burner on Tyson, Malakai pressed the button that activated his Bluetooth, answering his cellular.

"What's up, momma?"

"He's here! He's here, baby!" she said hysterically, breathing funny, like she was having an asthma attack.

"Who momma? Who?" His face balled up, wondering what had her so excited.

"Malakai, man!" Chief Sams shouted, looking from him to his rear where police cars were hastily approaching.

Malakai's face balled tighter, and he threw up a finger for him to give him a minute. The conversation with his grandmother had his undivided attention.

"Showtime, that bastard killed your brother, baby! He murdered our Blessyn!"

"Where is he?"

She gave him Big Willie records CEO's location.

"I want chu to get him, Malakai. You kill that son of bitch for me!"she told him. "I tried to kill 'em but I couldn't bring myself to do it."

"It's alright. I'm on it, momma, you just stay on 'em. I'll be right there."

***

Mrs. Williams disconnected the call and wiped the tears trickling from her eyes with a curled finger. She sniffled and blew her nose with a tissue. After balling up the tissue, she looked up at the windshield at ambulance that had just loaded up Showtime. It was pulling through the gates of the mansion and onto the street, making a left turn. Mrs. Williams fired up her Benz and drove off after the emergency vehicle. She played it from a safe distance as its sirens wailed and its lights flashed. Driving, she looked from the ambulance to the screen of her cellular as she texted Malakai messages, letting him know the streets as they past them.

***

Disconnecting the call with his grandmother, Malakai tucked his banger while keeping his eyes on Tyson. He didn't say a word as he jogged off and climbed inside of the chief's trunk. The old man slammed the trunk shut, hopped back inside of his ride and peeled off.

Seeing the Crown Victoria fleeing the scene, Tyson looked around on the ground for his .45. Recovering it, he pulled himself upon his feet by a parked car's tire just as several police cruisers were bending the corner. He glanced over his shoulder and took off as fast as he could, half of the vehicles coming after him. He was running as hard as he could, but his wound had slowed him down tremendously. He ducked off into a nearby alley bringing the cars along with him. The headlights of the cruisers illuminating the dark path making him look like a silhouette as he ran.

"Haa! Haa! Haa! Haa!" he ran, occasionally taking glancing over his shoulder while holding his side. When he looked ahead and saw a brick wall he knew he was fucked. "Shit!" he threw his back up against the wall, facing the speeding cruisers whose lights was shining on him. He held his freehand over his brows to see what was going on. Hearing movement at his back, he looked up to see a silhouette above extending something.

"Come on, son!"

He peered closely and made out his father who was outstretching his hand. His cracked a smile and stashed his weapon on his waist. He grabbed his pop's hand, and he pulled him over the wall. Tyson jumped down to the ground inside of another alley, hopping into an awaiting car. Henry slid into the whip behind the wheel, throwing his arm over the front passenger seat's headrest, and flooring it out of the alley. The car swung out into the street and peeled out.

Urrrrrk!

"You all right, son?" he asked concerned.

Henry looked from the windshield to his son who was lying back in the seat, still holding his bleeding side.

"I'm doing okay, pop. Slide me out to Treasure's spot." he took his hand from the hole in his side, looking to see how bad it was. "Grrrrr!" he gritted to combat the raging fire in his side.

"You okay, Tyson." Trenton leaned over from the backseat, staring down at his bloody hand.

"I'm straight, lil' homie, how are you?" he managed a smile, his forehead beaded with sweat.

"I'm good." He frowned, examining his crimson stained hand closely. "You sure you're okay? You're bleeding kind of bad."

"Uh huh, this is just a paper cut." He lied convincingly. With that the little dude sat back in the seat.

"Son, that looks pretty bad, you don't want me to take you to the hospital?"

"Nah, nah, nah." He shook his head no. "Take me to my lady. I wanna be with her if this is to be my last night on earth."

"Son, I really think you should…"

"Pop…please," he eyes begged for him.

"Okay." He reluctantly agreed.

Henry's cellular rung and vibrated with a text message. He pulled it out of his pocket and looked at the screen. Moon, his oldest son's name, was visible with the message. It's done. Henry texted a message back: Ok. Meet us bk @ the house.

Once Moon texted back that he was on his way out to Treasure's place, Henry sat his cellular aside and focused back on the streets ahead of him. Although he and his son had failed their mission it was alright with him because they both were still alive.

Meanwhile

Inside of the trunk was pitch black save for the glow of Malakai's cell phone's screen as he laid on his side texting his grandmother. About five minutes later the car was skidding to a stop, the driver side door was opening and slamming shut, and feet were hurrying around to the trunk. He heard keys' jiggling as the trunk was being unlocked and before he knew it, he was looking up at Chief Sams silhouette.

"Come on and…"

Bloc!

The chief's head snapped back from the impact of the bullet, and he fell out in the street. Malakai climbed out of the trunk and stood over his twitching form. With arched eyebrows, a scrunched nose and while biting down on his bottom lip, he clapped that ass twice more.

Bloc! Bloc!

Each shot echoed throughout the night, creating golden orange flashes. His head snapped from left to right, checking the streets for any possible witnesses. Once he didn't see anyone he jumped behind the wheel of the Crown Victorian and drove all. Malakai had whacked out Chief

Sams because he was corrupted. Between what had gone down at Club Nocturnal and the attack that was launched on The Sheridan, he was expecting major heat. Heat that was going to put pressure on the chief to get some answers and he was going to have to deliver. That would leave him no choice but burn Malakai at the stake.

"Fuck 'em," Malakai spoke to no one in particular as he drove along. "Better him than me."

A couple of minutes later an ambulance came blowing past his line of vision with its lights flashing and its sirens crying aloud. He saw his grandmother in her Benz following behind the emergency vehicle at a safe distance. He activated his Bluetooth and spoke into the small microphone. "Momma, I'm on 'em, stay close by though. I'ma leave the scene with chu. Alright." He disconnected the call. Right after, his eyes lowered, and he clenched his jaws. "I'ma ram this mothafucka!" he spoke of the ambulance and strapped his safety belt across him. He then mashed the gas pedal to the floor, sending the stolen car flying at the back of the emergency vehicle.

Vroooom! Crash! Vroooom! Crash! Urrrrrrk! Screeeech! Boom!

The ambulance fishtailed out of control and slammed into a light post, wrapping around it and slightly bending it.

Urrrrrrrrrk!

The Crown Victorian jerked when it came to a skidding halt. Malakai blinked his eyes and then shook his head, trying to shake off the dizziness from crashing into the back of the ambulance. Once he pulled himself together, he grabbed his head bussa off of the front passenger seat. He checked the magazine, making sure it was fully loaded before smacking it back into the butt of the gun. When he peered up and saw his grandmother's Benz pulling up on a residential block which was dimly lit, so its bright headlights looked like florescent orbs moving in the darkness. Malakai threw open the door and hopped out, slamming it shut with his elbow. Looking from where his grandmother's Benz was parked to the ambulance; he ran over to the driver side of the emergency vehicle and looked inside. The driver, who was also one of the EMT's, was slumped over with his bloody face lying against the steering wheel, barely conscious groaning in pain. Malakai's gloved hand opened the driver's door and he leaned the injured man back against the seat. Reaching over, he unlocked the double doors of the ambulance. While doing this he heard Showtime and the other EMT groaning in pain, also. Leaving the driver's door open, he stepped to the back of the vehicle and pulled open the twin doors. Inside he found Showtime on the gurney which was lying on the side with him half way out of it. His head bobbling as he looked through hooded eyes. The CEO of Big Willie records touched his fingers to his forehead and his finger tips came away bloody. The other EMT lay beside him on the floor of the ambulance with a nasty gash in his forehead. His eyelids fluttered as he tried to keep the blood out of his eyes and see who it was at the rear of the van.

Malakai couldn't give two shakes of a rat's ass about the EMTs. Fuck naw, his attention was solely focused on the cock sucker that murdered his brother. When Showtime saw him climbing into the back of the van, he gasped and looked alive. He meant the younger brother of his late recording artist didn't mean him any good. His head snapped all around in a panic looking for someone to save him or someplace to escape. Finding neither of the above he decided to talk his way out of his situation.

"Now, come on, man! What chu wanna kill me for? I—"

Bloc! Bloc! Bloc! Bloc! Bloc!

After handling the last of his business, Malakai jumped down out of the ambulance and slammed the twin doors shut. He retreated across the street to his grandmother's car and hopped into the front passenger seat. She busted a U-turn on the residential block as police car sirens were sounding off in the distance.

"You got 'em?" Mrs. Williams glanced over at him. He gave her a nod. Shutting her eyes, she took a deep breath and exhaled. "It's over. It's finally over."

Malakai gripped his grandmother's hand emotionally. He then lifted it up and kissed it tenderly, with affection a man could only show his mother.

"Momma, something went down at my…" he trailed off knowing he'd almost said traps and looked away, hoping she wouldn't get in his ass.

"Drug house?" she glanced at him. "There's no need for you to hide your dealings in the streets. I know all about them; people talk. Besides, I asked you to kill someone. I'll be damned for that but I could not sleep another night knowing that man was still alive after murdering Blessyn.

"You're right, momma. I need you to slide me by my trap so I can see if my dudes are alright. Cool?" he looked at her with raise eyebrows that also posed the question his lips had asked. She nodded yes and he gave her the address. When they coasted by The Sheridan the front of the place was light up by red and blue flashing lights from police cruisers and ambulances. The last of two gurneys were being rolled out with dead bodies beneath blood stains white sheets. Malakai saw the dread locks hanging out of one of them and a limb wearing a prosthetic arm with a knife attachment. He already knew that this was Bizeal and Crazy but he had to be sure so he hit them up through his cell phone. As Bizeal's cell phone rang, he looked back to The

Sheridan where a detective was toting a Ziploc bag containing two cellular phones that were identical to his closest homies. One of them lit up. He quickly disconnected the call and called Crazy's cell. The second phone in the bag lit up. The detective looked at the bag just as the ringing stopped.

Malakai's eyes became glassy realizing that his niggaz had been murdered. He wished he had smoked Tyson then but he wanted Showtime so bad that he broke his neck trying to get out of the streets so that he could get to him before he got away. Mrs. Williams face wrinkled with concern seeing her grandson in emotion pain. She reached over and squeezed his hand affectionately.

"Yeah, ma, I'll be alright. Both of my homeboys are dead." He informed her.

"I'm sorry, son. I'm terribly, terribly sorry." She looked into his sorrowful eyes.

"It's okay, ma, it's all a part of the game."

"Where would you like me to go now?"

"Home." He told her. "I'ma get my wife and whatever lil' money I have and we're leaving L.A. I done out here, momma. Me and mine gon' start from scratch somewhere else, I'ma have my own family and just live righteously."

"That's good, son, really good." She smiled.

"Momma, I was thinking you come with us."

"Really?" she looked at him like Are you serious?

"Yes, can't start a family without a grandmother."

"Okay, alright, I'll go with you."

"Alright then, we'll scoop up wifey and head to the L.A.X. We'll get on whatever flight that's leaving next when we get there. I don't care where it's going if it gets us far away from Cali."

Still holding his grandmother's hand, he kissed it and gave her a smile. He looked on out of the window as the Benz drove along through the streets. He'd thought about tracking Tyson down and murking him out but changed his mind. After he killed him, he was sure that his people would come looking for revenge. That only meant that the cycle of violence would continue until everyone was wiped out. He was tired of all the senseless killing. He was going to throw in the towel and try living a different lifestyle. He only hoped that this new one was better than his old one.

CHAPTER TEN

Skylar lay on the couch asleep with a blanket wrapped around her shoulders. The fireplace crackled and popped as the logs inhabiting it were cooked by the flames. The golden orange illumination from the fire shone on her face, casting a shadow on the wall behind her. In her slumber she was none the wiser to the twitching of the front door's knob as it twitched every so often. Suddenly, the knob settled and then it was being turned as the door was being pushed open. The door squeaked open, and a chocolate face emerged, individual braids laid to one side of her head. Her eyes moved from left to right, inspecting the living room for anyone else that may be present. After noticing that Skylar was sleep, he tip-toed inside and closed the door shut behind her. She started to pull out her head bussa and put one in her head, but she thought it would have been colder for homegirl to wake up and find her dead. A devilish smile crept across her lips when she noticed the big fluffy pillows on the couch. With the stealth of a cat, she made her way over to the couch and grabbed one of its pillows. For a time she stood there staring at Skylar and watching her breathe. Satisfied that she wasn't getting up any time soon, she went on about her business.

Dakeemia crept up the steps calm and easy with the couch pillow, being as quiet as she possibly could. She had one task in mind, and she was determined to carry it out. Finding where Treasure was laying her head really wasn't that hard to do. Since it was a public rumor that Treasure was shacking up with Showtime, Dakeemia paid a fee on a site online that gave her every home address and telephone number on him. She discovered that he had two addresses out in Los Angeles. That was the mansion and the modest house that Treasure and Tyson were holed up. She didn't know what it was that told her to try this address, but she was glad that she did. She had hoped to catch Tyson, Treasure and Showtime there so she could finish them all off at once, but to her surprise, so far there wasn't anyone there. Her reasoning for going on the dummy mission was to score brownie points with her man. See, she wanted him to know that he had a down ass bitch on his team willing to do anything he needed her to do. To her, killing all of these mothafuckas would have Malakai really feeling the love she had for him.

The Amazon threw her hair over to the other side of her head as she made her way down the corridor, gripping the pillow with both hands. Making it to the beginning of the door, she eased her head inside of the doorway. An evil smiled crept upon her face when she saw Treasure peacefully asleep, her chest rising and falling gently. Snickering like a fiend, she turned the corner of the doorway striding toward her bed. Murder poisoned her thoughts. Her intentions were to hold the pillow over the R & B diva's face until she took her last breath.

As Dakeemia advanced in her intended victim's direction, her shadow casted on the floor and over the bed. She took the pillow in one hand and leaned down, kissing her tenderly on the lips. When her lips came back from mashing against hers she smiled evilly again.

That's The Kiss of Death, she thought and took the pillow into both of her hands. The pillow was an inch above Treasure's face when she felt a hard whack across her back that made her grimace. When she turned around she found Skylar bringing the firewood poker down again, face balled up in anger. Whack! She held up her arm to block the assault and hollered out when she was struck again. Skylar was about to bring the poker down again but she kicked her hard between her legs. She dropped the poker and grabbed her aching coochie, doubling over. Right after she felt a blow across her jaw which knocked her to the floor, landing her on her hands and knees.

"Gon' brang yo' lil' skinny ass up in here with a firewood poker and whack me with it? Bitch you must done lost yo' mind." She kicked and stomped her until her face was bloody and she was spitting blood. Breathing hard, she grabbed the back of her shirt and dogged walked her ass to the beginning of the staircase, kicking her in the ass hard as shit. With little effort, she went tumbling down the steps fast and furious. Once she landed, she lay there on her back wincing and holding the lower half of her back. When she looked up and saw Dakeemia hustling down the staircase, she scrambled to her feet panting. She whipped around with her fists ready to get busy and was rewarded handsomely.

Bwhrack!

The Amazon kicked her square in the face.

"Ughhhh!" Skylar flew into the wall bumping her head up against it and wincing. Sniktt! Hearing Dakeemia pulling a knife from the sleeve of her coat, her eyelids peeled open just in time to see it flying toward her. It looked like a white blur spinning around fast as it was intended to. She made to duck it but it caught her in the shoulder, burying half way into it. "Ahhhhh!" her eyes bulged and her uvula shook she screamed so loud. Dakeemia grabbed her by her wrist and threw her over her back, sending her into the glass cocktail table. Boom! The table exploded and sent broken glass flew everywhere, littering the carpet. She lay there on her back, eyes hooded and head moving about, moaning.

"Like I said, this ain't what chu want." Dakeemia looked down on her. She whipped her gun from the small of her back and went to finish her off. Boom! A chunk of the door's frame went flying across the living room as it was kicked open. Dakeemia lifted her head bussa up and swung it around, pointing it. Standing in the doorway was Tyson and Henry. Their blazers were pointed right at her ass poised to fill her with something steaming hot.

Seeing the Amazon standing there with that banger on them and a defeated Skylar at her feet, made Tyson grateful that he'd left Trenton inside of the car. Something had told him that there may be trouble inside and he'd be damned if he was.

Dakeemia and Tyson were locked into an intense gaze. "Haa! Haa! Haa!" Her chest jumped up and down, breathing hard. Her face and shoulders shined with sweat from the fight.

"Drop your piece!" Henry ordered.

"The only thing I'll be dropping is yo' old ass!" she spat back, pressing her sneaker down on the kilt of the knife in Skylar's shoulder.

"Ahhhhhhh!" she screamed aloud; eyes squeezed shut. Blood oozed from her wound.

"Stop goddamn it!" Henry belted.

"Only one way you can make me." Dakeemia cracked a wicked smile.

"Pop, there's only way this is gonna end." Tyson winced, sweating from his wound. It was wreaking havoc on him.

"I know, son, born to live, bred to die!"

They all went to pull their triggers when a sound made them pause.

Briiiing! Briiiing! Briiiing!

The skin of the Amazon's forehead bunched together, and she checked to see who it was banging her line. A smile curled the corners of her full lips when she saw the person's name. She pressed the button on her black Bluetooth, answering the call.

"Hey, baby." She cooed, happy to hear from her boo. "I'm not at home, sweetheart, I'm actually at Showtimes place. Yep, he's not here, but Treasure and Tyson are. Say what? Leave 'em be?" she frowned. "Babe, I've got 'em right here though." She sighed and rolled her eyes, looking down at Skylar. Her face was swollen and covered with tiny cuts. The girl's nose had a red ring around its bridge from being broken and her lips were busted. "Oh, alright, I'll be home in a second, love you, too. Muah!" She disconnected the call. Her eyes lingered Tyson and his father before she dropped the hand that was pointing the gun at them to her side. Tyson and Henry did the same and moved from out of the doorway, giving her a clear path to the outside. Tucking her steel at the small of her back, she walked on top of the broken glass en route out of the door.

"Check on her, pop. I'ma see if Treas is okay." Tyson stole a glance at Skylar as he walked past her, heading up the staircase.

Henry helped Skylar from off the broken glass on the carpet and sat her upon the couch. Kneeling, he examined where the knife was embedded, narrowing his eyes.

He placed his hand on her shoulder and looked up into her eyes. "On the count of three, I'm gonna yank it out, okay?"

She closed her eyes, huffing and puffing to prepare herself from the pain that was to come. Nodding her head rapidly, she said, "Okay, alright."

"One, two!" He yanked it out ahead of time.

"Ahhhhhh, fuck!" She squeezed her eyes shut and bellowed, throwing her head back. "I thought you said three."

Tyson staggered up the staircase and fell to his knees, crawling the rest of the way up. When he reached the doorway of Treasure's bedroom, he pulled himself upon his feet. He took a couple of deep breaths and gathered himself before entering. The last thing he wanted was for her to see him on the brink of death. Tyson crossed the threshold into the bedroom cool, calm, and collected. Looking up into the mirror of the nightstand, he saw that his face was still shiny from the agony of his wound. He wiped his face down with his gloved hand, before landing his eyes on his lady.

"Baby." He called out to her.

"Oh my God, Tyson, where have you been?"

"It's a long story, baby, I'll tell you all about it later."

"Skylar!" she panicked; eyes big. "Dakeemia, Malakai's girlfriend broke in here, they were fighting and…"

"Shhhhhhh!" he hushed her with a finger to his lips. "Skylar is absolutely fine, sweetheart. She's a lil' banged up, but she'll live. My old man is taking care of her."

Treasure shut her eyes and took a deep breath. "Thank you, Jesus."

"You okay, Love?"

"Uh huh." She nodded. A line went across her forehead; something looked a little off to her about him. "Baby, are you, okay? You don't look so good."

"I'm straight, Lover." He leaned up against the closet door, folding his arms across his chest. When he went to do this he winced feeling the fresh wound in his side.

"You sure?"

"Yes, sweetness." He nodded.

"Babe, there's something I gotta tell you, but first I need you to open that closet for me."

"Okay." He did as she asked.

"I want chu to take out that big hat and that trench coat. Then bring it to me." He brought her the items and sat down on the bed beside her. "Reach inside of the pocket of the coat."

"What is this?" Tyson inquired, holding up the device.

"It's a voice distortion device, baby."

"Oh, really?"

"Yes."

He brought the device to his lips and held down the button as he spoke. "I love you, babe." He smirked, hearing how eerie he sounded through the distortion device.

"I love you, too."

"What's up with all of this stuff, though?"

Closing her eyes, she took a deep breath and swallowed hard. She then went on to tell her story.

***

"Did you tell 'em what I told you to?" the man's voice came through a distortion device. He was dressed in a big black hat and a trench coat which was tied tight around his waist.

"Yeah." Tyrone nodded, rubbing his hands together, ready to be blessed. He'd just came back from telling Malakai that Showtime was the one that had murdered his brother, Blessyn. It was for this favor that he was told that he would be handsomely rewarded. "I told 'em exactly what you told me to tell 'em, nothing more nothing less."

"How'd he take it?"

"He was shocked. Shiiid, how you expect 'em to take it with what I laid on 'em?"

"Right, right." He nodded his understanding.

"Well, you got my blessing?" His eyes were bugged and his mouth was salivating thinking about the treat he was in for.

The man reached inside of his trench coat and pulled out a Ziploc bag full of tan crack rocks. Before he knew it, the fiend was snatching the bag from out of his gloved hand. He hurriedly pulled a black scorched and scratched up glass stem from out of the small pocket of his jeans. The mysterious stranger watched as he stuffed the stem with rocks and set fire to the end of it. The drugs sizzled and crackled as the bluish orange flame cooked the crack inside of the glass. He sucked on the end of it blowing puffs of thick white smoke. Tyrone became so occupied with getting high that he wasn't any longer paying the stranger any mind.

"I trust that this whole thing stays between us?" He gave him a look like You better say yes.

"Yeah, yeah, yeah." The junkie closed his eyes and tilted his head back, blowing out a cloud of smoke. He wasn't trying to do much more talking. All that lip service was starting to bring his high down.

"My man, you have a good one." The mysterious man patted him on the shoulder as he passed him.

Sssssssss!

The rocks sizzled as they were cooked at the end of the stem. Tyrone was holding the flame of his lighter to the glass and sucking on the opposite end of it.

Choot!

The top of Tyrone's head splattered, and he hit the ground hard. Thud! The man extended his gloved hand down at the twitching fiend and exercised his trigger finger.

Choot! Choot! Choot! Choot!

He lowered his weapon to his side. After he took the time to admire his handiwork, he brought his head up and looked around. His white breath misted the air as he breathed heavily. The mysterious man dropped his gun beside the lifeless body. As he turned to walk away, he pulled his collar up to combat the cool air. The stranger retreated to a Honda Accord and resurrected it, its headlights illuminated the back of a Nissan and it pulled off. The man pulled off his black leather gloves with his teeth, revealing his manicured hands. He tossed the gloves into a Nordstrom's shopping bag as well as the big hat he was wearing. Looking from the windshield to the rearview mirror he untied his trench coat. He looked himself over and combed his fingers through his long hair. The mysterious man was Treasure.

She removed a cellular from the pocket of her jeans and placed a call to a taxicab service, requesting a vehicle to pick her up from a specific location. Once she disconnected the call, she sat the device down on the front passenger seat. Next, the R & B diva pulled off the trench coat and stuffed it into the bag along with the other items before sitting it on the floor. Pulling upon an unusually quiet block, she found a parking space and murdered the engine. She took a scarf from out of the glove box and wiped everything she had touched down. After she hopped out of the Honda, she walked two blocks down and glanced at the address on the house she'd chose to post out in the front of. This was the same address she'd given the taxicab service. About thirty minutes later she was being whisked away from where she stood. She paid the driver and left him a nice tip once he pulled up to Showtime's mansion. Treasure unlocked the door and crept in with the Nordstrom's shopping bag in hand.

"Tyson? Tyson?" She called out seeing him lying in bed fast asleep. Once he didn't move, she figured that he was in a very deep sleep and wouldn't be waking up anytime soon. With that in mind she crept to the closet, open the door and hung up the big hat and the trench coat, sliding the distortion device into its pocket. She kept a close eye on her boo as she pushed the door closed gently, careful as not to wake him up. Once the door had clicked shut, she tip toed over to the bed where she slid in beside him and lay on her side. Suddenly, his eyes peeled open, and his forehead deepened with creases, he turned over in bed to face her and found her back to him.

"Babe…" He nudged her. "Babe…" He nudged her again and again.

Treasure stirred a little and responded back groggily. "Yes, sweetie?" she kept her eyes closed.

"Were you just up and moving about just a minute ago?"

"No, baby, I haven't left this bed since you put it on me. Now, let's get some sleep." She grabbed him by his wrist and pulled his arm around her. He nestled his head against the back of hers and kissed her tenderly on the back of her neck.

***

Tyson had a shocked expression on his face after listening to what Treasure had told him.

"Why though?"

"Why did you have the smoker fool tell Malakai that Showtime was the one that popped his brother?"

"Fuck Showtime!" She spat perturbed. "That was get back. I knew I couldn't be the one to get up on 'em and do the deed 'cause the first people the police look to are the ones closest to you."

"Why you gotta hard-on for Show?"

"'Cause I'm fucking broke Tyson, I'm flat fucking broke…and it's all his fault." She broke down crying, tears outlining her eyelids and running down her cheeks. Her nose threatened to drip snot and she snorted it back up. "He gave me that shitty ass 360 deal. He owns all of my publishing. The only money he allows me to get is when I do a walk through at a club or host events. That's why I do so many. Other than that I'm struggling, living from pay check to pay check like your average Joe. Babe, why do you think I'm living here with him? I can't afford to have my own place, at least not one that my fans or media are expecting me to. You know in this industry you have to maintain this image." She began whimpering, closing her eyes and snorting. Seeing her distracted, he took a peek at his wound, more of his blood had absorbed his shirt and he started to feel woozy. He blinked his eyes a couple of time but managed to keep consciousness. Wincing, he leaned forth grabbing the end of her bed sheet and wiping the tears from her eyes. When he was done, he let the sheet fall and kissed her on the lips.

"When Malakai made it inside of the club that night I knew he'd planned on murdering Showtime, but I didn't expect to get caught up in the crossfire." She sniffled and swallowed spit. "I—I—I did this to myself, baby." Her body rocked uncontrollably as she broke down sobbing violently, snot bubbling in her left nostril.

"It's alright, babe." He pulled his glove from his hand with his teeth, and threw his from his mouth to the floor. Afterwards, he took her hand into his and caressed it with his thumb delicately. "Outta curiosity I have to ask, did Showtime really knock off Malakai's brother?"

Treasure closed her eyes and sucked in her lips, forming a tight line. She shook her head no, tears cascading down her face. When she peeled her eyelids open, her eyes were glassy and red webbed. Clearing her throat, she went on to tell the story.

***

"Yo' who dat?" Snaps leaned forth and narrowed his eyes when he saw a purple Lamborghini Gallardo pulled up in the Nickerson Gardens.

"I don't know, but you know the deal, we murk any thang purple that slides through here." Ace pulled a Beretta from the front of his sagging jeans. His man was right behind him, drawing a Tec-9, letting it hang at his side. They pointed them head bussas and were about to Swiss cheese the European whip when the driver side door lifted up. The hoodlums were about to get it popping when someone oozed out of the sports car, one red All Star Chuck Taylor Converse at a time. A jeweled hand grasped the door frame and Bless stepped out into view, clad in a red long sleeve T-shirt. He was sporting a red LA fitted cap backwards. Both his ears had square diamond earrings, and he had what looked like a hundred gold chains on, resembling Mr. T. On top of that he was rocking two gold presidential Rolex watches on both of his wrists which were on top of shirt's sleeves. The gangsta rap spitter was stunting harder than a bitch out in them projects.

"Blessyn? Blood, that's you?" Ace inquired.

"Who else, nigga?" He cracked a smile and closed the door of his expensive ride.

His homies tucked their burners, and he jogged across the streets, slapping hands with them.

"What chu been up to? I ain't seen you in the hood in eons," Ace asked. He and Snaps were taking a good look at their old friend. He was flamed up and rocking heavy jewels looking like a straight up rapper, live and in the flesh. That he was. He always told them that he was going to get it popping and they'd be damned if he didn't. They'd run the streets since they were pups and when his career took off he promised to come back and get them which was the reason why he was there now.

"Runnin' up that check, man, I just came off of tour." He explained to them. "Thought I'd come back and bless my niggaz."

"What chu mean, Bleed?" Snaps lifted an eyebrow.

"I came back to get you two niggaz like I promised I would."

"You bullshitting, dawg, don't be playing," Ace told him looking dead serious.

"That's on the Blood B, homeboy," he matched his nigga's serious look, banging the B to his chest. "I could always use some security, and I thought why not my niggaz, ya feel me?"

"Sho' nuff." Snaps nodded.

With that said, Blessyn took two chains each off of his neck and looped them over his homies' necks. He then took off a Rolex and slid them on their wrists. Next, he dipped inside of his pocket and pulled out four thousand dollars, giving them two grand a piece. They both thanked him and slapped hands, embracing their long time friend.

"Good looking out, my nigga Bless," Snaps told him.

"Ain't a thang, S, y'all been my niggaz since free lunch. Plus, I owe u that. I keep my word."

"True dat." He nodded.

"Y'all niggaz ain't got no choke though." He hit an imaginary blunt.

"Hell yeah." Snaps pulled a half smoked bleezy from behind his ear, cupping his hand around it as he fired it up, blowing smoke. He passed the blunt to his main man and he took flight on it, eyes narrowing as he sucked on the end of it.

"This shit off the hook." He took the bleezy out of his mouth and looked at it as if he couldn't believe how fire it was. "You got some mo of this shit? If so I tryna buy a pound offa you."

"Fa sho.'" Snaps nodded. "I got that. Just remind me before you raise up."

"No prob," he responded holding smoke in his lungs.

"Who this?" Ace went under his shirt again, seeing a bubble eyed Lexus pull up in the projects.

"I know that ain't who I think it is." Blessyn snaked his neck as he tried to id the car.

"Who?" Ace's head snapped in his direction.

"Yeah, that's my lil' bitch I be fucking with, hell she doing over here?"

"She looks like the singer broad, what's her face?" Snaps snapped his fingers trying to recall the young lady that had just hopped out of the luxury vehicle.

"Treasure Gold," Ace told him, eyes locked on her as she approached.

"That is her. Y'all take it to the store and get us some drank," he went to reach inside of his pocket, but Ace stopped him.

"Nah, I got it. We'll be right back. Come on, Snaps," Ace motioned for his man to follow him. Together, the hoodlums made their way out of The Bricks, eyes lingering on Treasure as they went along. The songstress gave them a smile and they sent some back before hurrying along on their liquor store run.

"Heeeey!" She greeted Blessyn as she stepped upon the curb.

"'Sup with it? Long time no see." He blew out smoke and dropped the roach end of the blunt on the ground, mashing it out underneath his Chuck.

"Yeah, I know. I needed the time off," she spoke of her taking time off from recording to go back home to East

Oakland. The life of a superstar, multiplatinum singer had become stressful to her, and she needed a break from it all. So she took it back home to be around the people that loved her the most.

"You couldn't pick up the phone?"

"Sorry about that. I was just tryna get my head together. This life we live is hectic, you know?"

"Shiiieet, who you telling?" He spoke the truth. He was having trouble adjusting to stardom as well.

"I gotta tell you something." She looked down at her fidgeting fingers.

"Oh yeah? What's on ya mind?" He rubbed his jeweled hands together.

"I can't do this anymore."

"What chu mean?" His brows furrowed.

"Us."

"Why?" He folded his arms across his chest and angled his head.

"Trip and I are getting back together."

"Fuck you mean?"

"Listen, don't go acting brand new on me now! I told you that if Trip ever got his shit together that I was going back to him!" Treasure's face twisted as she wagged a manicured nail in his face. "You know what? I'm done here." She turned to walk away, but he grabbed her by her arm and spun her around.

Treasure's high school sweetheart, Trip, had been out in the streets hustling like his life depended on it. He'd gotten hit with case after case and was looking at a life sentence if he didn't change his lifestyle. The singer had pleaded with him on several occasions to get out of the streets, but he wasn't trying to hear her. But once she had gotten kidnapped and held for a ransom by a couple of goon ass niggaz that knew how her man was getting it, she decided right then and there that if she lived through the ordeal that she was giving Trip an ultimatum: either stop trapping or I'm leaving you. Trip paid the hundred-thousand-dollar ransom and Treasure was safely return. She told him exactly what she swore she was, and he gave her his ass to kiss. He was a hard ass at first but after three months of not talking to or seeing his boo; he gave in to what she had wanted. He left the drug game and used the money he had stashed to open a laundry mat, a Roscoe's Chicken & Waffles, and Boss Life Customs, an auto body and detail shop, which also specialized in customizing cars. He co-owned this business with his best friend, Paco.

"Look me in my eyes and tell me that you don't love me anymore." Blessyn locked eyes with her, daring her to deny what he assumed she felt.

She hung her head and took a deep breath, looking back up into his eyes. "I got love for you, but I love my man. Besides, I'm pregnant."

He smacked his lips and twisted them; looking at her side eyed and waving her off like Get the fuck out of here with that bullshit. "Pleeeease, come again with that weak ass cap. I know you not carrying that bum ass nigga'z seed."

With that said, she unzipped her jacket and revealed her round belly. When he seen it his eyes misted and his lips peeled apart in shock. He couldn't believe his eyes so he had to touch it, pushing on it gently.

"See." She smirked, looking down at his hand poking her stomach and then up at him, seeing the hurt and water in his eyes.

"How many months?"

"Four."

Hearing that, he hung his head and massaged his nose, taking deep breaths trying to sustain his anger. He was more so hurt than anything. In her he had found the greatest love imaginable, and she was being ripped out of his life just like he had feared. Although she had told him that there was a possibility that she could get back with her fiancé he'd never worried about it. This was because she and her ex hadn't been together for the past year. He thought that they were officially done, but boy was he sadly mistaken. He and she had agreed to have a no strings attached relationship. Meaning they could both see whomever they wanted without having to worry about the others catching feelings or interfering. She didn't want to go along with it but he convinced her too. See, Blessyn was the hottest rapper out then and groupies were lining up willing to do any and everything he wanted sexually so he felt this was the perfect idea. He was regretting it now though. It had cost him what he believed was his future wife.

Damn, right under my nose though? How the fuck was she creeping with homie, and I didn't even notice? He thought, sighing and shaking his head like it was a goddamn shame. But then again, how could I see this shit coming though, when I'm out here on my hoe shit runnin' through these skeezas? Four months pregnant, shhhh. He took his hand from her stomach and stood upright, tears dancing at the corners of his eyes. He watched as she zipped her jacket up and wiped the tears from her eyes with a curled finger, sniffling.

"I'm sorry that things turned out this way, but we both agreed to keep this thing of ours open." She wiped her snotty nose with the sleeve of her jacket.

"I'm sorry Treasure, I know what we agreed upon then, but I can't let chu go through with this. Ahhh!" He sniffled and thumbed his nose, blinking back his tears.

She narrowed her eyes at him and coiled her head, placing her hands on her hips. "What?"

"I can't let chu go. I can't do it, boo."

"Shhhh!" She looked down blowing hot air from her mouth and kicking a pebble on the ground. She looked back up at him, eyes bleeding seriousness. "Blessyn, I'm begging you, please don't make this harder than it is. Just let me go."

"Nah, nah, nah." He looked down shaking his head, ears and neck on warming. He was growing hotter by the second. The nigga was on fire. "You and me gon' stay together. Once my girl always my girl, you feel me?" He pulled a .380 from the small of his back, letting it hang at his side. He looked up at her, eyes pink and tears sliding down his cheeks.

"Blessyn, please, I'm pregnant." She begged, holding her belly and fearing for the precious life growing inside of her womb.

"You think I give a fuck!" he raged, spittle leaping from off of his lips as he grabbed and yanked her into him. "Fuck that nigga baby, it ain't mine!"

"Ahhhh!" she hollered terrified, stumbling and almost falling from the strength he'd pulled her with.

"This is how its gon' go." He began bringing the hand he held the head bussa with around her back. He gripped her throat with his free hand and stared deep into her eyes, madness glinting inside of his own. "I'ma slide you up to this clinic and you gon' abort this nigga'z baby and we gon' be together. You understand me?" He gripped her throat tighter and shook her violently. Her long hair jumped up and down. Tears cascaded down her cheeks and she gagged and coughed. She was looking into his eyes scared and helpless. "You fuckin' hear me talkin' to you? Huh?" He gritted.

"Gaggg! Haaah! Yes! Yes! I understand you!" She managed to say through his stranglehold.

"Good."

"Yo', Bless, Five-Oh!" Snaps hollered out as he and Ace trekked up the sidewalk. He spat on the curb and nodded to an approaching police cruiser. Its headlights were off and it was flashing a light on everything on their side of the street.

Blessyn quickly released Treasure and tucked his banger at the small of his back. She gagged and coughed, massaging her throat. When he looked up the officer in the passenger seat shined a bright florescent light into his face, causing him to wince and hold a hand over his brows.

"What's going on out here?" the police officer asked over the loud speaker, having seen Treasure rubbing her throat and coughing.

"Ain't 'bout shit."

"Are you alright?" he questioned the woman. Treasure looked up and nodded. "Okay, the four of you beat it now. I don't wanna see your face around here no more, got it?"

"No, problem, officer." Blessyn gave him a weak smile.

Blessyn and his niggaz went to leave, but the officer's next order froze them in their tracks.

"Hold on! Don't chu guys have any manners? Ladies first." He looked to Treasure.

"Thank you." She said, making hurried steps across the street toward her car.

Once Treasure hopped into her ride and drove off, the officer killed the light. He made sure all eyes were on him before saying, "Watch your black asses!" With that said, his partner whisked him away in the police cruiser.

CHAPTER ELEVEN

As soon as the cops were out of his sight, the pleasant smile on his face converted into one of hostility. "Punk ass mothafuckaz." He spat on the ground just as his niggaz came to stand on both sides of him. They all watched the police car drive off into its back red lights disappeared.

"I hate them niggaz, man." Snaps eyes narrowed into as he twisted the cap off of a .40 oz of Olde English malt liquor and took it to the head guzzling it, his throat rolling up and down his neck as he drunk.

"Fuck 'em," Ace spoke his piece before turning to Blessyn, tapping him. "So, what's up wit ol' girl?"

The superstar rapper shook his head sadly. "Bitch knocked up by this otha nigga, can you believe it?"

"Damnnn, that broad foul as all hell." Snaps tried to give his .40 oz to Blessyn, but he waved him off.

"Cold world," Ace replied, remorsefully.

"You gotta get even, homie. I know you ain't letting dude slide for that violation?" When he didn't say anything, he went onto plant the seeds that would hopefully give birth to violence. "Awww, man, don't tell me that rap shit done made you soft."

"Hell naw, fuck I look like?" Blessyn frowned, looking him up and down like he'd lost his mind.

"Okay then, let's find this nigga and smoke his ass." He gave him a serious ass expression before turning to Snaps. "I know you down to make this pussy bleed like it's that time of the month."

"You mothafucking right I am." Snaps sat the .40 oz on the ground before him and stood up, lifting his sweatshirt. Showcasing the Tec-9 he'd drawn earlier that night when Blessyn rolled up on him and Ace.

"You with it then we can hit this nigga in the next few days. I just needa get my hands on a G-ride."

"That's what I'm talkin' about." Blessyn smiled and dapped both up.

Three days later

Treasure was in the front yard talking to Skylar about names for the baby, while Grief played dominoes on the porch with the rest of the old heads. Trip was manning the grill and chopping it up with his homeboys when he heard tires screeching as an old white drop Malibu bent the corner. The first thing he noticed was the menacing eyes of the shooter who was wearing a bandana over the lower half of his face. He clutched an Uzi and rode the windowsill of the passenger door.

Everything seemed to move in slow motion to Trip. "Y'all get down!" He shouted a warning to his loved ones and everyone hit the dirt except for Treasure. She was frozen like a deer in headlights. Through her eyes she saw the car toting the shooters in color while everything else was in black and white like an old ass TV show. Things were moving in slow motion for her also. All she could hear was her heart beating inside of her ears, from it pounding inside of her chest so hard. Treasures eyes zeroed in on the bandana wearing nigga hanging out of the window pointing the Uzi about to light some shit up. Below his bandana she noticed a tattoo in red ink on his neck, Money Over Bullshit.

Oh, my God, that's Blessyn, she thought, eyes bulging and gasping. Her eyes focused in on the next shooter hanging out of the back window gripping a Tec-9. She noted the gold chain around his neck which held onto a .357 Magnum revolver piece. The only nigga she knew that rocked one of those was Blessyn's homeboy, Ace. Her eyes left him and paid special attention to the driver of the old school whip. He had a tattoo going up his arm. South Central. This was Snaps, her ex's right hand man. She couldn't believe they had come to murder her entire family. Treasure wanted to take off running, but her legs wouldn't move. It was like they were frozen stiff. All the poor girl could do was squeeze her eyelids shut and hold her belly.

Please, Lord, somehow make these bullets miss me and my baby, she prayed, hearing the screams and hollers of her loved ones as bullets flew like they were on Vietnam soil.

"Gahhh!"

"Ahhhh!"

"Arghhh!"

Several of Treasure's friends and relatives went down when hot slugs went through them, misting the air with their blood. In one swift motion, Trip pulled his strap and started dumping on the shooters as he ran for Treasure. Splocka! Splocka! Splocka! He squinted his eyes and gritted as he got busy with that mothafucking tool trying to flat line the entire car before they could steal the lives of his wife to be and his unborn child.

Blat! Tat! Tat! Tat! Tat! Tat!

Blawk! Blawk! Blawk! Blawk!

Blessyn and Ace were spraying the whole yard trying to lay everything down moving that wasn't already dead. When the superstar rapper spotted Trip sending heat their way he and his man focused their weapons on him.

"Yeahhhh, homeboy, yo' punk ass should have stayed gon'." Blessyn frowned and clenched his jaws, gripping his machine gun with both gloved hands. Together, he and Ace let loose on Trip sending hot shit hurling in his direction. He took one in the chest and shoulder which caused him to drop his strap. The young nigga fell on his hands and knees, bleeding and hurting. When he looked up and saw his pregnant fiancé and the cargo of shooters headed her way, he fought back the burning in his form, scrambling after her as fast as he could. Unbeknownst to him, the shooters weren't after his lady only him. The closer he got to Treasure the more bullets flew and the more they flew the more he caught, tatting him up. Only God knew how he could keep on moving with that many holes in him, but he was still in motion, determined to save the lives of his family.

"Haa! Wheeze! Haa! Wheeze! Haa!" his eyes were hooded, and he was breathing funny. With only five feet between him and his love, he used his last bit of strength to leap into the air. Arms spread wide and legs outstretched, he tackled Treasure to the ground, saving her life but crushing her belly in the process.

Urrrrrrrk!

Blessyn and his crew sped away from the murder scene hastily. Dead bodies littered the lawn while blood and gun smoke lingered in the air.

"Ughhh!" She grimaced when she hit the lawn under the weight of her lover. Blood shot out from between her legs as she lay between her man screaming for the lives of him and their baby. "Ahh! Ahhh! Ahhh!" she wailed louder and louder, tears pouring down her cheeks and her head vibrating from all the screaming. Trip lay upon her long dead. His eyes were rolled to their whites and his mouth dribbled blood onto her blouse. Grief and the rest of the old heads came running down from the porch with their guns at their sides. When the OG turned his future son in law over, he was no more than bloody flesh occupying a T-shirt and Jeans.

"Damn, son." Grief shook his head sadly, hating to see the young man in a bad way. His eyes moisten and tears wanted to fall but he held onto them. Now wasn't the time to grieve, he'd do that after the repast. "God Almighty, please."

His forehead creased when he saw all the blood staining his daughter's blouse he panicked, thinking she'd taking a couple in the drive by. "Baby girl were you hit?" he asked concerned, worriment in his voice.

"No. The baby! Oh, my God, daddy, the baby!" Treasure panicked and screamed, hands trembling. "I have to get to the hospital."

"Somebody call an ambulance!" Grief's homie Fat Rat yelled out.

"Fuck the ambulance," Grief scooped his only child up into his arms. "I'll take her myself. Fat Rat, open the backdoor of my truck."

Fat Rat opened the backdoor of the SUV for him and stood aside as he deposited Treasure into the backseat. He slammed the door shut and when the OG went to cross his path he grabbed him by the arm.

"What?" Grief frowned.

"What about him?" He nodded to Trip who was laid on the lawn, his riddled body a bloody mess.

Keeping his eyes on him, the old school gangsta took a deep breath and said, "There's nothing we can do for the kid, the Lord's got 'em now." He crossed himself in the sign of the crucifix and mouthed Thank you to the young man that saved the life of his daughter before running around the enormous white truck and climbing in behind the wheel. He sped off with police sirens filling the air.

When the doctor told Treasure she'd lost her baby, she was devastated. She didn't eat, sleep, or bathe for days. All she did was stare out of her bedroom window into the street hoping that Trip would come walking up with their baby boy in his arms. Her father had convinced her to see a therapist, but once she was in the office she just sat there like a deaf mute.

Realizing that both her fiancé and their son were dead and weren't coming back, Treasure became overwhelmed with grief and knew that she wouldn't be truly happy until she was reunited with her family. She pulled a .44 Magnum revolver from a bookshelf full of books, knocking literary works to the floor in the process. Treasure dropped down to her knees and checked the chamber of her revolver. It was fully loaded. As tears ran down her face, she slid the pistol in between her lips and into her mouth. Applying pressure to the trigger, she caught something in the corner of her eye. She looked and found The Holy Bible opened to a page: Exodus 21:24 Eye for an eye, tooth for a tooth, hand for hand, and foot for foot.

Seeing this as a sign, she dropped her weapon and crawled over to the Holy book. She picked up the thick brown book and held it to her person, reciting the passage to herself. As she continued to say this repeatedly, she wiped away her tears and sniffed snot back. Treasure allowed these powerful words to soak into her mental and gave them her own meaning. To her they meant that she should seek revenge against those that had murdered her fiancé and son. Suddenly, she closed her eyes and flashes of white exploded inside of her brain. Right there on the spot she relived the worse day of her life. She saw the tattoos of the shooters and remembered the chain hanging from one of their necks.

A couple of days later

The door swung open in the men's room allowing the loud music of the club to spill inside as an intoxicated Snaps came in with a platinum haired cutie in a fishnet dress that left very little to the imagination. Snaps locked the door behind them and led platinum hair into a stall. He swallowed an X-pill and placed one on platinum hair's tongue. He then unzipped his pants and pulled out his meat, allowing it to hang out of his zipper. He leaned his head back against the wall of the stall, licking his lips and spewing obscenities as platinum hair blessed him with a blowjob that would have put Monica Lewinski to shame.

"Easy, baby, easy," Snaps whispered feeling platinum hair's teeth graze the shaft of his dick. "Ouch! Shit, take it easy with the teeth now. Ssssss, you…" That was as far as he got before his eyes went wide and glassy. Veins formed in his forehead and neck, his face turned beet red. His lips peeled apart quivering and he unleashed a blood curdling scream. "Ahhhhhh!" He grabbed what was left of his dick, his head shaking like it was about to erupt like a volcano.

"Shut the fuck up!" Bwap! Treasure punched him in the jaw, whipping his head to the right and silencing his screams of excruciation. He whimpered like the ho ass nigga he was as she gripped him about the neck and turned him to face her. Pulling her platinum wig from her head, she looked him dead in the eyes with hatred twinkling in her pupils. The blood from her biting off his dick slicked her chin and dripped on the yellowing piss-stained floor. "Trip sends his love." She spat blood in his face and held up his flaccid, severed dick for him to see it. Next, she dropped it into the commode where it made a splash, sounding like a turd hitting water. With the deed done, she flushed the toilet like she'd just finished using it. She released his neck, and he slid down to the filthy linoleum, squeezing his eyelids shut and holding onto whatever was left of his privates. Round and round his limp meat went in the swirl of water in the bowl until it was sucked into the hole to be lost forever.

Treasure peered down at her lifeless victim with no remorse. She then looked up to the ceiling and smiled victoriously. "Two more, baby, and you can finally rest in peace."

The rest room door rattling from knocks startled her and she stepped over her kill's body, unlocking the stall's door.

"Hey, hurry it up in there, man! A nigga gotta piss, shit. I done had four glasses of Henny and Coke," a clubber complained outside of the locked door.

Hearing other people pounding at the door along with the impatient man, Treasure opened the small window of the men's rest room and wiggled her way out to salvation.

A week later

"Haa! Haa! Haa!" Ace breathed huskily as he broke through the woods butt naked, dick and balls swinging as he occasionally glanced over his shoulder to see if the huntress was still on his heels. His forehead glistened with beads of sweat and he heaved heavily as he made tracks through the trees, scratching up his legs and arms as he went along. Needing a breather, he stopped at a tree and hunched over trying to catch his breath. The hoots of an owl and the howling of wolves startled him and soon he was on the move again. "Haa! Haa! Haa! This bitch is crazy! This bitch is crazy!" His socked feet smacked against the damp dirt as he flew passed the trees, trying to put as much distance between himself and the huntress that was on his heels. *Shhhhhhh! Thoomp!* He got about ten feet before an arrow pierced the back of his skull and came out of his right-eye socket. Ace staggered forward, moving like a reanimated corpse before collapsing to the ground. The horror he experienced was etched across his face.

For a time, there were only the hoots of an owl in the woods and then came the rustling in the trees. Something was moving within them disturbing their branches and leaves. A moment later, Treasure emerged from them, stepping forth one booted foot at a time with a bow gun in tow. She straightened out her skirt and pulled her bra strap back upon her shoulder. She approached Ace cautiously and nudged him with her foot to make sure his black ass was dead before grasping the arrow in his head. With a grunt and two good tugs, she was able to pull the arrow out of his skull. After taking the time to admire her handiwork, she walked back from where she came being swallowed by the trees.

A few months later

Treasure and Blessyn spent the next couple of months consoling one another after the murders of their loved ones. It was during this time that they both fell back in love with one another. The rap star popped the question, and she accepted. They were engaged now and made plans to get married next year. Their relationship now, like their previous one, was kept secret to any and everyone, even their friends and family. They wanted to surprise them all with invitations and airline tickets to Puerto Rico where they planned to get married. Blessyn's eyes were focused on the street as he blew through the stop lights like a speed demon, leaving debris in his wake. The city reflected on the spotless windshield of his purple Lamborghini. The illumination of the light posts lining the curbs shining in on him and Treasure's faces. The R & B diva was perched in the front passenger seat rubbing the back of his neck and head, as she stared at him lovingly.

"I love you, Blessyn." She smiled.

"I love you, too, baby."

Treasure leaned closer and locked lips with him. He turned his head as they kissed hard and sensually, keeping his eyes on the streets. Remembering his 11 P.M. meeting with Showtime that night at the park, he looked to the clock on the dash. It was 10:45 which gave him fifteen minutes to get there if he wanted to be on time. When Treasure settled back down in her seat, Blessyn switched gears and mashed the gas pedal further. *Vroooooom!* The vehicle looked like a purple blur as it swept through the streets. Its headlights were bright and seemed to be glowing, shining on the paved road as it raced through the avenues.

It was exactly eleven o'clock when Blessyn pulled up to the park banging Scarface's Smile in his European whip.

"I'll be right back, beautiful. Let me just see what this nigga Show wants and then we can breeze, alright?" he tilted her chin up with a curled finger so she would be looking into his eyes.

"Alright, baby," she replied before receiving his kiss.

Blessyn executed the engine, grabbed his lemon Snapple, and hopped out clad in camouflage fatigues and matching cap, swagged the fuck out. He took a drink of his Snapple as he advanced in Showtime's direction, his iced out cross and Jesus piece swinging from left to right. The lights of the park hit the jewelry and made its diamonds twinkle like the stars in space.

He stopped before Showtime and took another drink of his beverage. He screwed the top back on the bottle and slapped hands with the CEO of his label.

"What's up, fam?" He addressed him.

"Who that you got with you?" He narrowed his eyes and tried to peer through the windshield of the Lamborghini.

The gangsta rap writer shook his head and said, "Ain't nobody, I'm solo out in these streets."

"You know the streets are talking," Showtime changed subjects, massaging his chin with a jeweled hand. "And they're saying you're severing ties with Big Willie after this next album." He cleared his throat with a fist to his mouth. "Now, I'm not one to take what a few niggaz say and run with it 'cause that ain't never been my style. Nah, I'd rather hear it straight from the horse's mouth."

Blessyn looked him dead in his eyes without so much as blinking. "Yeah, I plan on making a move." He spoke as if it wasn't a big deal.

"Say what?" The multimillionaire's forehead wrinkled. He couldn't believe that one of the biggest stars on his label was saying that he was about to cut out on him, especially since he'd given him his big break.

Blessyn looked Showtime directly in his eyes, speaking loud and clear. "After this next joint I'm out. I took a few meetings with A1 Entertainment and they're talking about: two albums, 1.5 mill. I keep all of my publishing and my masters."

"So, you leave me to find out about it like this, through word of mouth?" Showtime asked hurt, eyes having grown glassy. He looked at the rapper like he was his little brother so this revelation cut him deeper than any scalpel could. "I thought me and you were 'pose to be better than this. I thought we were family."

"I was gone tell you, my nigga, but with us celebrating this new album going double platinum. And seeing how happy you were, I didn't know how to come at chu about it, ya feel me? I was just waiting for the right time for us to sit down and chop it up, real spit."

Showtime nodded and gripped Blessyn's shoulder, placing his hand on the back of his neck. "Come here." He managed a weak smile as he embraced him, tears streaming down his cheeks. "You broke my heart," he whispered into the rap star's ear and pecked him on the cheek. Right after, he shoved him backwards and walked off.

Hearing movement at his back, Blessyn whipped around and met a dark figure. He held his arm over his brow trying to see the face of who it was standing in the darkness, straining his eyes. Abruptly, the mysterious person pointed something at him that he couldn't make out, but his heart told him that it was a gun. Realizing that his life was in danger, Blessyn's eyes bulged, and he gasped.

"Fuck you doing!" Showtime smacked Keith's arm upward as he pulled the trigger of his .45, making the shot go wild.

Poc!

"Fuck you mean what I'm doing, nigga?" Keith mad dogged his nephew as they stood face to face.

"You tryna kill the mothafucka?" Showtime fumed, clenching his fists ready to fire on his uncle.

"You said we were coming out here to handle some business."

"Right and I just did." Showtime stared him down with a hard face. "If that nigga doesn't wanna stay down with Big Willie, fine, he can walk. I'm onto the next big thing, feel me?'

"Right, I feel you." Keith tucked his gun inside of the holster underneath his armpit.

"Don't you ever point a strap at me again, mothafucka!" Blessyn was scowling with his .380 pointed at Keith, his Snapple lay in broken glass at his boot, soiling the ground.

Showtime spun around and hastily approached the rap star, with his hands up.

"Whoa! Whoa! Whoa! Easy there, killa, ain't no need for anybody to get murdered." The CEO of Big Willie records reasoned. "Ain't no need for anybody to get murdered."

Blessyn and Keith's threatening eyes lingered on one another for a time, before the three-time platinum rapper walked off, burner clutched in his hand.

"I'm outta here."

Showtime and Keith watched as he trekked off, heading back to his Lamborghini.

"You, alright, babe?" Treasure's forehead wrinkled.

"Yeah, I'm good," Blessyn said as he stashed the gun in between the console and the seat.

"You sure, baby?" She looked him over, feeling over his chest to make that he hadn't been shot.

He fired up the Lamborghini and sped out of the parking lot, tires squealing.

"Bitch ass nigga, gon' pull his strap out on me." Blessyn slammed his fist into the steering wheel, occasional glancing out the side view mirror as he turned into the other lane. He wasn't speaking to anyone in particular. More so he was just ranting and venting. "I can't believe this shit! Fuck Blood think, that I just write gangsta shit? Mothafucka I lived it, don't make me have to show you a rerun out this bitch." While he went on and on, Treasure just watched him. Seeing her moving around, his head snapped over into her direction as he held a half smoked blunt to his blackened lips. "What chu doing?" He frowned. When he looked down he saw her hand grip and squeeze his leg, caressing it to calm the beast in him.

"Nothing, Blessyn, I'm just worried about chu is all."

"Don't be, ya man gon' be alright. I can't say the same for yo' boy Keith though. 'Cause that old ass nigga is definitely living on borrowed time." His eyes darted from the blunt in his mouth to the windshield as he took the time to light it up, blowing clouds of smoke.

The screen of Treasure's cellular lit up as a text was sent to it, its bright display glowing blue. The R & B singer settled down in her seat and held her cellular close to her, responding back. While she was doing this, Blessyn was looking from the windshield to her with curious eyes.

"Who that?" he asked, eyebrows arching.

"Skylar, she's flying out here tomorrow to come see me." She kept her eyes focused on the screen.

"Oh." His face softened once he found out that she was only chopping it up with her best friend.

Blessyn mashed the brake pedal at a red light. Hearing laughter coming from Treasure, he looked at her and she was cackling at a message that was sent.

"What's so funny, big head?" He tried to look over into her lap to see the message that was sent, but she turned away not wanting him to see.

"Move nosey." She chuckled.

Looking up at the front passenger side window's glass, he narrowed his eyes when he saw someone dressed in a black hoodie running up behind him in the reflection. He looked over his shoulder and saw them almost on top of him. He went to grab his .380, but Treasure snatched it before he could.

He gasped realizing that the entire scenario was a setup.

"You fuckin' bitch!" He lunged for the gun, grabbing its barrel and her wrist. They struggled for control of the weapon. Both of them balling their faces and clenching their jaws.

"This is for my brotha, mothafucka!"

When Blessyn heard that hostile feminine voice at his back, he whipped around and met a face he couldn't make out because it was in the shade of the hood the person was wearing. The gunman threw the hood from off of his head and revealed their identity. It was Skylar. Her eyelids were rimmed red and her eyes were pink from crying, cheeks slickened wet from tears of grief. She clutched her P-89 with both hands and took aim.

"My brotha, Trip, wanted you to have these!" Her eyes bled her mortal hatred as she snarled, licking shot after shot.

Blowl! Blowl! Blowl! Blowl!

The gangsta rapper grimaced as his body absorbed the shots, doing a funny dance in his seat. He killed over and slumped, sliding off to the side. His head leant up against the driver side door.

Skylar took a cautious scan of the area to make sure no one had seen her lay her murder game down. There wasn't a soul in sight besides a stray dog that was eating something out of a discarded McDonald's bag.

She dipped her head down into the driver side window where she found Treasure breathing hard and clutching Blessyn's .380. Her hair was wild, and her clothes were ruffled.

"Treas, are you alright?" she asked in a hushed tone.

"Uh huh." She nodded rapidly, taking a hold of the gun with one hand and wiping her sweaty forehead with the back of the other.

The sounds of police sirens made them look alive; their heads darted in every direction looking to see police cruisers pulling in from every angle. They were rookies when it came to murder, but this had to be done.

"Shit, we've gotta hurry up!"

She tucked her burner at the front of her jeans and reached inside of the driver's window, unlocking the door. She opened the door and Blessyn fell halfway out. His eyes were staring off at nothing and his mouth was open, clothes soaked with blood. Skylar ran through his pockets taking his money and leaving them inside out. Next, she snatched the chain from around his neck and relieved him of the rest of his jewelry, stuffing it all in her pockets.

"Alright, sis, you know what's next." She whipped her gun out again.

Treasure wiped her fingerprints off of the .380 and stashed it underneath the driver seat. She then turned her arm so that it was facing Skylar in full view. Turning her head, she squeezed her eyelids closed and bit down on her fist as hard as she could.

Skylar aimed the banger at her sister from another mother's arm. Closing one eye and turning her head slightly. "Alright, momma, brace yo' self."

A couple of seconds passed, and a single shot resonated throughout the night, ringing out like a lone bell.

"Arghhhhhh, fuck!" Treasure's face morphed with excruciation; she pounded her fist on the dashboard feeling fire rip through her arm. Tears bled from her eyes as she looked to the arm of her jean jacket which was expanding with blood from the black hole there. "Ahhhh, shhhhhiet! Mmmm." She mashed her lips together hard.

"You, okay?" Skylar asked concerned, hoping she hadn't hurt her homegirl too bad.

"I'll be fine, just get the hell outta here!" Her eyes rolled to their whites, and she bit down on her bottom lip hard to fight back the pain.

"Okay, I love you. I'll be at the hospital as soon as I can." She kissed her palm and blew her a kiss before fleeing into the night. Treasure could hear a car somewhere far off being started and then peeling off. She knew without a doubt that, that was her girl making her getaway. Looking ahead and seeing a host of police cruisers speeding in her direction, she threw open the door and hopped out. She ran out into the street jumping up and down, waving her good arm for their attention.

Two days later

Treasure sat in a wheelchair with her arm in a cast. Showtime pushed her from behind through the double doors of UCLA hospital. On the sides of them were Skylar and Keith.

"Alright, we're almost in the clear now. We've got old boy's funeral tomorrow so everyone turn out in their feelings, like you're devastated and shit. His family is going to be watching us, his grandmother especially. I'm hearing she already suspects that I had something to do with Blessyn's murder and she's even spreading the word."

"Fuck that old ass bitch." Keith frowned, spitting off to the side. He looked to Showtime. "Why didn't chu let me in on this plot of yours anyway?"

"That's what chu tight about?" Showtime asked, pushing the wheelchair through the parking lot. "Nigga, I didn't let cho trigger happy ass in on what was going down 'cause I didn't want chu jumping the gun and popping old boy. Just like you tried to, ya hot head. Shit, I needed it to go down just like it did. This way, Blessyn will die a legend and this next album will go diamond. Baby girl stands to gain from this, too. An R & B singer with some street cred, her next album is destined to go triple platinum."

"Mrs. Williams really thinks you are the one that brought it to Blessyn?" Treasure looked up at him, seeing under his chin and his nostrils until he peered down at her.

"Hell yeah, lil' does she know I wasn't even the one that pulled the trigger." Showtime cut his eyes at Skylar's bubble ass. Lil' momma was looking right in those jeans. He smiled wickedly and poked his gold fangs with the tip of his tongue. "Anyway, ya'll copy that?"

"Yeah," Keith responded under his breath, gnawing on a toothpick.

"Roger that," Treasure answered.

"I got it," Skylar said.

This was a secret that they all vowed to take to their graves.

CHAPTER TWELVE

Present

"Ssssss." Tyson repositioned himself as he gritted, then wiped his sweaty forehead with the back of his hand.

"Baby, what's wrong with you?" Treasure's face balled up. She was seriously worried about him.

"I'll… I'll be alright, sweetheart."He shut his eyes and bit down on his bottom lip, fighting back the pain in his side. "Just…just…just finish telling me the story."

"Showtime overheard me and Skylar planning to kill Blessyn. He wanted in on it 'cause he was pissed that he was leaving Big Willie for A1 Entertainment. He said that although Blessyn made him a truck load of money, he was worth far more dead. I'll be damned if he wasn't right. His last couple of albums went diamond."

"Why didn't Show just let Keith nod him at the park?"

"We all agreed to let Sky pull the trigger since it was her brother that Blessyn had killed. This way everyone would be satisfied."

"Right."

"Baby, I hope…I hope you don't stop loving me for what I've done." Her eyes dared to drip tears. She sniffled and bit down on her bottom lip before releasing it.

"No, sweetheart, I'll never stop loving you." Her brows meshed in a long lump that extended above both of her eyes when she saw the bleeding hole in his side and the blood on his hand. "You were down for your man, a straight up rider. I don't blame you for what you did. I respect chu for it."

"Babe, what happened?" Treasure inquired, tears sliding down her face. She couldn't take her eyes off of the bleeding hole in his side.

"Shhhhh!" He held a finger to his lips hushing her, his eyes blinking like he was struggling to stay awake. "Never mind that, I've gotta question to ask you."

"What is it?"

He went to hold her hand with his other hand, and he fell off to the side, hitting the floor. Slowly he got upon his knees, taking her by the hand again.

"What's going on in here?" Henry asked, holding his head bussa at his side. Skylar was beside him with her shoulder wrapped up in an Ace bandage. "Oh shit, Tyson." He went to attend to his son but when he threw up a hand it stopped him in his tracks.

"It's—it's okay, pop, I got it," he said, looking like he was on the brink of death. Eyes hooded, face shiny from perspiration. From his appearance it looked like he had a bad case of the flu.

"Son…"

"Pop, please, let me do this."

Treasure's head darted between her man and his father. "Babe, what's going on?"

Tyson dipped his hand inside of his pocket and pulled out a red velvet box. Using his thumb, he flipped it open revealing a twinkling, ten karat, platinum ring, with a canary yellow diamond and baguettes outlining the sides. The diamond was six karats alone.

Tyson sat the box on the bed and plucked the ring from where it was embedded. Treasure's face contracted. Her eyes wrinkled at their corners, her bottom lip trembled, and tears poured down her cheeks. She knew exactly what his intentions were.

"Baby, you're…you're the greatest thing to have ever happened to a thug ass nigga like me. I thank God each day for placing you in my life. I am nothing—I mean, absolutely nothing without you." Tears rolled down his face, dripping and splashing on the bed. He took the time to take a deep breath and blinked his eyes several times, feeling himself about to pass out. "Treasure, will you…will you…"

"Yes, Tyson, yes, I'll marry you!" She sobbed and whimpered, snot peeking out of her right nostril.

He took her by the hand and slipped the engagement ring onto her finger. Grasping her hand with both of his, he kissed it lovingly.

Skylar stood by the door watching the entire thing, tears rolling down her face as she silently sobbed and wiped her eyes with the back of her hand.

A crooked smile curled Tyson's lips and he rose to his feet, leaning over her. His lips met hers as he angled his head, slipping his tongue inside of her mouth and kissing her long, hard, passionately and romantically. He pulled back and whispered into her ear.

"I love you, Treasure Jones," he croaked.

Fresh tears coated her cheeks, and she sniffled. She swallowed the ball of hurt in her throat. It was because she was experiencing happiness and overwhelming fear of losing the man she loved more than life itself. Still, she managed to fight those emotions back and tell him the words everyone wanted to hear back that had said them first. "I love you, too."

With that, he fell out on the side of the floor wearing a smirk on his lips.

"Help him, please, help him!" Treasure shouted to her best friend and her man's father.

"Call 9-1-1!" Henry shouted to Skylar. She didn't waste any time doing like she was instructed while he attended to his son. He got on the floor and pulled him in between his legs, resting his head in his lap. He leaned over staring into his face and slapping his cheek. "Come on, son! Come on, son! Stay with me now!"

"Pop, I love you...I love you, man. I'm sorry, pop. I'm so sorry I wasn't a better son."

"You were the greatest son, Tyson. The greatest son an old man could ask for." His eyes threatened to trickle tears, he wiped his face with the back of his fist. "You hear me? You and your brother are my hearts, my reasons for living; you kept me fighting every day to keep on going in this God forsaken world. Now, you've gotta fight, baby boy. You must fight and make this beautiful girl of yours the happiest woman on earth."

"I'm…I'm tired, pop. I'm so, so tired."

"Nooooo, Tyson, don't leave me! Don't leave me, baby, I love you, sweetheart! I love you so much!" Treasure pleaded. "I can't live without you, babe. If you go, I wanna go with you! Please, haa! Haa! Haa! Haa!" She broke down hollering, body rocking as she sobbed.

"An ambulance is on the way," Skylar informed them, pressing end on her cellular. She ran over to look at Tyson and tears instantly came running down her face. She cupped her hands to her nose and mouth, weeping. She hadn't known him that long, but she knew that he was one hell of a guy, especially to have won her girl's heart because that wasn't an easy task to do.

"Pop, what's going on?" Moon came running through the bedroom door and over to his father and brother. He got down on his knees beside them, taking his sibling's hand. His eyes pooled with tears. "Stay with us, bro bro, you gotta fight that shit! You stronger than death! McGowan's don't die, we multiply."

"I'm…sorry." He finally shut his eyes.

***

Belinda was sitting up in a hospital bed with her bare feet in steel stirrups. The light above her head beat down on her form causing her to sweat as she was straining trying her damnedest to push out her second son from her slick womb. Belinda's face was shiny from perspiration and her hair was stringy and matted to her face. Veins rolled up her neck and forehead as her brows furrowed, dripping sweat. The slick goo covered; bloody head of her baby peeked out from her middle. Her husband stood beside her gripping her hand affectionately and giving her encouraging words as she struggled to give the world what was going to be their youngest child.

"Come on, I can see his head now." He looked from her to in between her legs. "Push! Push!"

"Arghhhhh!" Her eyelids squeezed shut and she hollered, intensity measured on her face as she strained to force out baby Tyson.

"Okay, that's it, Mrs. McGowan, he's coming out. Keep at it now!" the doctor ordered, sitting between her legs with his latex gloved hands prepared to receive her baby. The doctor grabbed a hold of the baby and pulled on him as he oozed from out of his mother's womb.

Henry and Belinda wore joyous expressions seeing their son in the doctor's hands. He was covered in slime, but he wasn't moving nor was he making any noise. The parents were worried, but once they saw the concerned look on the MD's face, their stomachs sunk.

"He's not breathing!" the doctor called out, alerting the nurses.

"What? Henry, what's going on?" A scared Belinda's head whipped around to her husband.

He shrugged and said, "I don't know."

"He's a stillborn!" the doctor announced.

"Tyson, I love you, don't leave me!"Tyson heard Treasure's voice.

"Come on, son, come on!" his father said.

"Come back to me!"He heard Treasure again.

"Real niggaz don't die, fuck death!"Moon spoke.

"We need you, Ty, you've gotta fight!"Skylar egged him.

The voices that Tyson heard sounded like they were coming from down a long narrow tunnel, a tunnel that he could see. The floor of the tunnel's path was wet and at its end there was a bright light. He could see himself as a ten-year-old boy, running down that tunnel into its white rays.

"Haa! Haa! Haa! Haa!" Young Tyson breathed, running with all that he had. He'd seen in movies that it was best to stay away from the light because going into it meant that you were crossing over into the afterlife. Although he acknowledged this, he still kept right along running. He could see the side of his sweaty face, the darkened area of his T-shirt from perspiration and his sneakers making hastily tracks. There was also the husky breathing in his ears, sounding like it was coming from a surround sound stereo.

"Haa! Haa! Haa! Haa! Haa!" his chest jumped up and down, as he moved forward, his legs looking like flashes of denim in his Levi's. "Hold up, wait a minute, don't leave me!"

"Hurry up, you've got to hurry…before it's too late!" a voice hollered out to him.

"I'm running as fast as I can, just don't…"

"Cleeaar!" A nurse called out.

The doctor pressed the handled pads of the defibrillator to Tyson's chest. Boom! His bare chest jerked violently from the electrical jolts sent through his heart. "Damn, turn it up!" he called out over his shoulder then pressed the pads against the thug's chest again. Boom!

Beeeeeeeep!

The green line ran from both sides of the heart monitor, flat line.

"That's it, he's..." a nurse started, but was quickly cut off.

"He's not dead, goddamn it, I haven't lost a patient in my twenty-five years, and I sure as shit not gonna lose this one."

"Come on, McGowan!" the doctor spoke in a tone that only he and Tyson could hear.

"Clear!" a nurse yelled.

Boom!

Tyson's body jerked again from the shock of the pads.

"Clear!"

Boom!

He jerked once again.

"Goddamn you, I've never lost one, notta one!" he said down to Tyson with an attitude, pissed off that he may make him lose his first patient ever. Fifty-three surgeries and he hadn't lost a man, woman, or child yet.

"Clear!"

Boom!

Another time.

Besides the noise that the medical machines made, all was silent inside of the room. The doctor stood over Tyson holding the handles of the pads. Chest rising and falling, as he stared down at him; his forehead beaded with sweat.

"Come on, come on, come on." He said again so only his patient could hear him. And then it happened...the green line started moving with a zig zag and beeping every so often.

Tyson's eyelids peeled open; he took a breath, the first of many. Through hooded eyes his pupils moved about, seeing the blinding florescent lights above and making out the shapes of the hospital staff as they moved around him.

"He's back, we've got 'em!" the doctor yelled, smiling behind the surgical mask. All the medical staff in the room started smiling. Some of them hugged one another, others high fived while the rest did fists pumps.

Nine months later

The physical therapist rolled Treasure out of her room into the hallway of the hospital. She was wearing a solemn expression across her face until she saw her man at the opposite end of the corridor. He stood there smiling in a red Cardinals snapback with his hands tucked inside the pockets of his red Dickies. The moment she laid eyes on her baby, her face came to life, and she was smiling so hard that it looked like it hurt.

"Hey, baby," he called out as he pulled his hand out of his pocket and waved to her.

"Hey, baby." She blushed and waved back. See, she had usage of her upper body, but her legs weren't fully functional yet. She could wiggle her toes but that was it. Twice a day the physical therapist would bring her out into the hallway where they would practice her walking for half an hour. The activity was strenuous and left her exhausted once they were finished, but she was determined to walk again, not only for herself but for her man as well.

"How are you today, sweetheart?"

"Fine, now that my baby is here."

Tyson smiled harder, his dimples defining his cheeks.

"You laying down that G, I see. Play on playette, I ain't mad at chu." He nodded, biting down on his bottom lip and massaging his chin. "You plan on getting up outta that chair and walking for me today, beautiful?" He inquired once he saw the therapist place the walker down before her.

"Uh huh." She nodded, watching as her therapist stood in front of her walker. Treasure grasped the handles of the walker firmly and took a few deep breaths. She closed her eyes and expelled her last breath, standing to her feet. Her legs wobbled a little, but she stood strong afterwards. Dedicated and determined, the R & B crooner was going to walk today, if it was the last thing she ever did. The therapist stood beside Treasure with her hand at the small of her back just in case she needed assistance.

"You sure you're up to this today, Ms. Jones?" Angela, her physical therapist, asked.

"Yes. Today is the day," she assured her with a nod and then stole a glance at her smiling lover.

"Alright, let's do it," Tyson said, ready to see his lady walk for the first time in months.

"Okay." Treasure took another deep breath. She moved the walker forward and went to move her right leg but it wouldn't budge. When she looked down and saw this, she tried harder wincing. Her foot slid forward. Then came her left leg, gradually. "I did it, baby, I did it!" she smiled brightly, casting that angelic smile of hers that so many people around the world knew and loved.

"I see, baby, you wanna try to make it to me?" he smiled excitedly.

She looked down as she was thinking about it.

Angela looked at her and seen the doubtful look in her eyes. "You don't have to if you don't want to, Ms. Jones. Today was progress enough. We could always…"

"No!" Treasure spat sharply. Staring into her eyes, she said, "I'm going to walk down there into my man's arms and I'm gonna give him the biggest kiss in the world. Then he's going to hold me in his arms and tell me he loves me."

"That's right, boo. I'm right here, let's get it." Tyson twisted his cap to the back and hunched over, rubbing his hands together, and his eyes bleeding his seriousness.

"Now, if you'll excuse me, I think my man's looking forward to that kiss." Treasure looked back to Tyson, she moved the walker forward and moved to inch her foot ahead of her. "Grrrr!" She squared her jaws, forehead beading with sweat. Her foot moved an inch, then two inches, three, four….it landed where she'd aimed it. Chest jumping up and down, she moved her other foot forward, gritting her teeth, moving it inch by inch. "Grrrr, ahhh!" She threw her head back and tears ran from her eyes, but her left foot landed where she wanted it. "Haa! Haa! Haa! Haa!" She looked down, face drenched in sweat, falling like tears from off of her chin. A smile spread across her lips.

"Come on, boo. Left, right, left, right, left, right, left!" Tyson chanted, hunched over like an umpire now.

"Left, right, left, right, left, right, left!" Face masked with concentration, Treasure chanted along with him, taking step after step.

"That's right! That's it, baby, you got this!" he licked his lips and clenched his fists tightly. His eyes were fixed on her. The physical therapist, the hospital staff, no one existed there beside him and his lady.

"Oh my God." Angela cupped her hands to her face, tears building up in her eyes. It was like seeing a miracle happen before her very eyes.

Tyson looked to Angela, who was wiping her eyes with the back of her hand. He gave her a nod, signaling to her to join in on the chanting to encourage his woman. She returned the gesture and assisted him.

They chanted together. "Left, right, left, right, left, right, left!"

Treasure moved along with the assistance of the walker, walking a little faster than she was before, but walking none the less. Having grown cocky, she tossed the walker aside.

"That's what I'm talking about, baby! Now come on, walk to me! Come to your man!" He smacked and rubbed his hands together; eyes having become glassy seeing her progress. As many times as he'd been to the hospital to see how she was doing, getting up to walk had always been her most difficult task. He was disappointed many days. He didn't know it but she seen it in his eyes, and every time she felt like she had failed him. This was why she had to do it this time. She had to walk to show him that their love could conquer all.

"Left, right, left, right, left, right!" They continued to chant, egging her to walk. She took six steps and fell to her knees.

Seeing this, Angela went to help her, but Tyson throwing up a hand and shaking his head no, froze her in her tracks.

"She got this!" He looked to Treasure. "Tell her, baby, tell her you got this."

"I got this." She looked up at her physical therapist, face sweaty and chest thumping hard. The chest of her shirt had darkened from her perspiration.

"Alright, soldier, on your feet, front and center!" He smacked his hands and rubbed them together, before placing them on his knees. Placing her hand on her knee, she pushed up from where she was kneeled and stood straight up.

Treasure stood right where she was, eyes shut, mouth a tight line as she balled her fists. She was mentally preparing herself for this one. She couldn't let her boo down again. Huffing and puffing, she worked herself up before she began. Having gotten ready, she peeled her eyelids open and looked straight ahead.

"Here goes nothing," she said loud enough for only her ears.

"Left, right, left, right, left, right, left!" The inseparable couple chanted aloud together, before long they had drawn a good amount of the hospital staff into the hallway. They were all staring at them. Some of them were crying, others eyes pooled with tears, while the rest wore solemn expressions. They all knew the songstress and her struggle to walk again, so seeing it happen before their eyes was amazing.

Treasure walked toward Tyson, slowly at first, but then she began moving at a regular pace. This brought tears to her man's eyes. His vision became blurred, and tears came sliding down his cheeks.

"Come on, baby, I'm right here." He stood up and spread his arms.

Tears rolled down her cheeks, too. Her shoulders shuddered and she made an ugly face, walking. As she proceeded forward, her own song played inside of her head, Bulletproof Love.

Bulletproof loveeeee…they can't break it, there's no mistaking/bulletproof loveeeee…it can't be faded, baby, we gone make it…

Treasure took one last step which placed her before the love of her life. She fell into his arms, and he embraced her, lifting her off of her feet. She hugged his neck and wrapped her legs around him. Cheeks pressed against one another, they cried their eyes out, wetting their faces.

"I knew you could do it, babe. I knew you could." His voice cracked with raw emotion.

"I couldn't have done it without you, bae. Our love can conquer any and everything this world throws at us." Her voice cracked as well.

"You are me…and I am you." He stared into her eyes, fresh tears accumulating in his.

"Together we are one; let no one…or nothing…come between this union." She sniffled.

They wiped the wetness from one another's faces.

"I love you so much, Tyson."

"I love you so much more."

Their lips mashed together, and they angled their heads, kissing. Once they stopped, he spun her around and around. They giggled and laughed.

The entire staff, Angela included, applauded and cheered the couple on. Treasure had beaten death, paralysis, and had gained love. She was victorious.

One year later in Jamaica

A pregnant Treasure stood looking Tyson directly in his eyes while they held hands, smiles plastered on their faces. She was in a beautiful white gown with see-through flower print sleeves and half of a top that made her cleavage barely visible. Her husband to be in a crisp white tuxedo. There they stood on the warm white sand of the island with the water crashing into the shores, the background lit by the golden orange marble known as the sun. A couple of seagulls flew across the sky squawking.

Skylar, her maid of honor, stood off to the side dressed in a sky-blue dress and pearls. Moon, the best-man, stood off to the side of his brother. He was dressed in an all-red tuxedo with bandana print on its collar. Taking up space beside him was Henry, donning a gray tuxedo and black tie. Little Trenton stood at his rear with fresh cornrows and a tuxedo that matched his adoptive father's. He was smiling appreciatively at his parents.

Also in attendance were Cody, Whispers and Grief. The shot-caller and his lieutenant were dressed in tuxedos and wore shackles. Surrounding them were police officers in windbreakers and holding shotguns. Despite all this Grief was smiling seeing his baby girl happy. The wedding was exactly how Treasure had imagined it back at Cynthia's when she and Tyson had tried on the wedding gown and the tuxedo.

The guests of the wedding looked attentively as Tyson and Treasure exchanged vows. Some of the people in attendance wore tear-streaked faces hearing the powerful and heartfelt words by the bride and groom. What the two people before them had was nothing short of amazing. No one could ever say that their love was made up for publicity. Not only could the guests see their love they could feel it. It was real.

"I do." Tyson responded to the minister's question.

"You may now kiss the bride." The minister told him.

Tyson and Treasure kissed.

They then went on to live happily ever after.

THE END

My self-published books

BLOODY KNUCKLES
THE DEVIL WEARS TIMBS 1-7
ME AND MY HITTAZ 1-6
THE LAST REAL NIGGA ALIVE 1-3
A HOOD NIGGA'S BLUES
A SOUTH-CENTRAL LOVE AFFAIR

My books published under LDP

BURY ME A G 1-5
THE DOPEMAN'S BODYGUARD 1-2
FEAR MY GANGSTA 1-5
THESE SCANDALOUS STREETS 1-3
THE REALEST KILLAZ 1-3
THE LAST OF THE OG'S 1-3
A GANGSTA'S EMPIRE 1-4
GOD BLESS THE TRAPPERS 1-3

Coming Soon

BLOODY KNUCKLES 2
THERE'S NO PLACE IN HEAVEN FOR THUGS
THEY MADE ME AN ANIMAL

www.ingramcontent.com/pod-product-compliance
Lightning Source LLC
LaVergne TN
LVHW012015060526
838201LV00061B/4316